DEFINED

FADE INTO YOU BOOK 2

DAKOTA WILLINK

DRAGONFLY INK PUBLISHING

PRAISE FOR THE FADE INTO YOU SERIES

"Dakota Willink gives you all the feels and stolen moments you crave!"
~ **Crystal's Book World**

"A beautifully written novel about first love and heartbreak."
~ **Tamara Lush, RITA Finalist**

"This is a book that will stick with me for years to come."
~ **Magic Beyond The Covers Book Blog**

"I have so many parts of this book that stuck with me. I find myself recalling them and getting emotional all over again!"
~ **Audiobook Obsession**

"The characters had me swooning and on the edge of my seat at times, with the twists, the drama, and the angst!"
~ **Once Upon a Romance Blog**

"I will say that this is one of the best conclusions to a story that I have read in a very long time."
~ **Moonlight Novels**

"Sigh... what a beautiful duet! The conclusion to the Cadence Duet is stunning."
~ **Next Book Review Blog**

DAKOTA WILLINK, LLC

This book is an original publication of Dakota Willink, LLC

Library of Congress Cataloging-in-Publication Data
Paperback ISBN: 978-0-9971603-8-3
Paperback ISBN: 978-1-954817-17-3
Defined | Copyright © 2019 by Dakota Willink | Pending

Cover design by Dragonfly Ink Publishing
Copyright © 2019

To all the women who've been told they can't...
Actually, you can.

PART TWO

"Life is about choices. Some we regret, some we're proud of. Some will haunt us forever."

- Graham Brown

1

Washington, D.C.
PRESENT DAY

CADENCE

I sat back in my office chair and shook my head. I just finished reading another news article that made my stomach turn. Climate change, healthcare, school shootings, immigration, government scandals—there was no escaping it. Some days I wished I could just shut out all the noise, politics, and injustices in the world. But then there were the days when I saw good defeat evil, reminding me of why I do what I do. Whenever I saw the good guys chalk up a point, it made everything worth it.

I looked up at the giant cork board hanging on the wall above my computer, filled with pictures of smiling children and families and thank you notes. There were letters of appreciation written to me and my colleagues at Dahlia's Dreamers, expressing gratitude for our work in keeping their family whole.

Yes. It's worth it. THEY are worth it.

I smiled to myself just as a knock sounded on my office door. Turning my gaze away from the pictures, I called, "Come on in."

Joy Martin, my best friend since our days at Camp Riley and current scheduler-in-chief, poked her head in. She was smiling broadly, her white teeth a vivid contrast to her smooth, cocoa colored skin. I returned her smile, always appreciative of the contagious grin that never failed to brighten even the darkest of rooms. The name Joy was fitting—she emitted it everywhere she went. That quality made her a true asset at Dahlia's Dreamers. The people who walked through our doors needed all the smiles they could get.

"Sorry, Cadence. I feel like I've been stuck on a billion conference calls today. I meant to check in before now. How's the day shaping up?" Joy asked as she plopped down in the chair across from me.

"Not too bad. I made a little progress on the Álvarez case after the family left but not as much as I would have liked. But then again, I became distracted by a news notification that popped up on my phone."

"Girl, how many times have I told you? Ignore it before it makes you go crazy."

"It already has," I laughed. "Anyway, I still need to go over my notes for my meeting with Simon Reed. He's due here at three o'clock. He'll get cranky if I'm not prepared."

"Actually, that's what I came in to tell you. He just called to say he's stuck in court and can't make it today. He asked if he could come in to meet you tomorrow morning at nine."

"Of course he wants to meet on a Saturday," I grunted and rolled my eyes. "I mean, I get he's doing the work pro-bono, but he's a royal pain in the ass sometimes. If he wasn't such a great attorney, I'd drop him from our list."

"Now, now, have patience," Joy said in a sing-song voice.

"You know he's only a pain because you refuse to go out with him."

"Whatevs," I waved off, deliberately using one of my daughter's favorite terms because I knew it would get under Joy's skin. She hated the way the younger generation shortened words. "You know how I feel about the argyle sweater vests he's constantly *not* rocking. They're hideous. Plus, I'm just not interested in him that way."

"Yeah, yeah, I've heard it all before," she muttered.

"Don't start the 'I need to date' crap. You sound just like Kallie. And speaking of which, Reed's cancelation means I can get home early and help her get ready for tonight. I wasn't sure if I would be able to before now."

Joy cocked one perfectly shaped brow in confusion.

"What's tonight?"

"Junior prom, remember? Can you even believe it? God, I feel old. It seems like I was just there yesterday, and now here I am sending my baby girl off to her own prom. Do you want to come by and join in on all the girly prep? I'm sure Kallie would love for her Auntie Joy to be there," I added.

"I wish I could! I hate to miss it, but it's my third wedding anniversary next month. Marissa will be out of town for work, so we decided to celebrate early and made plans for a little getaway this weekend instead. We're driving up to Philadelphia tonight."

"Wow! Has it been almost three years already?"

"June twenty-sixth, baby. A day for the history books!"

"It sure was," I laughed. "How could I forget the way you hightailed it out of here the minute the Supreme Court ruling came in? You and Marissa couldn't wait to tie the knot. The two of you were like teenage kids on prom night!"

As soon as the words left my mouth, visions of my sixteen-year-old daughter doing things I didn't want to think about sprang into my mind. I paled. Joy, on the other hand, slapped her palm against her knee and burst out laughing.

"Here's hoping Kallie's prom night isn't like my wedding night!"

"Not funny. Not funny at all," I scowled, but I had clearly walked into that one.

"Oh, and another thing," Joy added once she calmed from her fit of giggles. "Your publisher called while you were meeting with the Álvarez family."

I frowned.

"Please tell me it's good news. The delay is killing us. We need that book released soon if we want to keep the lights on around here."

"Everything is back on schedule and set to release in two weeks. The final files were sent to you for review. They should already be in your Dropbox folder."

"Awesome! That's a huge relief! Let's have a look at them, shall we?"

Joy came over to my side of the desk while I opened the link to my Dropbox. Sure enough, I found a little blue file labeled *And I Smile*—FINAL. I clicked on it as a thrill of excitement seeped into my veins. When the first image filled the screen, I couldn't stop the surge of adrenaline I always felt seeing my drawings come to life in digital format. The colors seemed to look sharper and more vibrant.

But, along with the thrill, there was also a nervous feeling. Even though I had hit multiple bestseller lists in the past, there was no guarantee I'd do it again with this particular children's book. Dahlia's Dreamers, the non-profit organization I established ten years ago, relied on the success of my stories and illustrations. The financial implications that came with a possible failure always weighed heavily on my shoulders. Since everyone here made the same salary, I also had to rely on a portion of the proceeds to substitute my personal income. Nobody was getting rich working for a non-profit.

"Wow, these look amazing!" Joy gushed. "And if I haven't already told you, I love the storyline for this one. It really hits home for me. I think you nailed it."

"Hmmm...maybe," was my only response. I stared contemplatively at the text that had been merged to flow with the illustrations.

"What's wrong?"

"I don't know. I mean, I happy with it, but I wonder if I took it too far or tackled too much at once."

"No, I don't think you did, not in the least bit." Joy shook her head vehemently. "*And I Smile* touches on every aspect, showing how prejudice is a learned behavior, yet you didn't do it in an in-your-face sort of way if you know what I mean. Don't second guess yourself. There should be more children's books like this in my opinion."

"I suppose I'm just nervous, that's all. Considering our federal funding just received a drastic cut, we can't afford poor sales with this book." I didn't add that I couldn't afford it either. Kallie's school tuition bill was due at the end of the month.

Joy moved back around the desk to reclaim her seat, then leaned forward with a knowing look.

"Cadence, have a little more faith in yourself. Everything always works out. Plus, don't forget about the upcoming gala. The tickets sold out so fast, I'm sure it will be a success. You've got an amazing thing going here. Just think of all the families Dahlia's Dreamers has put back together or all the young students who were given the opportunity to be something great. Those people would never have had a chance if it weren't for you. You're loved by so many, and the new book will do great because of that fact."

I pursed my lips tightly together but didn't respond.

Perhaps I was worrying too much. But then again, lives were at stake. People were counting on me and my team.

I glanced at the time on the top corner of my computer screen. It was going on three o'clock.

"Since Simon isn't coming, I'm going to finish up the few things I have left to do, then head out to be with Kallie. Do you mind holding the fort for the remainder of the day?"

"What are you waiting for?" Joy waved her hands in a shooting motion. "Go now! Prom is a special day for her!"

I laughed, thinking of Kallie's squeal after she had finally found the 'perfect' dress.

"Yeah, it is. She's so excited for it too," I added and began stacking the printouts of information about the Álvarez case. "I'll leave in a just a bit. I just want to get this disaster all over my desk cleaned up before I go."

"Well, don't take too long." Joy stood to leave. "Have fun beautifying tonight—not that Kallie really needs it. That girl has the face of an angel!" She smiled, but then her face drooped a little, regret evident in her eyes. "You'll text me pictures of her, right?"

Joy had never even so much as missed a birthday party for Kallie. I knew she was feeling a little bad about missing out on tonight. I offered a smile of reassurance, silently telling her I understood her predicament.

"Joy, it's your anniversary. Enjoy it! You know I'll text you. Hell, you can probably count on me to blow up your phone with a play-by-play later on. It will be just like you were there. Now, get out of here so I can wrap things up," I told her with a wink.

Once she was gone, I added the piles of papers I had collected for Simon Reed to a manila folder and placed it in the age-worn file cabinet drawer with our pending cases. Still left to sort were three other cases. Two of them were still in process, and the outlook was grim. However, the third one had closed yesterday, and it had a happy ending. I thought about the little boy who, after spending months apart, had been reunited with his parents. Their file went into the drawer labeled only with a smiley face. That was ultimately our job—to create smiles.

When I turned back to my desk, I noticed a legal document poking out from under a spiral notebook. It was an offer letter that came to me over a week ago. In an instant, all of my excitement about Kallie and her prom disappeared and I felt my stomach plummet.

I pulled it out and stared at it, the text nearly burning a hole through my heart. That's what happened every time I looked at the offer. It was for the last parcel of land my parents owned in Abingdon, Virginia. The property—all one hundred forty acres —had been left to me upon their passing over ten years ago. It had been their life and their dream until they died.

I sighed as a wave of sadness came over me.

"I still miss you so much, Momma," I whispered to the empty room.

I was barely twenty-four when my mother passed, my father following her less than a year later. Their deaths nearly crushed me, especially once I realized I lacked the knowledge and resources to keep their camp running. I was a single mother struggling to stay afloat. I had to prioritize. Unable to afford the tax burden, I eventually began to sell off pieces of the land bit by bit. I used some of the money to pay off my student loans and to start Dahlia's Dreamers. Later on, I sold more land to buy a modest house for Kallie and me, but the school district hadn't been the greatest. More land was parceled off so I could afford to send her to private schools.

Now there was only thirty-seven acres left. Kallie's school tuition and the fate of Dahlia's Dreamers hung in the balance. Despite the uncertainty of my financial future, I was hesitant to sell because of one major stipulation. The interested buyer refused to divide the property, which included the summer cottage I had lived in with my parents and the nearby lake.

My lake.

That was the real reason I couldn't bring myself to sign on the dotted line. It wouldn't just mean losing my childhood summer home. It would also mean giving up the lake. As good as the offer was, the thought of giving up my secret spot and the place where I'd matured from girl to woman nearly broke me. To me, it would be like selling a piece of my heart.

I'd always loved the lake. It held a certain layer of beauty and mystery that drew me in. I found the sultry summer air and sunsets to be magical. The way I had romanticized the place, it was no wonder why it was far too easy to fall in love there.

Suppressed memories tried to resurface. I struggled to push them away, but the effort was in vain. As much as I wanted to deny it, deep down, I knew that's what was stopping me from agreeing to the sale. A final sale would give me the closure I wasn't sure I was ready for. It would mean finally giving up *him*. It would mean all the memories we made together would end up being just that—memories.

2

FITZ

I was sitting outside of a popular Irish pub in D.C., staring absently at the Washington Monument in the distance. It was a clear day in early May. It was warm, but the high heat of summer had not yet descended on the nation's capital.

Senator Robert Cochran was sitting across from me, opening his second pack of Marlboro Reds. As he flicked his lighter to the tip of yet another cigarette, I was convinced he only wanted to meet here because the pub allowed smoking on the outdoor patio.

It really wasn't the ideal place for us to meet. I would have preferred someplace less public, such as a private conference room or a suite at the Jefferson Hotel. Cochran said my office was out of the question and I understood why he didn't want to be seen entering my building. None of them wanted to be caught there. It would signal to anyone who was watching trouble was brewing. If he was spotted, the dogs would start sniffing around. Questions would arise, prompting a headline that would read something like, "Senator Cochran Enters Office of Washington Fixer." Then I'd have an even bigger mess on my hands.

I looked around, taking stock of my surroundings. It was in between the lunch and dinner hour, so the normally crowded restaurant was near empty. Other than Cochran and me, the only other patrons were two women seated four tables away from us. They looked young, probably fresh out of college. They were professionally dressed in pantsuits and heels, smiling and talking animatedly. I could barely hear their chatter, but I heard enough to know they were discussing politics. I shook my head.

Nothing to be excited about, ladies.

The young ones were always so eager. Little did they know, ten years in D.C. would harden them. They'd lose that fight— all that hopeful ambition that made them believe they could change the world.

I glanced at Cochran. He'd noticed them as well, but he wasn't eyeing them warily as he should be. No, instead of being worried about the implications of us being seen together or the possibility of our conversation being overheard, this asshole was busy checking them out. The look on his face was all too familiar—he was trying to sum up which one he wanted to bag first.

Disgusting.

He was old enough to be their grandfather.

"Eyes over here," I hissed quietly. "That wondering eye is what you got into trouble in the first place."

Cochran looked at me, his expression stoic.

"Boy, don't lecture me. I can handle myself," he drawled out.

"If that were true, we wouldn't be sitting here right now. While I don't particularly care who you're popping Viagra for, your wife does."

That wiped the smirk off his fat, arrogant face.

Robert Cochran wasn't anything to look at, but that didn't matter to a high-priced hooker. His money had them all vying for their turn in the sack. Patricia, Cochran's wife, was not a stupid woman. After thirty years of putting up with his philandering ways, she finally had enough and hired a private investigator. Cochran was sloppy, so it didn't take any sort of stellar investigative skills to find out what he'd been up to. In a matter of days, the PI collected hundreds of incriminating photographs—ones Patricia had no problem leaking to the press if her husband didn't pay up. For a cool five million, she'd give him a quiet divorce and the Republican Party would avoid an embarrassing scandal. The problem was, Cochran didn't want to give her a single cent.

"That's why I want to hire you and your firm to fix the problem," Cochran explained. "Your father said you're the best. He brags about his son, Fitzgerald Quinn, as being the Washington Fixer. I can't let my soon to be ex-wife fuck this up for me. She's a bitch, and she knows what's at stake. It's an election year, and we can't afford to lose a single seat."

I eyed him coolly, not caring for the way he spoke about his wife, the mother of his two college-aged sons. From what I knew of Patricia, she seemed like a nice woman. She was involved in the community, actively promoting a literacy program with the wives of other U.S. Senators. In the public eye, she appeared to be the model wife of an elected official. While I may not know what it was like to be married to her, I did know appearances were everything. Because of that, I also knew there was no way I could put a positive spin on Cochran's indiscretions.

"My father is correct, I am the best. But he failed to tell you I won't take on clients who cheat on their wives with whores. I'm sorry, Senator, but you've come to the wrong guy."

I stood up to leave, but Cochran grabbed my arm.

"Don't give me that bullshit," he said in a loud whisper. "I know you've helped your father get out of a few jams in the past. Get off that high horse of yours!"

I nearly winced at his words but had been in the business long enough to know how to keep my poker face in place. I knew the jams he was referring to, but who my father was fucking wasn't any concern for Cochran. I pulled my arm away and brushed my sleeve like I was swatting away a fly. Reaching for my wallet, I tossed a twenty on the table to pay for the gin and tonic I had ordered but never drank.

"Have a good day, Senator Cochran," I said. Not giving him a second glance, I casually strolled away from the table. I was sure the old man was fuming, but I didn't look back and hailed a taxi.

"Where to, sir?" the cab driver asked.

"East End," I told him.

The driver took me along the Potomac, past the elaborate memorials, and entered the heart of the city. He slowed to a stop near The White House in order to allow a group of tourists to cross the pedestrian walk so they could gawk at the pristine white exterior. I had seen these sights a countless number of times, so for me, they had lost some of their luster.

Still, I always felt D.C. had a quiet strength, a force which was a constant reminder of being the home of the country's most powerful executive seat. With its vast monuments, lush green lawns, politicians, and hopeful wanna-be candidates crowding the cafes and streets, Washington sat proudly as the most dignified city in the nation. I knew the city by heart. While I could appreciate and understand its pulse, I also hated it. Yes, there was beauty, but there was also an underlying ruthlessness that couldn't be matched anywhere else. One had to understand that in order to survive here. Anyone who didn't would eventually become bait for the sharks.

As we got closer to the East End, I instructed the driver to pull over in front of my building on the corner of New Jersey Avenue NW. I paid the fare and climbed out. Crossing the pavement in a few short strides, I pushed through the double glass doors and went straight to the offices of Quinn & Wilkshire on the seventh floor.

When the elevator doors opened, our newly remodeled interior came into view. A fountain sat in the center of the waiting room, emitting the calming sound of running water at all hours of the day. Everything was pristine, including the black granite top reception desk and sleek leather furniture. The muted grays, creams, and burgundy accents gave the PR agency an air of confidence and power, matching that of the many clients who walked through our doors. From politicians to movie stars to prominent sports figures—we worked hard to promote our clients, making them appear successful, honest, relevant, and as exciting as possible.

Unfortunately, people rarely came to us when things were going well. Our clients usually came knocking *after* shit hit the fan. It ranged anywhere from a rising actress getting caught on camera snorting lines of coke to an athlete who may have celebrated too much and got a DWI. Despite what people say about there being no such thing as bad press, the reality proved time and again it wasn't true. Bad press was never good. Our job was to get them out of the negative spotlight with a positive public relations campaign. We did it, and we did it well.

As I approached my office, my secretary was there to greet me.

"Afternoon, Angie," I said with a small nod.

"Hello, Mr. Quinn. Um," she began nervously. "The other Mr. Quinn, your father, he's here to see you. He's in your office."

Of course, he is. Fucking Cochran probably called him.

But I didn't voice the words aloud. She might know I wouldn't be pleased to hear my father had come here unannounced, but she didn't need to know what went down today.

Appearances. It's all about appearances.

Instead of saying more, I gave her another nod and continued on through my office door. When I entered, I saw my father standing near the large, black-stained, maple bookshelf on the far-left wall. He appeared to be perusing the titles which I found to be extremely odd. I'd never seen him read a book in his life, despite his position with the United States government.

My father, Michael Fitzgerald Quinn, Senator of the Old Line State, strived for perfection. It often came out during public speaking events where he never failed to engage a crowd with the meticulousness of his words. That precision extended to his appearance as well. His cropped gray hair never went more than two weeks without a cut and his face was always smoothly shaved. Even his suit was always impeccable. Maryland, a state that normally voted democratic, seemed to buy this polished façade hook, line, and sinker. To anyone who truly knew him, it was nothing but a costume to hide the predator beneath the surface.

"Dad," I said, striding past him and taking a seat behind my desk. I refused to give him more courtesy than he deserved.

"Robert Cochran called," he said, not wasting any time getting to the point of his visit.

"I assumed that was the reason you got off your perch on Capitol Hill to come see me."

"Why aren't you handling this, Fitzgerald?"

"Because I don't want to," I stated matter-of-factly.

"Where's Devon? He's not as soft as you are. Put him on it."

It never failed. The man rarely spoke more than two sentences to me without throwing a cheap shot. I tossed him a look of impatience while I mentally counted to ten.

"Devon is in the Caribbean on a much-needed vacation, not

that I need to explain the whereabouts of my partner to you. He's been working his ass off. I won't call him back here for this bullshit, nor will I put another member of my staff on it. Fixing a mess for a slimeball politician who can't keep his dick in his pants will never be on the firm's agenda."

"Your job is to fix negative publicity. If this goes public, the whole Party will suffer!"

I sighed, annoyed he was wasting my time and fired up my computer.

"You may have painted a picture of me as Washington's Fixer, but believe it or not, my company adheres to a code of ethics," I shot back as I watched the little apple icon light up. I wasn't about to get into it with him—been there, done that. He knew why I would never take on a client like Cochran even if he'd never understand or support it because his hands were just as dirty.

"Ah, forget it. It's time for Cochran to give up his seat anyway," he conceded. "He's been getting heat from both sides of the aisle on unrelated issues a lot lately. Sure, we don't want a scandal, but at least it gives us an excuse to push him out."

I looked up, shocked he was giving in so easily. My father never went down without a fight.

"So that's it then?" I asked incredulously.

"Why argue about it? I know how you think. You're weak, despite all my efforts to toughen you up. The only reason you refuse to take his case is because of what happened between your mother and me."

My blood began to boil at the mention of my mother. The fucking bastard never missed out on a chance to bring her up. I still hated him for what he did to her, yet he loved to remind me about it at every goddamned opportunity.

"Oh, do you mean how you left her high and dry after she got sick?"

He laughed, the sound unforgiving and cruel as he sat down in the chair opposite me.

"You need to let it go. She's been gone for almost thirty years. You think I'm no better than Cochran, but there are some things you'll never understand, son."

My fingers tightened around the computer mouse under my palm.

"Get out," I hissed, fighting the instinct to shout. I was normally calm, rational—except when it came to my father. He always knew how to push the right buttons. I loosened my grip on the mouse and pretended to click through emails, needing a distraction before I pummeled the old man.

Unfortunately, he continued on.

"You think I don't know how you feel? I know you better than you care to admit, and I know how loyal you were and still are to your mother's memory." He paused and rubbed his chin contemplatively. "But then again, we could use that to our advantage. Lost your mother when you were only a child... voters may prove to be sympathetic. We'd have to conduct a poll of course. That combined with—"

"What are you talking about?" I interrupted. His ramblings were wearing on me. I just wanted him to get to the point, then get the hell out of my office. "The voters don't care about me. They only care about the politicians who end up as my clients."

"They will care a lot about you in November."

November?

I eyed him warily. My father always had a self-serving agenda, and I was beginning to think he didn't come here solely for the Cochran issue.

"Why did you really come to see me today?" I questioned cautiously.

"It won't be long before Cochran announces his resignation. His attempt to hire you was simply a last-ditch effort. He knows he's out. Once he officially resigns, there will be an open seat in Virginia. You'll be the one to fill it."

I shook my head, my suspicions confirmed.

Not this again.

He'd brought up the subject of me running for office a few times before, but I hadn't taken him seriously. However, there was something different about his expression this time around that made my insides turn cold.

"I've already told you before, I have no interest in politics."

"It doesn't matter what your interests are. You don't have a choice anymore."

I ignored his comment and waved him off.

"Doesn't Bateman already have an itch to run?" I asked, recalling an interview I caught on one of the local news channels a few months back. "Let him do it."

"Bateman is an idiot. He's too easily swayed to the other side and he's not the for sure win. I've already talked to other members of the Party. You're the sure thing, not Bateman. You have the past and family connections to support it. People vote for those who make them feel comfortable. You're it, Fitzgerald."

"I'm happy doing what I'm doing. Devon and I have a successful and lucrative business I won't neglect. Even if I wanted to, it would be impossible. The primaries are in two months. I can't put together a campaign in that short amount of time," I insisted.

"We've already got the numbers from the exploratory committee I put together," he continued on as if he hadn't heard a word I said. "The National Republican Senatorial Committee has agreed to back you. They don't want Bateman, but they also don't want to appear biased. If he decides to throw his hat into the race, they won't stop him, but he won't get their full endorsement either. Once Cochran resigns, it will be as if the race went uncontested."

"Even without my consent, you went ahead and got the ball rolling." Feeling incredulous, I sat back in my chair and shook my head. "You're really unbelievable sometimes. You think you have this all figured out, don't you?"

"Your biggest worry will be in November. Polls are showing some woman from Richmond will win the Democratic primary. She's the only one getting in the way of you taking Cochran's seat."

I leaned forward, splayed my hands across my desk, and looked him squarely in the eye.

"I'm not running," I said for the second time in under five minutes. "And if I had any desire to do so, it certainly wouldn't be for your team."

My father stood and slammed his fist on the edge of the desk.

"Damn it! Don't try to toy with me! It's time to fucking grow up, Fitzgerald!" he shouted. "Your little business is only successful because I saw to it. I let you have your fun, but game time is over! Let Devon run the show for a while. You will do this for your country and for the Party—the Party you're registered with!"

"Or else?" I asked with a cocked brow. He could rage all he wanted. I refused to show an ounce of intimidation.

He folded his arms across his chest and tilted his chin up. His anger slowly dissolved into something icy—sinister almost —as he stared down his nose at me.

"Then I'll leak your little mishap with that girl during your years at Georgetown."

I narrowed my eyes at him.

"That was years ago, and it was a tragic accident. You know it as well as I do. I'm not a kid anymore. You can't threaten me and continue to hold that over my head."

"Can't I?" He smiled a wide, toothy grin. "I think the press will eat up a story about a poor girl who drowned because of you whether it was an accident or not. Can you imagine? Washington's Fixer couldn't fix his own mess. Daddy had to bail him out. Your life will be ruined. Your business will sink. And your son will suffer from the fallout."

I paled as a feeling of dread began to seep into my bones. I didn't give a shit about what he did to me, but my son was another matter entirely. He was my life. My responsibility. My whole reason for living.

"You wouldn't do that to Austin. You can't."

"I can, and I will. And speaking of your *son*," he spat out, emphasizing the word as if it left a bitter taste in his mouth. "It's about time you find yourself a new wife. Bethany's been gone for almost eleven years now. The voters will want to see you show strong family values. More stability."

My stomach plummeted. It was as if I were watching a rerun of my life, the past constantly on repeat. I wouldn't let him do this to me again. I rolled my eyes in a weak attempt to show I wasn't rattled by his threats.

"You've got to be kidding me. Old age must be screwing with your mind. With everything I have going on, I barely have time to date, let alone think about getting married."

"Barely? When was the last time you took a woman out?"

My gaze narrowed.

"That's none of your business."

"Well, I'm making it my business now. Don't try to play me for a chump. I know why you haven't dated. You're still pining over that girl from—how long has it been now? Sixteen years? The girl from—"

"Stop. Now. You have no idea what you're talking about," I growled. "I don't date because of Austin. He doesn't need to be confused by women coming in and out of my life. You taught me all too well what that's like. I won't follow your example."

He snorted and let out another cruel laugh.

"I have a meeting scheduled with the leaders of the RNC tomorrow night. I'll have my secretary send you the details. Make sure to be there. We need to discuss campaign strategy. The clock is ticking," he warned as if I hadn't said a word. He moved toward the door to leave. The asshole actually looked unperturbed. Confident even.

Then...he left. In his eyes, the matter was settled. I sat at my desk, feeling relatively stunned as I contemplated what in the hell had happened.

I rubbed my hands over my face, the five o'clock shadow rubbing harsh against my palms. I got up from behind my desk, moved over to the wet bar, and poured myself a stiff drink. Throwing back a swig, the Johnnie Walker Black Label burned going down and warmed my insides. Now alone with my thoughts, I walked over to the window that made up the back wall and absently stared out at the traffic.

I had no intention of running for office, but my father's threats loomed. I had to think of Austin. While I managed to shield my son from my father's cruelty, I knew he wasn't stupid. At fifteen years old, I could see so much of myself in him— some good, some bad. There was a rebellious side to him that made me worry. While I felt I had a good relationship with him, we'd been at each other's throats as of late.

Goddamn teenagers.

Either way, I may be able to weather the embarrassment from a near twenty-year-old scandal, but I wasn't sure if Austin, an impressionable teenager, could handle it. I also didn't think a rigorous political campaign and the public scrutiny that came with it was a better alternative.

"Fuck this," I whispered and threw back the remaining contents of my drink. I stared at the empty glass, fighting the urge to pour another. Alcohol wasn't the answer, a fact I understood all too well.

What am I doing?

At that moment, I needed a way to push through all the madness but drowning myself in booze wasn't the answer. A brisk jog around the National Mall was the only thing that would truly clear my head. Normally, I ran in the morning when the temperature was cooler, but a good sweat would be the perfect therapy after listening to my father's ultimatums.

Loosening my tie, I headed into the private bathroom attached to my office to change into running gear. As I stripped out of the button-down Calvin Klein dress shirt, I caught sight of my upper arm tattoo in the mirror. I stared at it as my father's words from earlier filled my mind.

"You're still pining over that girl..."

When he said it, I almost laughed. He didn't know about the many nights I wasted after Bethany died, drowning in a bottle of scotch and fucking any nameless body who was willing. I wasn't mourning the death of my wife like I should have been. Instead, I used the women and booze like they had the power to erase what I had truly lost. It didn't take long for me to realize I would never rid myself of the emptiness I'd felt ever since the day I left behind my first and only love.

Memories I struggled to suppress for years came to the forefront—memories of Cadence. The image of her face clouded my vision. As much as I tried, there was no forgetting a face like hers.

Our beginning may have been common and possibly forgotten if it had been anyone but her. With her long golden hair and the spark in her striking emerald eyes, no one could say Cadence was pretty. She was too stunning to use such a mundane word. Cadence wasn't just pretty. She was beautiful. And unlike most women I had come across in my thirty-nine years on this earth, her beauty wasn't only skin deep. She was unapologetic and had an enthusiasm for life that could match no other. She was delicate, yet so driven and determined.

Even at twenty-two, I knew she'd be the woman I'd spend the rest of my life looking for, but never be able to hang onto. She was exquisite—and she was still my biggest regret. We were so young, and our time together had been too short. It was one summer. That's all I was able to have with her. But it was the summer that had changed my life.

3

CADENCE

"Oh, Kallie! Just look at you!" I choked, blinking back the tears welling in my eyes. "You look so pretty!"

My beautiful daughter smiled as she descended the stairs of our modest Cape Cod style house. Her hair was swept up into a French twist, leaving just a few strands of blond hair to curl around her face. Her makeup, although she had spent an hour perfecting it, was subtle and accented her already stunning features.

After stepping off the bottom step, Kallie slowly spun in a circle. Her pale blue gown twirled around her, making the tiny sequence details sparkle in the light shining in through the bay window of the living room. If she had wings, one would swear she was an angel sent from heaven.

"Don't move," I said and quickly moved to the end table. I wanted to capture her just as she was, needing to freeze this moment in time. I opened up the drawer and rifled through the contents. TV remote controls, old batteries, and power cords—

none of which I was looking for. "Damn it. I could have sworn it was in here."

"What are you looking for?" Kallie asked.

"My good camera. I think it might be upstairs in my nightstand."

"Mom," Kallie whined. "Like, you already took a hundred pics with your phone. My friends will be here any minute."

"Yes, but the phone quality isn't as good. Let me just go upstairs and grab my camera. We have time. The limo isn't supposed to be here for another ten minutes."

"Ugh," she grunted.

"Oh, shush. It will only take me a second to grab it," I told her and raced up the stairs to my bedroom.

Sure enough, as soon as I opened the drawer, I found the expensive Nikon laying on top of a bunch of other paraphernalia. It had been a rare splurge for me, an impulse purchase I made when Kallie had begun high school. It came from a sudden realization I was running out of time. It was strange. When she was little, I used to wish for her to grow older. I wanted her to talk, walk, and feed herself. The days always seemed so long, yet her childhood had gone by remarkably fast. Now, I would give anything to have that time back. Soon she'd be a legal adult, ready to embark on the next phase of her life. Photographs would never replace the memories we shared together, but at least I would have the pictures to look back on.

I picked up the camera and was about to close the drawer, but what had been under the camera caught my eye. I paused and reached for it. It was a Mother's Day card Kallie had made for me when she was in elementary school. If memory served me right, she was eight years old when she made it.

Slowly lowering myself to sit on the edge of the bed, I stared at the faded pink construction paper. I suddenly felt very old even though I was barely thirty-five. It seemed like it was only yesterday when she came home from school with this card. She had been so excited. It had been a Friday, but she couldn't hold out until Sunday to give it to me. However, she quickly found herself disappointed come Mother's Day when she realized she didn't have a surprise to give me. Determined to make it up to me, she almost started a toaster fire attempting to make me breakfast in bed.

I smiled at the memory. It was so like Kallie. Even as a child, she always put other people first and I was proud to call her my daughter. It was hard to believe she was headed off to her first prom. Although she assured me her date was only a friend, I still worried. She was growing up way too fast.

"Mom! The limo just pulled up!" Kallie called, breaking me away from my thoughts.

"I'm coming, I'm coming," I answered and stood to make my way back down the stairs. "Hold your horses. Don't go rushing out the door. Your date should come in and introduce himself."

When I reached the bottom of the steps, I caught Kallie rolling her eyes.

"You know I love you, mom, but geez-Louise. You call yourself a feminist, but you have some really old-fashioned ideas sometimes."

"There's nothing wrong with being courted properly. It's a sign of respect," I countered.

"You did *not* just say 'courted,' did you?" Her eyes went wide with disbelief.

"Okay, okay! You got me there," I laughed. "Maybe I am a little old fashioned at times. What can I say? I'm your mom and you're going to prom. It's my job to worry about whether a boy is treating you with respect."

"I've told you like a thousand times. He's only a friend from my French class. He's doing me a favor because I didn't have a date. Besides, he's a year younger than me. I can't date a sophomore! It would be like breaking the rules or something. Girls aren't supposed to go out with younger guys!"

Tongue in cheek, I smirked.

"Is that so?"

"Yes, my friend Gabby said—"

The doorbell rang, interrupting whatever she was going to say. I barely had a moment to react. Kallie was at the door in a flash.

"Hi," I heard her say after she opened it.

"Hey, Kallie. Wow, you look great!" said a male voice. I couldn't see his face because Kallie was blocking him from view. I moved over to the door, needing to take stock of the boy who was here to take my baby girl out. When Kallie heard me come up beside her, she made the introductions.

"Mom, this is Austin. Austin, my mom."

"It's a pleasure to meet you, ah...Ms. Riley," he said with a shy smile.

I began to return his grin but faltered. There was something familiar about him. It was strange. He reminded me of...

I blinked twice, trying to shake off an unsettling sense of déjà vu. I slowly extended my hand to shake his.

"Austin, it's nice to meet you too."

My words were hesitant, cautious. I knew his face from somewhere. Those eyes. Piercing gray with flecks of dark. That crooked grin. The hair was a shade lighter, but...

No. It can't be. I'm just feeling nostalgic from stumbling upon the Mother's Day card.

"My mom wanted to take more pictures," Kallie said to him. "Let's go ask everyone to get out of the limo so we can get a group shot."

I blinked again.

Yes, pictures. I need to take pictures.

I shook my head to clear it and followed Kallie and Austin outside. After the group of twelve teenagers from St. Aloysius

Prep assembled into a line, I snapped a few pictures of them all dressed up in their tuxedos and gowns. They stood formally for some while others were posed so I could capture silly shots of them jumping or making goofy faces at one another. With every picture, I tried discreetly to get a better look at Austin through the viewfinder. It was so strange, I felt like I had been catapulted through some sort of twisted time warp. A sensation of dread began to settle over me.

Kallie and her friends started to get antsy, eager to begin their big night. I had stalled them long enough. I lowered the camera and shooed them off toward the limo.

"Have a good time!" I called out to the group as they began to climb back into the waiting car. Kallie flashed me a beaming smile which only intensified the knot forming in my stomach. On impulse, I motioned for her to come over to me.

"What's up?" she asked hurriedly.

"Have fun. No drinking. Behave and be safe." I pecked her cheek with a light kiss.

"Come on, mom. You know me. I always behave."

"It's not you I'm worried about," I said, glancing over at Austin. Kallie caught the direction of my gaze and rolled her eyes.

"Relax. You don't need to worry about Austin," she tried to assure.

"You'll be home by eleven?"

"On the nose!"

She gave me a brief hug before turning back to join her friends, but I caught her by the arm. I had to know if I was just imagining things.

"Kallie, what's Austin's last name?"

Her brow furrowed in confusion at my question.

"Quinn. Why?"

My stomach plummeted to my feet and my heart began to race.

No. No, no, no!

The odds had to be a million to one.

It was inconceivable.

The chances were just too great.

A picture from a newspaper clipping I had saved years ago flashed in my mind. I knew Fitz had settled somewhere in the D.C. area, but I stopped following his whereabouts after Kallie was born. I had to. It was the only way I could survive emotionally.

But now this.

It could just be a coincidence, but deep down I knew it wasn't. It was possible—even probable. The similarities in physical appearance between Austin and Fitz were too close to dismiss as being a fluke. And they shared the same last name.

This can't actually be happening to me. Not now. Not after all this time.

As far as Kallie knew, I didn't know who her father was. I lied to protect her, and I didn't know how to tell her the truth at that moment. We were close, but she may not forgive me for this. It was her prom night, and the seventeen-year-old secret was about to ruin it and destroy every other belief she held dear.

"Mom, are you okay?" Kallie asked, her concern evident.

I looked at my daughter. So young and innocent. Just like I was once upon a time.

God help me. What do I do?

I gripped her forearms tightly, fighting the overwhelming urge to vomit.

"Kallie, promise me that Austin is just a friend."

Her eyes widened as if I had just grown antlers.

"Yeah! Chillax, Mom. You're way too wound up about this. It's only prom. What are you going to do in a couple of weeks when I go away to Montreal for the French class trip? I'll be fine tonight and be back before you know it."

A flash of what she said earlier about Austin came to mind. In a split second, my already frayed nerves seemed to completely tear apart.

"Kallie, you said Austin was in your French class. Is he going on the trip too?"

"Mom, stop. Maybe when I get home tonight, we can stay up late and watch an old musical or something. With popcorn? Just like we used to when I was a little kid? After all, I am sixteen going on seventeen..." she trailed off in a sing-song voice, repeating the lyrics to a song from *The Sound of Music*. She leaned in to hug me once more, but neither her words nor her embrace made me feel any better.

I looked at the limo. All of her friends had already piled inside, just waiting on Kallie.

"Sure, honey. Sounds like fun," I responded absently, feeling like I was in the Twilight Zone.

I didn't stop her when she finally stepped away. Perhaps I should have, but I didn't know how to explain it. There was no good way to tell my daughter, out of all the people in the whole wide world, she was going to the prom with her half-brother.

4

CADENCE

Once the limo pulled away, I went back into the house. Feeling as though I were in a trance, I somehow managed to put one foot in front of the other and lumbered to the kitchen. I thought about calling Joy since she knew the truth about everything, but I didn't want to be a burden while she was celebrating her anniversary. Instead, I went to the fridge in search of a drink—preferably a strong one.

Unfortunately, all I found was a half empty bottle of champagne that was left over from New Year's Eve nearly six months earlier and a few bottles of beer normally reserved for guests. I sighed and made a mental note to start stocking more alcohol in the house. Deciding a beer would be better than flat champagne, I popped the cap off and made my way upstairs to my bedroom.

On the way, I stopped in Kallie's bedroom to turn off the light she had left on. As usual, it looked like a hurricane had blown through and left clothes strewn about in its wake. I navigated through the maze until I reached the lamp. As I went to turn it off, I caught sight of the worn old teddy bear sitting at the foot of her bed. She'd hung on to it ever since she was a little girl, never once feeling teenage embarrassment over keeping her childhood companion in her bed. Love and adoration for my daughter pumped through me. She was so strong, never willing to compromise herself to please others, and it made me so proud. That pride brought a smile to my face as I reached to turn off the lamp switch before heading back out to my own bedroom.

Once there, I pulled open the door to my closet and reached for the shoebox tucked away on the top shelf. I needed to be absolutely sure before I had a full-blown panic attack over what might just be a coincidence or a faulty memory. Inside the box were letters I had written to Fitz while I was pregnant with Kallie but never mailed. I don't know why I kept them over the years. Perhaps I knew I'd be faced with something like this one day. The letters were the only proof and justification I had for keeping such a secret. Kallie wasn't the only one in the dark.

Fitz didn't know about her either.

Settling onto the bed, I placed the beer on the nightstand and blew the dust off the top of the box. Slowly, I lifted the lid. A bundle of envelopes secured in a rubber band lay on top. I pulled out the stack and set it to the side. Underneath were newspaper clippings and the playbill from *Singin' in the Rain*. I opened it up and flipped to the back to find the group photo of all the staff members from Camp Riley. Having memorized Fitz's location in the photo years ago, I easily located him and ran my finger over his image. I stared at the yellowing photo for a long while. It was a face I hadn't seen in so long, yet never managed to erase from my memory. Then tonight, that same face showed up on my doorstep to take Kallie to prom.

I placed the picture back inside the box and sifted through the other contents, spotting a folded square of paper.

Chinese Fortune Teller.

I didn't need to open the origami Fitz had given me on that final day to know what each fortune said. I had memorized the words he had written long ago.

Sunsets will always belong to you.

When it's dark, I'll remember you to find the light.

You will forever hold my heart.

Leaving you will always be my biggest regret.

Swallowing the lump beginning to form in my throat, I reached for the stack of envelopes. The rubber band, brittle from age, snapped apart when I tried to remove it, causing the letters to fall over my lap. It was no matter. Although they'd been stacked in the order they were written, I remember dating each and every one of them. I opened the envelope resting on top of the now messy pile. Pulling the lined paper from within, I began to read. It was the last letter I had written to Fitz.

To the keeper of my heart,

I shouldn't start out this letter by addressing you that way, especially since this is more like a Dear John than anything else. Or maybe it's not a Dear John since we aren't even together. Either way, I can't help but still call you the keeper of my heart because that's who you'll always be to me—no matter what life has dictated for us.

Our daughter came into the world one week ago today. I named her Kalliope because the sound of her cry on the day she was born was like music to my ears. The name comes from Greek mythology and means "beautiful voice". Perhaps I'm more in tune with my mother's musical talents than I had originally thought.

Kallie, as I've come to nickname her, is the prettiest baby I've ever seen. I wish you could meet her, but just as sure as I'll never send you this letter, I know you'll never get to. I saw a picture of you, your father, and your wife in the paper today. It was taken at a political function in support for your father. From the sounds of it, you'll soon be the son of a United States Senator. You looked so proud in the photo, and I felt my heart bursting with admiration for your strength to endure a life you had little choice over. But the photo also made me sad. You see, I also couldn't help but notice your wife's small baby bump.

I wish things could have been different for us, but I accept the choice I've made. I will never regret the time I had with you. It was special and will forever be cherished. However, I've come to realize I can't keep holding on to the hope perhaps you'll rebel against your father and come back to me. I need to let you go. Being with me would only cause a scandal for your family. That sort of attention wouldn't be fair to you. You don't need your past mistakes thrown into the limelight—even if it what happened at Georgetown was a tragic accident. It wouldn't be fair to your unborn child, nor would it be fair to me or Kallie.

And most importantly, I realized you were right about me. I don't deserve to be "the other woman," and I certainly don't want Kallie to grow up with a cloud of illegitimacy over her head. That's why I will never tell you of her existence. That's why this will be my last letter. I have to think about Kallie now. My daughter. My new reason for living. She is my priority, just as your priority should be your new family. I need to provide a life for her even if it means creating a life without you in it.

Tears blurred my vision and I could barely read my own signature at the bottom. The letter slipped from my fingers and fell onto my lap. What I just read, while true, were ramblings of a broken-hearted teenager who had been forced to grow up too soon. I had been too open and trusting. First love was naïve. I didn't hold back on the love I gave but willingly gave him every ounce inside of me. And he took it all—leaving no space for another man to move in. My head swam with memories as I hastily wiped the tears away.

I searched through the shoebox once again, needing to locate the newspaper article that had forced my decision all those years ago. Now, the article could potentially be confirmation Austin was exactly who I suspected. It wasn't hard to find among the neatly folded clippings. The bold headline shone like a beacon in the night.

SENATOR QUINN PUSHES FOR LANDMARK TAX REFORM BILL WITHIN FIRST 90-DAYS

I skimmed through the article, not particularly interested in recapping details about a bill that ultimately threw our country into a recession. I was more interested in the details about the photo alongside the article.

My eyes scanned the picture. The freeze frame was of Fitz, his father, and Fitz's young pregnant wife. Reporters were all around them with microphones trained on Senator Fitzgerald as they descended the steps of the Capitol Building. My heart constricted as an age-old jealousy welled up in me from seeing her again. She was definitely pretty, but that's not why I resented her. I didn't like the dark-haired woman because she got to have the life I had only dreamed about.

What was her name again?

As sharp as my memory was about that time in my life, I somehow managed to block out that little detail.

Forcing my gaze away from the photo, I ran my finger along the text of the article, stopping when I found the passage I was looking for.

"I CAN TELL YOU WE HAVE A CONTINUED INTEREST IN BUILDING ON THE SUCCESS OF THE BILL. WE ARE DEDICATED TO IMPROVING THE TAX CODE FOR HARDWORKING FAMILIES AND AMERICA'S SMALL BUSINESSES," QUINN SAID IN A STATEMENT. WHEN PUSHED FOR FURTHER DETAILS, NONE WERE FORTHCOMING. INSTEAD, SENATORIAL CANDIDATE QUINN DEFLECTED TO HIS SOON-TO-ARRIVE GRANDSON, USING THE OPPORTUNITY TO BOAST ABOUT HOW

MUCH THE REPUBLICAN PARTY IS INVESTED IN THEIR CANDIDATE. "WHILE I'D LOVE TO TALK MORE ABOUT THIS, I HAVE A PRIOR ENGAGEMENT TO GET TO. MY SON'S WIFE IS EXPECTING A BABY BOY IN A FEW MONTHS. THE WIVES OF SENATE REPUBLICANS ARE EXCITED ABOUT LITTLE AUSTIN AND HAVE PLANNED A BABY SHOWER."

Austin.

That was all the confirmation I needed. There was no denying it. The boy who had shown up on my doorstep was, in fact, Fitz's son. I closed my eyes, took a deep breath, and pinched the bridge of my nose. Exhaling, I slowly looked up to the ceiling.

Did I make a mistake all those years ago? Should I have told him? Should I have fought harder for Fitz?

I didn't know what the answers were, but I was suddenly faced with having to justify my actions. I thought I had done the right thing at the time. I had my parents to help me through everything while Fitz had no one. My parents supported my choice. I thought I had taken the unselfish path, but now I wasn't so sure. What I once viewed as a noble decision looked like it was about to blow up in my face.

I glanced down at the now lukewarm bottle of beer I hadn't touched and followed the lines of condensation pooled around the base. A small stream of water was slowly making its way to the edge of the nightstand. There was no rhyme or reason to the pattern. It just moved closer to the edge. Water always found a way. I wished my life could be as simple, to have that gravitational force to push me toward a destination.

I was so confused. Seventeen years ago, I relied on my parents for advice. Now I sat alone, searching for guidance that would never come.

5

CADENCE

I sat at my desk on Monday morning with Joy sitting across from me, her face aghast as I finished telling her about the weekend. The knot of dread that had formed in my stomach on Friday night was still there, but it was worsening with each passing hour.

Kallie had come home from the prom on time, just as she promised, and we had stayed up until after two in the morning watching our favorite musicals. I picked out *Newsies* to watch first, the story loosely based on the New York City Newsboys' Strike of 1899. The way I looked at it, nobody could resist a young Christian Bale. She picked the second musical of the night—*Mamma Mia!* Of all the things she could have picked... That was just my luck. I squirmed uncomfortably through the entire second movie, the plotline hitting way too close to home. Now I couldn't get the damn theme song from the movie soundtrack out of my head.

There were plenty of opportunities between then and now

to tell her about Austin and the truth about her father, but I chickened out every time the words began to form on my tongue. I just couldn't tell her. As a result, I got to listen to a lecture from Joy.

"Cadence, this is bad. Senator Quinn is his father—the man who stands firmly against everything Dahlia's Dreamers stands for. When he finds out about Kallie and discovers what you do for a living, I'd like to say maybe he'd soften his stance, but the man just seems ruthless." Joy paused and shuddered. "Political implications aside, you need to go to Fitz. It's long past time."

"And say what? 'Hey, remember me? That stupid girl you banged one summer seventeen years ago? Well, you're my baby daddy.' Come on, Joy. He probably doesn't even remember me. I don't need to go to Fitz, but I do need to tell Kallie."

"So, why haven't you yet? She has to know before something crazy happens. Sweet Jesus! Can you imagine what would happen if she ended up dating Austin?"

I pressed my lips together in a tight line.

"Trust me, it's all I've thought about for days. I just don't know how to tell her. I went for a run yesterday morning. I needed some 'me time' to clear my head. It didn't work, so I went for another run in the afternoon. I'm sure the guys tending to the lawn around the Washington Monument thought I was nuts. I must have passed them twenty times."

"What were you doing all the way over there?" Joy asked with a furrowed brow.

"There's construction in my neighborhood and they have all the sidewalks blocked off. Running the Mall has been easier. Anyway, I was all set to tell Kallie when I returned home, but then I froze up."

Joy shook her head.

"I still think you should tell Fitz. It's not only Kallie. Austin should know too. What if he has feelings for her?"

I dropped my head and banged it on the desk.

"Did you have to remind me of that too?" I groaned.

"Hey, I know you're in a tough spot. I'm just trying to help you see it from all angles so that—"

"Hello? Is anyone there?" a female voice called from outside my office door. Joy stopped speaking and we both turned to see who it was. When nobody came in, I stood and walked out into the corridor.

A woman with a little girl was peering into the worn wooden office doors down the hall. The tiny child held a raggedy looking doll tightly to her chest. She looked around, seeming confused as the woman who held her hand dragged her from door to door.

"Can I help you?" I asked.

"Oh!" she startled. "I'm sorry. Nobody was at the desk, so I decided to see if I could find someone in one of the offices. I should have made an appointment first, but I-I couldn't wait. I need to speak with someone right away."

She had a subtle accent I couldn't quite place, but it sounded Spanish in origin. It was hard to tell with the way her voice cracked. Her expression was panicked, desperate almost. It was a look I knew all too well.

"Please, come in and have a seat," I told her. Once she stepped inside, I motioned for her to sit at the small round table in the corner. "I'm sorry there wasn't anyone to greet you. My secretary is currently out on maternity leave. The rest of the staff has just been handling things while she's out. What can we do for you?"

The woman looked back and forth between Joy and me.

"My...my name is-is Emilia Garcia," she stuttered.

Afraid. They always come in here afraid.

"It's a pleasure to meet you." I took a seat across from her at the table. Over the years, I'd found it less intimidating for new clients if I sat here, rather than behind my desk. It seemed to make them feel more like we were on equal turf. I stretched out my hand for her to shake, hoping to put her more at ease. It was cool and clammy, a sure sign the woman was a nervous wreck. "I'm Cadence Riley, and this is my colleague, Joy Martin."

She nodded to Joy, then began to fiddle with the hem of her bright pink shirt.

"I, um...I'm from Richmond, Virginia."

"You're quite a way from home," I noted. If the look of anxiety on her face wasn't already enough, knowing she traveled over two hours, with a small child, without a scheduled appointment told a story about how desperate she was.

"Yes, I am," she admitted. Then she looked at me with terrified dark brown eyes, reminding me of a deer caught in headlights. "Again, I'm so sorry for showing up unannounced. I–I just don't know where to begin."

"Ms. Garcia, every person who walks through our doors comes here for one thing. Why don't you just start from the beginning?"

She looked down nervously at the little girl.

"Oh, um. My daughter. I don't like to..." she trailed off.

I looked at the little girl sitting on her mother's lap. She couldn't have been more than five years old, and I understood her hesitation. I stood up from my chair and knelt down in front of the child.

"What's your name?" I softly asked.

"Mayra," she responded shyly.

"Why, hello Mayra. It's so nice to meet you. My name is Cadence. How old are you?" She held up five fingers.

"No, no. You're not five yet," her mother chided, bending Mayra's thumb down so she only held up four. "You don't turn five for another few weeks."

I smiled, recalling how Kallie always liked to pad her age by a few months.

"Almost five? Wow! You're practically a big girl! You're not too big to color though, are you?" I asked. Her brown eyes widened with excitement as she shook her head. "Well then, if it's okay with your mom, would you like to go with Ms. Joy to find a coloring book and crayons?"

She looked up at her mother expectantly.

"Go ahead. Remember your manners," Emilia told her with a nod.

Mayra beamed and jumped off Emilia's lap. Joy walked over to her and took hold of her little hand. Once they were safely out of earshot, I returned to my seat and reached out across the table to take Emilia's hand in mine.

"Ms. Garcia," I began.

"Please, call me Emilia."

"Emilia, I can tell you're nervous. Don't be. Whatever it is, we're here to help you."

She afforded me a small smile.

"I've heard others talk of your kindness. That's why I knew I had to come here. You have to help m–me." Her voice cracked again on the last word, and it broke my heart. My only hope was that I *could* help her. Sometimes, it was too late.

"Why don't you start from the beginning, and we'll go from there?"

She swallowed and took a deep breath.

"It's about my fiancé. My daughter's father. They-they took him!"

Then she began a tale I had heard a countless number of times. With each time, the names and places were different, but the story was always the same.

Emilia's fiancé, Andrés Mendez, moved from Ecuador to the United States with his family when he was three years old. He, his younger sister, and his parents were all undocumented immigrants—a fact Andrés never knew until he was seventeen years old and preparing to attend college. He needed a social security number to apply for student loans. That was when his parents first told him the truth about where he came from.

"Andrés is so smart," Emilia said with pride in her voice. "As it turned out, he didn't need to get loans. He was awarded an undergraduate academic scholarship to attend Harvard."

"That's amazing!"

"Yes," she agreed, but then her tone turned sad once again. "He applied for a student visa and was all set to head off to Massachusetts. But that summer, I became pregnant with Mayra. I urged him to still go, but Andrés refused to leave me. He ended up going to Virginia Tech to study engineering instead. My parents were furious, but his parents didn't understand what he was giving up. They never even heard of Harvard until Andrés was accepted into the school."

I reached over to my desk and grabbed a notepad to begin taking notes. I scribbled down a few basics.

Smart. Accepted to Harvard on scholarship. Mayra.

"Emilia, are you undocumented as well?"

"No, I was born here. My mother was born in El Salvador, and my father was born in the States. She eventually became a naturalized citizen years after they were married."

"Did Andrés end up finishing college?"

"Thankfully, he did. It wasn't easy though. While he attended school, I lived at home. My parents watched Mayra while I worked to pay his school bills. Andrés usually took the Metro bus to his campus, but sometimes I would drive him when I wasn't working. At the time, because of his immigration status, he couldn't get a license."

No license. Has family support.

Having worked my way through school as a single mother, I wasn't sure if I could have done it without my parents' help. I recognized the importance of family support better than most.

"I can imagine how difficult it must have been. So, what happened next?"

"Right before Andrés graduated, we made plans to move in together. We wanted to get married first but couldn't afford a nice wedding with only my income. Andrés needed to find a job. The Dream Act had just been passed a few years before. Since he qualified, I encouraged him to fill out the DACA paperwork. I thought it was a good idea. It would mean he could get his driver's license, apply for work, and we wouldn't have to fear possible deportation anymore—and I would get to have my dream wedding. Maybe that part was selfish of me. I don't know. It took some convincing, but he finally did it. Now, I can't help but feel like it was the wrong thing to do."

"Why is that?"

"With all due respect, you know what's happening in the world. Too many in this county don't care about people like Andrés although I'll never understand why. He's a hardworking man—a good man," she spat out bitterly.

"I'm sorry about what's happening in our country, Emilia. I hope you know not everyone thinks that way. Did he get a job after he graduated?"

"Oh, of course! He's a mechanical engineer at Advanced Solutions—or at least, he was. I'm not sure what will happen now." She sniffled, and I could tell she was fighting tears. "Anyway, Andrés hated that I worked to pay his school bills, but he also knew finishing college and getting a good paying job was the best way for us to provide a good life for Mayra. He applied and the DACA application was approved. Shortly after, he landed his job at AS and got his driver's license. We found an apartment in Richmond, and he insisted I quit my job to stay at home to care for our daughter. Things were finally looking up. Until..."

Engineer. Holds a job. Recognizes family stability. Contributing member of society.

I scribbled the notes while I waited for Emilia to go on. She shook her head, seeming lost in thought and looked down at her lap. She began to fidget with the hem of her shirt again as a single tear trickled down her cheek.

"Until what, Emilia?"

"Andrés, Mayra, and I took a day trip to Andrés parents' house in Fairfax. It was Sunday and his mother was making pupusas, Mayra's favorite meal. We were running late due to traffic on I-95 which caused us to be in a rush to get there. Andrés was the driver. He rolled through a stop sign on his parent's street. Unfortunately, a police car was coming in the opposite direction. The officer saw it happen and pulled us over."

I knew where her story was going before she even finished. She was from Virginia, the second state in the nation to implement an agreement with the Federal government to participate in Immigration and Customs Enforcement Secure Communities program. The program was designed to create coordination between local law enforcement and the Department of Homeland Security. If an arrest was made, fingerprints were automatically run through the databases of the FBI and Homeland Security.

In the end, it would show Andrés was a DACA recipient.

"Emilia, where is Andrés now?"

She choked back a sob.

"The officer interrogated us about being so far from home, and Andrés was brought down to the police station for more questioning. He was released within a few hours but was given a traffic ticket and a court date. I went with him to court. Andrés was found guilty of the traffic violation for failure to come to a complete stop. He was given a fine to pay, which we paid before leaving. When we exited the courthouse, a man in uniform called out to Andrés by his first and last name. We didn't expect the man to be an ICE agent. There were three of them in total, just waiting for us. Andrés was detained right then and there." She stared back at me with a look of bewilderment, almost as if she couldn't believe her own story. "It took me two weeks to find out where they had taken him. Currently, he's being held by the D.C. Department of Corrections. Deportations proceedings have already begun—and all because he failed to stop at a stop sign."

6

FITZ

My alarm went off at five on Tuesday. After ensuring Austin was set for school, I headed out for my morning run, leaving myself plenty of time to be to the office by eight. As my feet pounded the pavement, sweat beaded on my neck and dripped down the length of my spine. I paused at the Lincoln Memorial to stretch my calf muscles before beginning the second lap of the four-mile run. Old Abe looked lost in thought, basking in the light of the early morning sun as he stared across the Reflecting Pool at the Washington Monument. I imagined his expression matched my own. My mind was in turmoil, conflicted over my father's threats. I didn't know if he had the balls to follow through and there was a lot at stake.

I was supposed to meet with members of the RNC this past Saturday night. I bailed, and now my father was on a warpath. It didn't matter. He might think I'm weak, but he was sadly mistaken. I was no longer the pushover I once was. I had allowed him to inflict enough damage on my life and I wasn't about to let history repeat itself.

I saw a flash of movement in the corner of my eye and glanced up from the lunge position I was in. From around the corner, a blond wearing tight running gear emerged, jogging in the opposite direction from where I had come. It wasn't uncommon to see another jogger. Many people ran the Mall this time of the morning. I returned to finishing my stretch, then stood to shake out my arms. Ready to begin the next lap, I started out in a measured pace, slowly closing the distance between me and the female jogger.

As I passed her, my steps seemed to falter. I blinked, struggling with the image of the woman who had just run by me.

I stopped running and looked back. She hadn't slowed her steps, but she was looking over her shoulder—at me. When she saw I had stopped, she quickly turned away and seemed to increase her pace.

"No, it's not her," I said aloud to myself.

I shook my head. The stress I was under was causing me to see things. But still, as I watched her petite form get further and further away from me, I couldn't shake the nagging feeling it *was* her—the girl who had haunted my dreams ever since I was twenty-two years old. Impulsively, I turned and began to run after her. I had to know. If it wasn't her, I'd just make up some excuse about mistaken identity and be on my way.

She was fast, I'd give her that much. I was in a full out run and I'd barely closed the gap between us. Much to my dismay, she veered off the path and ducked around the wall at the Korean Memorial, disappearing from sight.

Fuck!

When I approached the wall, I looked around. Early rising tourists roamed the area, snapping pictures of the statues created to commemorate the forgotten war. I scanned the area again. She was nowhere to be found. It was like she vanished off the face of the earth.

I'm chasing a goddamned ghost.

Convinced I had completely lost my mind, I decided to abandon the rest of my workout routine. I'd left my Audi parked off 14th Street. The shortest way back to it was to cut along the path that would take me through Ash Woods.

And that's where I found her.

She was approaching the steps of the D.C. War Memorial. Careful to stay out of sight, I crept around to the opposite side of the round monument. I watched as she sat down on the steps and pulled out what appeared to be a cell phone. From this angle, I couldn't see her face, only the back of her head. Her hair—the color a golden blond that brought me back nearly two decades—was pulled back into a braid. Another thing that brought me back. Staring at the woven shades of pale yellow and gold, I knew it had to be her. Only *she* had hair like that.

I could hear her speaking to someone on the other end of the call. She had the phone on speaker mode, so the conversation was loud and clear.

"For the love of God," said the voice on the other end of the line. "Girl, do you have any idea what time it is?"

"Oh, shush," the blond said. Her voice was crisp yet feminine. And so fucking familiar. "I know it's early but listen up. This is major. I saw him."

"Saw who?"

"Fitz!" she hissed my name, making me all but certain this woman was, in fact, the woman from my dreams.

"Okay, now I'm awake. What do you mean you saw Fitz? Are you sure?"

"Yes–er, well. No. His hair was a bit longer but... yes, I'm sure it was him."

"Where did you see him, Cadence?"

Bingo. It is her.

A wave of satisfaction came over me before another thought hit me in the chest like a sledgehammer.

Cadence. It's really her, flesh and blood and just a few steps away from me.

Memories of hot summer nights flashed before my eyes. I saw her again, by the lake with her green eyes sparkling and hair shimmering beneath the light of a fading sunset. I could almost feel her in my arms—even now. The warmth of her embrace, the way she whispered my name when I kissed her...

Cadence began to speak again, ripping me away from a time long past.

"I'm on my morning run," I heard her explain to the person on the phone. "He was out running too. I ran right by him, but I'm not sure if he knew it was me."

"Did you talk to him?"

"Are you crazy?" Cadence shrieked, then seemed to catch herself. She glanced around nervously for a moment and I had to duck down to stay hidden. When she spoke again, her voice was noticeably lower, and I had to strain to hear her. "Seriously, Joy. What are the odds of seeing him jogging the Mall after all this time? And especially now!"

Joy. The African American girl who worked at the store with Cadence.

I smiled to myself, pleased for some strange reason over the fact they'd remained friends after all this time.

"This is spooky—as in you-need-to-go-see-a-psychic kind of spooky," Joy said. "I don't know, hun. The stars seem to be aligning in a really weird way. It doesn't matter how long it's been. You need to tell him."

"Oh, God. I don't know if I can do this!"

"Well, something is telling you it's time. There have just been too many coincidences."

"You're right. I can do this. No sweat," Cadence replied, but her tone was bordering on sarcastic.

"Good. I'm glad it's settled. Now I'm going back to bed. I don't need to be at work for another two hours."

"Wait, Joy–" She stopped short, looked down at the phone, and swore. "Damn it!"

She stood up and rapidly began to pace back and forth, appearing lost in her thoughts. I followed the lines of her petite body. She looked good, really good actually. Her curves were more pronounced, her breasts and hips shapelier than I remembered yet still slender and fit. The body I was looking at belonged to a woman, not the young girl I had fallen in love with. Still, despite the years that had passed, I itched to reach out and touch her.

I shouldn't have eavesdropped on her conversation, but the minute I heard my name, I couldn't help myself. I was curious about what they were talking about and what it was she was supposed to tell me.

And I was very curious about her.

She was the girl who had rocked my world seventeen years ago so much so, I'd rarely thought about another woman since —and that included the years I spent married. As I debated over coming out of my hiding spot to reveal myself, I realized the irony of the current situation. I was spying on her, just like I had on that first day I saw her by the lake. Now here I stood today. Perhaps history does, in its own way, repeat itself. It was up to me to change its course.

"Cadence," I called out as I moved from behind the monument.

She jumped a mile and spun around, her hand going to her chest.

"You scared the shit out of me!"

"I'm sorry. I didn't mean to," I apologized as I approached her. My memory didn't do her justice. She was even more beautiful than I remembered, nearly causing me to gasp in disbelief. I didn't think it was possible for her to be more stunning than she once was. I cleared my throat. "I must say, it's fancy meeting you here."

Recovering from the shock of my sudden appearance, she seemed to remember herself.

"Yeah, ah... fancy that. I um..." she faltered. "I actually need to be off. I was just about to start my jog back."

"Wait," I said and reached out to grab her arm. When my palm made contact with her skin, she froze. So did I as the very air seemed to sizzle. I almost couldn't speak or unscramble my brain enough to move. It was the first time I'd touched her in more than seventeen years. My throat became ridiculously dry, and I had to clear it before I could speak again. "It's been a long time. How are you?"

She shrugged her arm free and rubbed the area where my hand had been. The action didn't seem to say she was offended by my touch, but rather the contact had made her feel the same way I did. Her green eyes sparkled like emeralds in the early morning sun.

Had they always been so vibrant?

"I've been good," she replied. "You?"

I went to speak again, but the words didn't want to come out. It was as if I was still absorbing the disbelief of seeing her again. I had to remind myself she was real, and not a crazy dream that had played on repeat for the past seventeen years.

"Not too bad," was all I managed to say.

"Well, that's good. But um, like I said. I need to get going."

She seemed nervous, but I couldn't let her walk away—not again. At least not until I found out what her phone conversation was about. When she tossed me a small wave and turned to jog away, I ran ahead to fall in step beside her. She tilted her head to eye me curiously but didn't say anything.

"Do you live around here?"

"I'm in the D.C. area, yes." Her response was cautious. I could appreciate that. After all, it had been a long time. For all she knew, I grew up to be a psychopath. Still, I needed to continue the small talk.

"I live in Alexandria, but my office is over in the East End. The Mall is convenient, and I jog this path almost every day. Strange I haven't bumped into you until now. Do you run here often?"

"No, I've only just started coming here because the sidewalks in my neighborhood are closed for construction." A strand of hair pulled loose from her braid as we ran. I wanted to reach out to tuck it behind her ear, but I refrained.

"I guess I should be thanking the DDOT then."

"For what?"

"For tearing up the sidewalks. It changed your routine and allowed us to bump into each other." She glanced sideways at me. Once again, she didn't respond, so I continued. "I couldn't help overhearing you on the phone."

Cadence stopped abruptly. When I turned back to look at her, I watched as her face paled. She looked like she had just seen a ghost. I stopped running and walked the few steps back toward her.

"You did?" she squeaked.

"Yeah, sorry. I should know better. After all, you did once lecture me on how spying isn't polite," I grinned, hoping to put her at ease by bringing up an old memory. "I am curious though. What did you have to tell me?"

"Nothing," she said, just a little too quickly.

Interesting.

Now I was really curious.

"Look, it's been a while, Cadence. As much as I'm enjoying this unexpected jog with you, I'd much rather talk when we aren't panting from exertion. Why don't we call it quits and go grab a cup of coffee? We can catch up."

She dropped her gaze and shook her head. When she looked up at me again, her eyes were pained. I reached out and took one of her hands, knowing instantly it was a mistake. She had always been a constant tug at my chest and the action brought me dangerously close to her. I looked down at her heart shaped lips. The urge to kiss her was undeniable.

Christ, man. Get ahold of yourself.

I don't know how it happened so quickly, but I shouldn't have been surprised. Even when we were younger, things had progressed fast. Now, with her small hand resting between my palms, I knew with absolute certainty, I wouldn't want to let her go. I couldn't force myself to step back.

For the first time in seventeen years, she was looking at me. I thought I'd gotten over her, but just holding her hand made me realize I hadn't—not at all. Somehow, over the course of one summer, Cadence had virtually ruined me for any other woman. I wished I could deny it, but if I tried, I'd only be lying to myself. Sure, I'd come across other beautiful women in my lifetime but none who flipped my switch more than Cadence did. The magnetic pull I always felt toward her was still there, just as charged as it was on the day we met. This could be my chance to explain myself—to apologize for not having the guts to stand up to my father all those years ago. She needed to hear me out and know not a single day went by when I didn't think of her.

"I don't think coffee is a good idea, Fitz," she whispered.

"Why not?"

"Because I..." she trailed off.

Then another thought occurred to me and I looked down quickly at the hand still in mine—no ring. I tried to hide my relief. I had been so wrapped up in seeing her again, it never occurred to me she might have given herself to someone else. Just the idea of her being with another man caused my gut to churn even if I had no right.

"It's only coffee, Cadence."

She pulled her hand free and took a step back. Her posture stiffened, and her gaze turned steely.

"Instead of asking *me* out for coffee, perhaps you should

consider taking your *wife*," she stated with acid in her tone. The way she emphasized the last word made me falter. I blinked, momentarily at a loss before the light went on.

She doesn't know.

"Cadence, I'm not married. My wife died eleven years ago."

Her eyes widened, and she began to laugh but not in a way that sounded even remotely happy.

"Of course she died! Isn't life ironic?" She dropped her gaze to the ground. When she looked back up, her gaze was wary. "Look, Fitz, I'm sorry about your wife—truly, I am. But I don't know what you're thinking. Doing anything together is a bad idea. Running, coffee. It's all bad. There's no catching up for us. It's been seventeen years. That ship has sailed."

"Has it?" I asked.

I stared intently at her as she raised her arms in exasperation.

"We bumped into each. Big deal. Let's just say 'it was nice to see you' and move on our merry ways."

Drawn like a moth to a flame, or perhaps I was just a glutton for punishment, I reached for her hand again. She didn't pull away.

"Have coffee with me," I insisted again. "Please."

Conflict raged in her eyes. What I wouldn't give to crawl inside her brain and pick apart her thoughts. All I knew was I felt like I'd been dreaming of green eyes, soft lips, and blond hair for way too long.

"There's a coffee shop within walking distance over on Maryland Avenue," she finally said. "I only have time for a quick cup. I have to work at nine, and I need time to go home and shower beforehand."

I released her hand and motioned in the direction she was referring to.

"Lead the way, sweetheart."

Her head snapped up to look at me. I winked and tossed her a cocky grin that silently said that's right—I remember.

By the time we finished this impromptu coffee date, she would know I hadn't forgotten about anything—and I hadn't forgotten about her.

7

CADENCE

W*hat am I doing? What am I doing? What am I doing?*
          I repeated the question over and over again in my head as I entered Café Aroma with Fitz. Yes, Fitz. If he hadn't been the person to hold open the coffee shop door for me, I wouldn't have believed it myself. I should have been running in the opposite direction, far away from the man who had destroyed my heart—from the only one I'd ever completely given myself to. However, I never expected seeing him again would bring a whole new problem to light. With just one touch, I learned this man still had the power to make me quiver and shake and question everything I thought I knew about myself. And I hated it.

I only agreed to have coffee because I knew Joy was right. My heart didn't belong to Fitz anymore. It belonged to Kallie. I had to tell him about her—maybe. He was now a grown man. I was sure he'd changed over the years, just as I had, and I wanted to find out exactly who this man was before I told him about our daughter.

I nervously stepped up to the counter and ordered my usual.

"I'll take a triple grande one-pump vanilla non-fat latte."

"That may have been the most complicated drink order I've ever heard," Fitz said with a laugh before placing his own order with the barista. "Breakfast Blend, black."

"Mock it all you want. It's way tastier than black coffee. Gross," I countered and stuck out my tongue in disgust. Then much to my annoyance, Fitz tried to pay. I waved him off. "I've got it."

While we waited for our beverages, I watched him out of the corner of my eye. I tried not to stare, but it was a challenge. He was as gorgeous as ever and still made me a little weak in the knees. His stance was confident yet easy with one hand inside the pocket of his running shorts. Fitz had always been fit, tall and lean with a mischievous smile. Today, he had grown into that body. Wide shoulders bulged beneath the blue t-shirt that seemed molded to his skin, accentuating the hard-muscled pectorals no t-shirt could conceal.

Yes, the years had been kind to Fitzgerald Quinn. He looked perfect standing there—even his dark hair was perfect, which was a remarkable feat considering we'd just been jogging. I knew my hair was probably a wreck. I could feel the loose strands from my braid brushing the sides of my neck.

After we collected our drink orders, we headed over to a small table in the corner. Once we were seated, a silence fell. He stared at me, almost if I were a mirage that would disappear at any moment. It was unnerving. I didn't know what to say, much less even know how we came to be here in the first place.

"So, are you going to tell me about your phone conversation?" he finally asked.

"Nope," I replied automatically with a decisive shake of my head.

"You're sure?"

"Positive. Sorry, Fitz. A girl has a right to her secrets."

And, boy, was mine a whopper.

Until I could get a better gauge on his character, my lips were sealed. I had to think of Kallie—and not his oh-so-snug blue t-shirt. Considering that, I should have been delivering The Spanish Inquisition, but it felt weird. Everything about him was so familiar—like I knew him. But, the reality was, I didn't know him at all. I didn't know what to say. I fiddled with the sleeve of my cup anxiously before taking a cautious sip.

"How's your triple vanilla whatever?"

"Latte. And it's good."

"I would have taken you for a strawberries and cream Frappuccino kind of girl. But then again, maybe your tastes have changed over the years."

"What do you mean?"

"Do you still like strawberries?"

"Um, yeah," I said, pulling my brow together in confusion.

"With a dollop of whipped cream if memory serves me right," he added.

All the air expelled from my lungs, my heart began to thud, and my stomach clenched from a mix of emotions.

Ten questions. Ten answers.

He remembered.

And I remembered.

His lips curved into a smile, and his eyes crinkled at the corners. I remembered that crinkle, the natural smile lines, just like I remembered the feel of the stubble on his jaw. Today, it was perfectly shaven, the smooth lines of his face just as chiseled and beautiful as they had once been. It was like every pore, every inch of me, remembered even the tiniest details.

We stared at one another for a long moment, and I found myself unable to speak. His eyes bore into mine, and I could swear he knew exactly what I was thinking. I tore my eyes from his, incapable of withstanding his penetrating gaze any longer.

"Fitz, the past is in the past. We should leave it there."

"What if I don't want to?"

"You have to." I paused, not wanting to elaborate further. I didn't want him to know his remembrance of such a small detail from the past affected me. Switching gears, I opted to ask about him, rather than discuss memories. I was supposed to be getting to know him after all. "So, you said you wanted to catch up. Tell me what you've been up to for the past seventeen years."

Fitz sat back in his chair contemplatively.

"A lot has happened, Cadence. Seventeen years is a long time."

I glanced down at my watch.

"You have thirty minutes."

"Well then I better get talking," he said and flashed me a lopsided grin I tried hard to ignore. "I suppose I should start with Austin, my son. He's fifteen. Good kid. People say he looks a lot like me."

Yes, I know.

But I couldn't say that without letting on about *how* I knew.

He didn't mention his wife or anything about how she died. I wondered if he had ended up loving her and if it was too painful for him to talk about. Instead, Fitz talked mostly about his partnership with Devon. He told me about the PR company they started a year after he left Camp Riley. He spoke about their successes but not in an arrogant sort of way. He simply sounded proud of what he and Devon accomplished together.

"The original plan was to represent corporations, but my father knows powerful people, and so does Devon's father. It didn't take long before the business model changed, and we found ourselves representing more individuals than corporations. Word spread, and business boomed. Plus, people are always in need of fixing. Who would have thought a couple of punks like us would be working to fix other people's messes?" he laughed.

"You were never a punk," I replied with a small smile.

"Right. I think my father would say otherwise."

There was no mistaking the shadow that crossed his face.

"How are things on that front? With your father I mean. Is he any better?"

"Nah. The old bastard is set in his ways. He still gives me shit. I just don't take it like I used to." He paused and lifted his coffee to his lips, studying my face carefully as he did so. His gaze was intense, and I felt a blush creep up my neck. Something somber and pensive filled his expression. Lowering the cup, he looked purposefully into my eyes. "I'm sorry, Cadence. For everything."

His apology slithered over my skin, a rich velvety sound tickling my senses.

"Sorry for what?" I asked, feeling a tremble rock through the question.

I knew what he was apologizing for, but I didn't expect to see the emotions swirling in his eyes—loss, regret, grief. He ran his hands through his hair nervously. At least I wasn't the only one feeling apprehensive.

"I realized years later, everything he did was nothing more than a scare tactic. He would never have allowed me to go to jail over that accident. It would have brought embarrassment to his good name. I should have seen through it all. I was a coward. Because of that, I walked away from you. I never wanted to hurt you. I loved you. Leaving you that day was the hardest thing I've ever had to do."

Apparently, small talk was over. He wasted no time getting to the heavy stuff. Little did he know, I felt like I'd waited to hear those words for nearly two decades. Trying not to appear shocked by his confession, I waved a flippant hand in the air.

"Hey, it was a long time ago. I'm over it," I lied. As of today, it was apparent I wasn't over it at all. However, my armor was stronger now than it was when I was eighteen. At least, I hoped it was.

I'd have to be dead to be unaffected by the gorgeous man staring at me. I wasn't delusional. If Fitz wanted to make something of our unlikely meeting, he would. After all, he once pursued me with a single-minded intensity that had made my young heart flutter. But unlike my teenage self, I knew better than to give in this time. Once a shell was broken, it can never truly be repaired. The cracks would always be present, no matter how strong the glue was.

"I noticed you don't wear a ring. Have you ever married?" he asked.

Gutting disbelief thundered through my chest like a dark and ugly storm. He had some nerve asking me that. It was none of his business.

"No, I haven't," I responded curtly. "Apparently, unlike you, it wasn't in the cards for me."

I knew it was a cheap shot, but I didn't particularly care. If he was offended, he didn't let on. Instead, he eyed me, almost as if he were assessing whether to believe my façade before he continued on.

"Right. Well, anyway...back to my father. He has this grand scheme going now. He wants me to run for political office—and a senator no less!" he laughed, like he found the idea ludicrous. "I have no intention of running for anything. I hate politics. I always have. It's all about a hunger for power and the party vote. I'm sure he thinks he can strongarm me into supporting his bills."

I raised one eyebrow.

"Could he?"

"Hell, no! I mean, assuming I ran and was elected, he'd be in for a rude awakening. I'm tired of seeing things get rushed through in the name of greed if you know what I mean."

"Trust me, I know exactly what you mean," I said warily. "I'm familiar with your father, or I should say his policies."

"Oh?"

"Unfortunately, yes. I own a non-profit organization that helps DACA recipients. Your father's voting habits tend to get in my way."

"So you did it, huh? It shouldn't surprise me—you always had your life goals all mapped out. You said you wanted to work non-profit, and now here you are. You actually started your own. Good for you. Although I imagined you'd be working with kids for some reason."

"I do work with kids sometimes. More often than not, DACA recipients have children of their own. When bad things happen, it's my job to make sure their families aren't ripped apart," I explained.

"I'm sure it's more complicated than that. They wouldn't be separated if they were abiding by our countries laws."

He said it so flippantly, my back instantly went up. Fitz was right about one thing—it was more complicated. However, his oversimplification for why someone would face deportation infuriated me. I'd heard similar sentiments all too often. I tossed him an icy glare.

"Are you sure you wouldn't vote for your father's proposals if you had the chance? Because that sounds a lot like something I've heard him say on the news." He flinched as if I had slapped him, but I didn't pause in my quiet rant. "Despite the popular rhetoric these days, the people I represent are not hardened criminals, drug dealers, or rapists. They're human beings. The things I hear and see every day would make you shudder. But then again, maybe not if you think it's just about abiding by the law."

Fitz held his hands up in surrender.

"Look, I didn't mean to imply anything. I'm sure it's exactly as you say. I'll be honest, I don't know much about DACA."

"That's the problem, most people don't," I spat out.

"Hey, I take back what I said, okay? I'll even be sure to read up on it more. I'm a firm believer in knowing the facts before I speak. Clearly, I was out of line there."

Beating back my annoyance, I took a deep breath and pinched the bridge of my nose.

"Look, I didn't mean to snap. Maybe what you said was completely innocent, but this is a really hot topic for me. It's a fight I have every single day."

"No need to explain. I get it. Really, I do."

I glanced at my watch again. We had been talking for close to an hour. Now, I barely had enough time to get home, shower, and get to work on time. Plus, I would need more than just a few minutes to process everything. Seeing him, talking to him, the electric current in the air—it was strange yet familiar. It was like seventeen years hadn't passed at all. I had walked into the coffee shop a nervous wreck, but we settled into easy conversation within minutes. And it truly was easy—outside of my little political outburst.

I was beyond confused. Seeing him again and knowing he was so close had me all torn up inside. My plan to get to know him seemed to have backfired. Not only was I was torn up over what to do about Kallie, but now my brain was muddled with images of a young Fitz and the man who sat across from me. So much time had passed. The crushing heartache I felt back then should have eased with time, but seeing him again made me realize I never truly moved on. He was the father of my daughter even if he didn't know it, and he would always be the keeper of my heart because of it.

"It's been great to catch up, but I really gotta run," I told him.

He reached across the table and took my hand, his fingers warm and strong, his grip feeling just right. When he pressed

Defined

his palm closer to mine, I felt something flat and smooth come
in contact with my skin. I looked down.

"All of my contact information is on this card. I want to see
you again, Cadence."

"Fitz, I..."

"Call me," he insisted as he stood up. His tone was firm and
completely unapologetic.

Leaning down, he pressed a light kiss to my forehead. I
sucked in a breath. Everything around us seemed to fade away.
All the other patrons in the coffee shop were nothing more
than a backdrop to him. The only thing I was aware of was the
tall, dark haired, broad-shouldered man whose lips were
touching my head.

The peck was brief, and he pulled away almost as quickly as
he'd leaned in, but his steely gray eyes lingered on my face. His
gaze was penetrating, drinking me in as if he were trying to
commit me to memory. I stared back, finding myself lost in the
endless universe held in his gaze. I shivered.

Then...he walked away.

I stayed there for another five minutes, looking absently at
the card he gave me, having just had my orderly world
completely flipped upside down.

8

FITZ

I arrived at my office late. To say I was rattled by the events of the morning was an understatement. Never did I think I would see Cadence again. Sure, I had thought about contacting her over the years, but then life seemed to happen. I became busy with Austin and building my company. Before I knew it, more than a decade had passed.

However, she had never been far from my mind. It had been seventeen fucking years, but memories of her never stopped plaguing me. She was my silent storm, the face that had tormented my dreams for so many years. I'd never forget her sweetheart lips when she looked up at me with nothing but a shy smile or the vulnerability shown in her emerald green eyes when she'd confessed she had never been properly kissed. Knowing I had been the first person to kiss the soft curve of her neck, to feel her tight nipples against my tongue, to hear the startled cry of her first orgasm never ceased to make me hard. Now that I had seen her again, the memory of what once was came harder and faster than ever before.

It only took a brief run in with her to make me realize our time apart didn't matter—at least for me it didn't. So much about her was still the same, yet she was also different. She still had a quiet strength about her with a level of vulnerability that contrasted with the confidence in her words. Her unsurpassed beauty only seemed to intensify over time, and her passion and sharp intelligence could still cut any man down with a mere look.

During the hour we spent together that morning, I saw all of that and found myself lost in her all over again. Now, as I stepped out of the elevator to my floor, I contemplated what I should do about that fact. One thing was for certain—I wouldn't be waiting around for her to call me. I knew I would need to go to her.

"Morning, Angie," I greeted my secretary.

"Good morning, Mr. Quinn. I have a few phone messages for you," she said, diving right into business. Angie was never one to waste time with idle chit-chat. "Your father called three times this morning."

Annoyed, I pressed my lips into a tight line.

"He also called my cell. I'm sorry he bothered you too. When you see him on the caller ID, just send it to voicemail until further notice. I'll handle him."

"Yes, sir," she said with a curt nod. "Jackson Dobbs also called. He said he's running a bit late and to expect him just after eleven."

"Looks like I'm not the only one behind schedule today. It's not an issue. We've already gone over the PR strategy for him. Today we're just finalizing the paperwork. However, I do need you to hold my calls between now and then. I have something I need to do, and it may take most of the morning."

"Will do."

I entered my office and walked over to the floor to ceiling windows on the back wall. Reaching into the inside breast pocket of my suit coat, I pulled out my cell to return my father's calls. There was no use putting him off any longer. I knew why he was calling as well as I knew my own name. He was pissed off because I didn't show up for the meeting with the RNC. It was no skin off my back, but I didn't want him harassing my employees because of it.

"Fitzgerald," he barked after the first ring. "Where have you been?"

"On a run, just like every other morning," I idly stated.

"I'm not talking about just this morning. You didn't return my calls from Sunday or yesterday. I'm a busy man. I don't have time to wait around for you."

I gritted my teeth and pinched the bridge of my nose.

"What do you want?"

"I'm calling about the damn meeting you couldn't be bothered to show up for," he bellowed through the line. "Do you have any idea how embarrassed I was to be sitting there with the heads of the RNC, having to make excuses about your absence?"

"Something came up," I lied. The truth was, I hadn't done anything of importance Saturday night unless you counted catching up with the Stark's and the Lannister's latest bloodbath on HBO as important.

"I'll not have you ruin this for me. There's an order to things, Fitzgerald. You have to show up and win this damn election. I need to get my people lined up if I have any hopes of gaining Senate Majority Leader."

A sudden awareness hit me, finally able to see his end game.

So, that's what this is about.

"Is that your angle? I knew there had to be one. You want me on the Senate so I can vote for you to be majority leader?"

"That's right. And you'll do what you're told. If you don't, you and I both know the Quinn & Wilkshire business will suffer. Half of your clients are politicians from the D.C. area. Plus, remember what I said. You need to think of Austin."

I sighed in annoyance. I'd had enough of him trying to use my son, his own grandson and flesh and blood, to coerce me into his convoluted agenda. But then I thought about Cadence and about how she'd followed her dreams to make a difference. It made me question myself and my own role in the world. I hadn't done much of anything to make an impact. Perhaps, just maybe, this Senate seat could be an opportunity to change that.

"You can't strongarm me with threats," I told my father. "If I do this, it won't be because you threatened me. You and I both know you won't follow through because that would mean outing Judge Perkins and his role in things. I didn't show because I needed time to think about it. Reschedule the meeting. I won't miss it, but I'm not making any promises."

"We'll see about that. I'll call you when I have a new date and location. You'd better not stiff this time."

The phone line went dead.

Asshole.

I returned the phone to my pocket and stared out the window. My office faced southeast and I was just able to see the top of the Capitol Building from my view. The painted cast-iron dome gleamed in the morning sun, the Statue of Freedom standing proudly with her sword and shield. I frowned, thinking of all the corruption and backdoor deals that went on behind the pristine walls. We may be free, but freedom always came with a price. I meant what I said to my father. I would consider, but I wouldn't commit just yet. A part of me worried if I did this, I'd be selling my soul to the devil.

I shook my head, refusing to allow my father's antics to get to me. I had more important matters to delve into. Moving to my desk, I sat down behind it and pulled out the key to open the file drawer to my left. My hands slid over the hanging folders inside. Each file contained client information, all arranged by last name in alphabetical order—all except one. I reached toward the back of the drawer and pulled out the file that had no label. It was the file for Cadence. I hadn't looked at it since the day I buried my wife.

There had been no love lost between Bethany Perkins and me. It was an arranged marriage, a fact she had reminded me of often. Although we initially tried to play the roles of husband and wife, consummating our marriage and making the best of a fucked up situation, it was only a matter of weeks before things fell apart. She was miserable. I was miserable. I think Bethany knew I loved someone else, and it was something I felt a little guilty about to this day. Perhaps I should have tried harder with her. If I had, maybe it would have changed the outcome of things. But I didn't try at all and Bethany had quickly turned back to her old ways.

After being married for only a few months, partying and drinking became a regular part of her life again. It was no small miracle I managed to keep her sober while she was pregnant with Austin. That had been the only time we ever really got along. After his birth, she went right back to the bottle. One day, she'd blame his colic for her behavior; another day, she'd blame me, saying I didn't love her. Although I never admitted it to her, she was right. I never loved her.

Before long, her drinking became more excessive. I had suspected drugs were in the mix but I never confronted her about it. A drunk Bethany was nasty and volatile. I didn't want to deal with it, but I did have Austin to worry about. My business had really started to take off, so I decided to hire a nanny for him. It may have been the best or worse decision of my life. A nanny gave Austin stability while I worked long hours, but it also gave my wife more freedom. She took it and ran with it until she drank herself to death.

My only saving grace after the whole shit storm was Austin had very little memory of that time in his life. He had been only four when she died. While he says he can remember flashes of her, his strongest memories were with me. I made sure of that.

After Bethany's funeral, I had come back to my office. Devon and I had just moved our offices from the tiny space in the West End to the building we were in now. I remembered the day like it was yesterday and could almost still smell the paint that had yet to dry on the walls completely. I recalled sitting down at this very desk, just as I was now, staring at a picture I thought I would tuck away forever. It was a picture of Cadence from the playbill handed out to everyone on the last day at Camp Riley.

The photos of staff members and students had been taken early in the summer, right after the cast was chosen. I ran my finger along the edge of Cadence's picture. She appeared happy. At this point, she was still completely unaware I was set to marry someone else. My picture told a different story. While I had smiled for the camera, there was dread beneath the façade.

Throughout my life, I learned more from my failures than I did from my successes. Failures were the moments that stuck with a person. If they didn't, one could never learn. Leaving Cadence was my ultimate failure. When I told her I was a coward for walking away, I never spoke truer words. After Bethany died, staring at the picture of Cadence made me realize all I had lost because I didn't stand up for myself. Since that day, I stopped rolling over to my father's demands. I vowed never again to be his whipping boy, and I've held true to that promise. I did it for Austin's sake as much as my own. Doing anything less would make me an unfit father and role model. Nobody would own me again.

I placed the program back into the folder and flipped through the remaining contents. It was mostly press releases about the happenings at Camp Riley. I looked for them every Spring, hoping one of them contained a picture of Cadence. None of them did and I wondered why I had kept them for all these years. The last one was about the closure of the camp after Jamison and Claudine Riley passed away. There wasn't a lot of details about the closing in the article, other than the fact the decision was made by Cadence. It mentioned she would be putting the land up for sale. Reading through all of this again caused a pain in my chest. Not for me but for her. Selling that land had to crush her.

I replaced the folder in its hiding spot at the back of the drawer and fired up my computer. Owning a PR company came with perks. It meant I had access to personal information most people had to pay to obtain. Finding the personal cell number for Cadence took less than a minute.

I scribbled the number down on a notepad and began a new search. I typed in her name and the words 'non-profit' and 'Washington D.C.' in the search bar. I wanted to find out more about her organization and what she did. I had clearly pissed her off in the coffee shop with my comment about DACA recipients breaking the law. I had some making up to do. If I had any hopes of doing just that, I would need to get an education first. I scrolled through the search results and stopped on the fourth one down the line.

Dahlia's Dreamers. That has to be it.

I clicked through to the website and was surprised at what I found. The site was full of resource links, past and current projects, and stories about their successes. However, the biggest shock was seeing she was a children's book author and illustrator. Portions of the proceeds from her books went to her non-profit. I sat back in my chair, feeling awestruck and a little proud of what she'd accomplished.

Buy links were included on the site, so of course I clicked on them and purchased every single one of the thirty-two books she had published.

9

CADENCE

Five o'clock in the morning came way too early. Normally, I'd set my alarm for six, leaving plenty of time to wash my face, get dressed, and head out for a run. I'd then come home, shower, and be to work by nine. However, with the construction on my street, taking my car to the nearest park added drive time I now needed to account for. As I turned the corner onto 14th Street, the sluggishness of the morning began to fade, and I started to feel anxious. I had barely slept a wink. I had tossed and turned, thinking about the Garcia-Mendez case, finances, book sales, and Kallie. In the end, my worry about telling Kallie the truth about Fitz always came back to the forefront. The problem was, I didn't even have the slightest clue about where to begin.

In a rare stroke of luck, I was able to find off street parking. After I parallel parked the car, I rested my head against the seat. If I didn't have enough concerns to keep me awake long into the late hours of the night, there was also the impromptu coffee break with Fitz. I tried not to think about it, just as I tried not to think about the voicemail he'd left me late yesterday afternoon.

Reaching toward the middle console of my car, I picked up my cell and played back his message for what must have been the twentieth time.

"Cadence, it's Fitz. It was really nice catching up with you this morning. I'd like to do it again sometime over dinner. Call me."

I didn't know how he got my number, but that was irrelevant. I couldn't muster up the courage to call him back. However, what I *did* decide to do was jog the National Mall again. I told myself I would have come here regardless of Fitz, but the reality was, I could have gone to a hundred other locations to run, yet here I was again.

After a good stretch on the curb, I plugged one earbud into my ear and tucked the other one into my shirt front before setting out. OneRepublic played in my ear as I passed the giant carousel and groups of people doing yoga on the lush green lawns. The sun pierced through the horizon, sparkling through the Cherry Blossom trees as I ran down what was quickly becoming my favorite running path. I smiled politely and nodded to the other joggers who passed me.

I wasn't scanning any of their faces in search of Fitz. That would've been silly. It wasn't like he'd consumed my thoughts since the day his son showed up on my doorstep. Those steely gray eyes and strong arms didn't haunt me in the late hours of the night, just as I hadn't slipped my hand under my bedsheets imagining it was his touch. Nope. I was just out here running for my own physical work out.

That was all a lie, of course, a fact that became apparent the moment I found myself disappointed when I didn't see his face among the people I passed. I began to assume he'd only called to be polite. Perhaps I only imagined the sizzling connection between us in the coffee shop and was getting caught up with feelings of nostalgia. Fitz was my first love after all. It was only natural for me to be nostalgic, but it had been years. People change—I'd changed. The boy I'd fallen in love with was not the man I'd had coffee with yesterday. It would be unfair of me to assume he was the same person.

"Morning, sweetheart," said a familiar male voice to my left.

My steps faltered and I stopped, bringing my hand to my chest.

"Geez, you need to stop doing that! You nearly scared me out of my skin!"

"Sorry. In my defense, I did call out to you several times," Fitz pointed out. "You must not have heard me because of the earbuds."

"Only one," I said, plucking the lone bud from my ear. "I never run with both in. It's not safe."

"Not safe?"

"Yeah," I said, fighting the urge to roll my eyes. It was so typical of a man not to understand the safeties women must adhere to day in and day out. "Being a woman, I need to think of these things. Creepers are everywhere, and I need to be able to hear if anyone approaches."

He raised one perfectly shaped eyebrow in amusement.

"Creepers, huh? You didn't hear me."

"True, but I was distracted."

"Distracted?"

My face flushed, not wanting to admit I had been thinking about him.

"Yeah, I just got a case at work that's bugging me," I said, giving him only the partial truth.

"Come on, then. Let's run and you can tell me about it."

I eyed him curiously for a moment. Going for another jog with him would only exacerbate my current predicament—that much was certain. But a run may also satisfy the unexplainable burning need I had to be near him again. Perhaps if I did this,

I'd be able to get him out of my system long enough to rein in my focus.

"Um, sure. Why not?" I agreed.

I started out, and Fitz casually fell into step beside me.

"So, Dahlia's Dreamers. The name's fitting."

I tossed him a sideways glance, trying to read his expression. He'd apparently done his research on me, and I worried about how far he'd dived in. However, if he knew anything about Kallie, he didn't let on. For that, I felt a small measure of relief.

"I thought so too. I was listening to all the political debate about the DREAM Act around the same time Dahlia had been put to rest. The name just sort of came to me. I started the company ten years ago. I have a small staff of five, including Joy. Do you remember Joy Martin from camp?"

"She worked in the store. Yeah, I remember her, but I thought she went to school for music."

"She did, but she couldn't find a job. When I offered her a spot, she jumped at it. She's good for Dahlia's Dreamers. It's become personal to her. It's hard to see her doing anything else now."

Fitz cut along the path that would lead us through Ash Woods, following the same trek we'd made yesterday. We moved as if we'd been running together for years, always seeming to know when the other was going to cut right or left along the path.

"Tell me about your case," he prompted.

"It's actually long and complicated, as they usually are, but this one is bugging me more because there's a little girl involved. The poor thing is barely five years old, and she has no idea where her daddy is."

I gave him a brief overview of Emilia's visit. He stayed quiet, seeming to absorb every word I said. When I finished, he sighed.

"I'll apologize again for assuming things yesterday, Cadence. After our talk, I read up on DACA. From what I gathered, I thought only a felony could revoke their status. I didn't realize a simple traffic ticket could send someone packing."

"It might not have three years ago, but new Executive Orders have changed all that. When I started Dahlia's Dreamers, our focus was to help individuals navigate through the DACA process so they could obtain legal status. Now all we do is help those very same people protect the legal status that was already granted to them. Sometimes we succeed. Sometimes we don't. Those are always the worst days," I admitted sadly.

"I mean, Christ. They have families and lives here. It just doesn't seem fair," he murmured. He shook his head and slowed his steps. When we came to a complete stop, he turned to face me. "Old Abe marks the halfway point. I usually stop here to stretch before I continue on."

Following his lead, I placed a foot on the first step leading up to the Lincoln Memorial and pressed down into a lunge. Fitz watched me, his gaze traveling from my foot, up my thigh until stopping on my face. His study of me was so intense, I became self-conscious, feeling like I was doing the stretch incorrectly.

"What? Am I doing something wrong?"

"No, sweetheart. You're doing everything right."

My breath caught, and I looked at him. His eyes were shining mischievously.

He's flirting with me.

If I couldn't resist those flirtations when I was eighteen, there was no way in hell I'd be able to keep away from the sinful, confident, and hot as hell man before me. Instantly, my face heated. Quickly, I returned to a standing position.

"Right, well...shall we continue on?"

"In a minute," he waved off dismissively and continued to

stretch. "I admire that you went into public service. I'm curious though. Why did you choose immigrants?"

"Honestly, my interest sparked when I read a story about five young undocumented activists who were trying to transform society's attitudes about immigration. I was inspired and found myself reevaluating what it means to be an American. Then I knew someone who was personally affected," I paused, not wanting to get into a story that wasn't mine to tell. "Things just kind of snowballed after that. What about you, Fitz? What inspires you?"

"You," he replied immediately. "Watching you. Listening to you speak."

I fought the flush that wanted to creep up my neck again and forced myself to push for his answer. After all, I was supposed to be figuring out who he was, yet all the conversation was about me. A flash of a memory resurfaced, reminding me of a similar situation seventeen years ago. I supposed some things never changed.

"I'm serious. Why go into public relations?" I pushed.

"It was one of my degrees, for starters. Plus, I had a knack for it. I knew what looked good in the eyes of the public and what didn't. I grew up with that. My father was always so concerned about appearances and what could negatively influence the voters. Other than my few years at Georgetown when I didn't care about much of anything, I can barely remember a time when I didn't have to be wary of public scrutiny."

Despite all the things I knew about his upbringing, I was surprised I never realized how difficult it must have been for him. He had always lived his life under a microscope because of his father's political status. He may still live that way for all I knew. That thought made me pause. I wasn't sure if I wanted to expose Kallie to that sort of life.

"It's a shame you had to live like that. I never realized. We were so wrapped up in our own private little cocoon at Camp Riley, it was easy to forget how isolated we were from the rest of the world."

Fitz stood to face me, settling those intense gray eyes on my face.

"I miss those days. I've missed you," he admitted huskily. "I still think about you a lot. All the time actually."

My body went rigid, unable to believe his words. I wasn't going to fall for it—not for a second. If he thought he could woo his way into my panty's again, he was sadly mistaken. I took a small step back.

"That's a line," I accused, feeling uneasy.

"No, it's not."

"Why on earth would you think of me still? After all this time?"

"It's simple. You were and still are my biggest regret."

I shook my head, needing to deny the words that nearly made my heart stop.

"It was a long time ago. I was a naïve girl with foolish dreams. I get why you did what you did. It was for the best," I rambled nervously. "We both avoided a painful goodbye that way. A lot has changed since then. There's no reason to hang onto any sort of guilt."

Part of my statement was true. I truly did think it was for the best, but we didn't avoid a painful goodbye—at least, I didn't. His cruel words, even though I knew they were false, had crushed me. There was no sense in rehashing the past.

I stared down at the ground and drew invisible circles with the toe of my shoe on the concrete sidewalk. I could feel his stare on me as if somehow it was its own entity. Panic welled up inside me, knowing he was slowly taking down my walls brick by brick, but I couldn't let him in. Not again.

"You'd always been so open and honest about your feelings. Whatever promises or decisions we made all those years ago doesn't change the fact that I'm here now–that you're here." He stepped toward me, his movements lined with power and purpose. He'd always moved that way, his profound presence hitting me like a bolt of lightning. "Look at me, Cadence."

My body stayed tense, but his tone nearly seduced me into compliance. Refusing to look at him would only make me look unreasonably stubborn or scared. The last thing I wanted to do was give Fitz a reason to believe our breakup mattered. He couldn't know I measured all potential lovers against him, always finding fault with each.

And I certainly didn't want him to know, as a result, there had only been him.

Drawing in a breath, I brought my eyes up to meet his.

"What do you want from me, Fitz?"

He took another step closer, wrapped his hand around the back of my neck, and tilted my head up to study my face. His eyes moved to my lips, then back up to meet my gaze.

"I want to kiss you."

Seventeen years ago, he had asked permission. Today, he didn't. Before I could react, he covered my mouth in a greedy kiss. He didn't ease inside or wait for me to accept him. No. Unlike the days from our youth, he prowled in.

I stiffened at first as my mind shouted instructions of protest. I was confused about whether I wanted this or not. Heat clouded my judgment, and my brain seemed to disconnect from my body. It took me less than a second to realize how much I longed for him—and that scared the hell out of me. I anchored my hands on his shoulders knowing full well I should end this madness, yet I didn't push him away. Without meaning to, I kissed him back and curled my hands around his neck. He plunged in again and I willingly opened, urging him closer and tangling my tongue with his. We had moved way too fast seventeen years ago, and it appeared as though the magnetic force that had once made us impatient lovers was another thing that hadn't changed with time.

My acceptance of his kiss encouraged him to press deeper into my mouth. Tasting. Possessing. I met every stroke of his tongue as he wrapped his arm around my waist, crushing my torso against his own. The kiss rocked me to my very core. There were so many reasons the kiss was wrong, yet none of them seemed to matter. This was what I needed. It felt so good. It had been too long. For the first time in nearly two decades, I felt complete. Something I thought was long dead seemed to come alive again and I began to wonder if I'd ever been truly feeling for years. Fitz was all that seemed to matter. Somehow, over the miles and years, he'd never lost his hold on me. Now, he was unexpectedly back in my life, and I knew this was what I'd been missing. He was the essence that haunted me. Him. Just him.

"Cadence, sweetheart," he murmured against my lips. His palm caressed the nape of my neck, gliding over the slope of my collarbone. I was drowning in sensation. I could hardly breathe as a wave of dizziness made my head swim. The masculine scent of spice and earth sent my body reeling. I knew this needed to stop, but his very touch made me feel powerfully female and desired in a way I hadn't experienced since the last time I was in his arms. My fingers found their way to his hair, tugging at the dark strands until a moan escaped me.

Almost intrusively, thoughts of my daughter popped into my head.

Shit. Kallie. What am I doing?

I tore my mouth from his, feeling guilty for forgetting about her. But worse, I was mortified over the twinge of resentment I felt toward her. Never once had I regretted Kallie or felt like I'd been cheated in some way. She was my life. Fitz, the boy who broke my heart seventeen years ago, was not. Yet just like my teenage self, I couldn't seem to hold back from him. Fitz was my downfall and probably always would be. He extracted too many memories that had long been buried.

I tried to focus on bringing my heart rate down to a normal rhythm. If one kiss triggered these sorts of feelings, I needed to find a way to stay far, far away. I wasn't ready for this. I staggered a step back.

"Fitz, I'm sorry. I shouldn't have let that happen."

He stared at me with glazed eyes and swollen lips. I was fairly certain his expression matched my own. He reached for me.

"We've finally found each other again. Why are you pushing me away?"

"It's not what you think. I have..." I trailed off, struggling to find the right words. "I have obligations. I can't shirk my responsibilities for a quick roll in the sack."

Fitz laughed.

"Putting the cart before the horse now, aren't you? It was just a kiss, Cadence. It's broad daylight. I don't think the D.C. police would take kindly to us fornicating on one their monuments."

I blushed. For some strange reason, the thought of defiling the sacred memorials was a complete turn on. I shook my head to clear the nasty thoughts.

"It's not that. You're screwing with my head. You don't get to come back into my life now, all these years later, mucking things up."

He laughed a low rumbling sound that coiled my insides up even further.

"Mucking things up? How am I doing that?"

"In just a few minutes, you managed to twist and confuse things in a way it should never have been," I said, my brows pinched in pain. I stared absently at the ground, not wanting to admit anything else.

"Have dinner with me."

My head snapped up to look at him. The intensity in his eyes grew and I felt like I'd been thrown back in time. For a moment, it was like I was eighteen all over again. The way he looked standing there—the assured grin he wore, his t-shirt and running shorts, the way his gray eyes expressed so many things he wouldn't say. The invitation to go out to dinner may as well have been an invitation to the lake. I had been so innocent and too idealistic back then. A lot had changed since the days at Camp Riley, not only in my life but who I was as a person. Loving someone the way I once loved him had changed me deep inside.

"I don't think that's a good idea, Fitz. We can't go back. We aren't kids anymore. Things aren't the same as they were before."

"One night. That's all I'm asking for, sweetheart."

Thankfully, a buzzing in the front pocket of my yoga pants gave me a much-needed interruption to the conversation. I pulled out my cell. Simon Reed's name showed on the caller ID.

Saved by the bell.

"Hey, Simon," I said. I looked at Fitz. His eyes narrowed suspiciously, and if I wasn't mistaken, I thought I saw a spark of jealousy flash.

"Sorry for the early call. I just figured you'd want an update. I started work on the Garcia-Mendez case," Simon said.

"What did you find out?" I asked anxiously.

"Judge Perkins has been assigned to the case."

My stomach dropped.

"Shit! He has a hardline stance on immigration. Every time we go up against him, we lose."

"I know. I'm currently looking into his past rulings. I might be able to petition the court for a motion to remove, but I'd have to prove allegations of bias. That's going to be tough. I'd be better off filing for a change in venue since the court is far from Emilia's home address. However, that means I'd have to travel to Richmond."

I knew what that meant. Simon Reed was doing this pro-bono. To ask him to travel almost two hours would be too much.

"See what you can do about having the judge removed first."

"I'll look into it," Simon promised. "Will you be at the gala next week?"

"Helping Lives Bloom? Yeah, I'll be there. I'm supposed to give a speech to kick things off. Wish me luck," I joked.

"I'll be there too. Are you bringing a date?"

I nearly groaned, hoping he wasn't going to ask me to attend the gala with him. Simon was a decent guy even if his clothing style was eclectic at best. It was hard to keep him at bay, yet still manage to maintain a professional connection to satisfy the needs at Dahlia's Dreamers. We needed to retain all the pro-bono lawyers we could.

But then again, perhaps this was the opportunity I needed to put a little distance back between me and Fitz. I glanced over at him. He stood there with his arms crossed, studying me intently, waiting patiently for me to end my call. As much as I didn't want to push him away as he accused me of doing, I knew I had to if I wanted to hang on to any measure of control. For Kallie's sake, I couldn't afford to get lost in old teenage dreams.

"Actually, Simon. I don't have a date for the gala. Do you want to go with me?"

I kept my eyes trained on Fitz. I saw a flash of something on his face, but I couldn't quite place it. Anger? Jealousy? Curiosity?

"That sounds great, Cadence. The gala starts at six. Should I pick you up at five-thirty?" Simon asked.

"Actually, make it five. I need to get there a little early."

After I ended the call, I replaced the phone in my pocket and looked at Fitz. His expression was still unreadable.

"I'm, ah...I'm going to head back to my car," I said nervously.

"Who's Simon?"

I tipped my chin up stubbornly.

"He's a lawyer friend."

"Are you going out with him?"

"I guess you could say that. We're going to a charity fundraiser together," I replied, trying to sound a hell of a lot more confident than I actually felt.

His eyes narrowed slightly, assessing me.

"Alright. I see how it is," he said with a slight nod. "Do you want to meet back here tomorrow morning for another run?"

"Another run? For real?"

"Why not? I like the company."

I couldn't meet him again. I already had a big enough mess on my hands. Kissing him only multiplied my problems by ten, yet all I could think about was doing it again. I could still feel the tingle on my lips from his demanding kiss and the warmth from his arms as they circled my waist. I longed to be back in his embrace, lost in the essence of him.

However, I didn't admit to any of those things. Instead, I hid the smile that wanted to curve on my lips and nodded.

"Okay, Fitz. Tomorrow then. I'll meet you at the Korean War Memorial."

10

FITZ

B *aby steps.*
      That's what I told myself as I sat down behind my desk to start the workday. My cell phone buzzed in my pocket and I fumbled for it.

"Shit," I muttered when the damn thing nearly slipped from my hand. It was a text from my father stating the new meeting time with the RNC. It was set for Saturday afternoon. I was going to have to deal with preparing for it sooner rather than later, but I needed to get my head on straight first. It didn't help my mind was all kinds of distracted, a pathetic fucker singularly focused like a dog after a bone—exactly what I'd become since running into Cadence. Pathetic.

For days, my stomach had been tied up in knots from the anxiety lining my insides. She had power and energy I hadn't realized I was missing. I didn't realize how much I missed her mouth. Her taste. I had kissed her like a man deprived, igniting a fire that went straight to my dick—another thing that missed her.

Still, I'd made progress with her that morning, but it was clear she was going to make me work to gain her trust again, and I'd make damn sure to bust my ass until I got it. The years didn't matter. She belonged with me, but she was right not to trust me. Despite what she said about having no regrets, I knew I'd crushed her. I was cruel even if things seemed to end on a bittersweet note. Now, it was up to me to prove I was a different man and no longer the spineless boy she knew at Camp Riley. A fake marriage, fatherhood, and time will do that to a person.

I pressed the intercom button on my desk phone and buzzed Angie.

"Yes, Mr. Quinn."

"I need you to secure a ticket to an event for me. It's called Helping People Bloom, or something to that effect. I can't recall the exact name."

As I spoke the words, I half wondered what the hell I was doing. Cadence had thrown me so far out of balance, I didn't seem to know my head from my ass anymore. Every action felt compulsive.

"Just one ticket, sir?" Angie asked.

"Yes, just one. And if you can, keep my name off the guest list until the last minute."

I heard the click of her nails on the keyboard before she responded.

"I've got it pulled up on the computer. It looks like the Helping Lives Bloom Gala is being held at the Roosevelt Plaza Hotel. It's being hosted by five different non-profit organizations to help children of immigrant families. It says it's sold out online but getting a ticket shouldn't be a problem. I've spoken with the event's manager, Eric Ledger, several times in the past. I'm sure he'll do me the favor."

"Perfect. Thanks. Let me know if you run into any issues."

"Will do."

I hit the button to break the connection, then dialed

Devon's cell. I hadn't touched base with my friend and partner in over a week. I wanted to let him enjoy his vacation in peace, but he needed to be brought up to speed on a few things.

"Devon, sorry to bug you on vacation, man," I said, pausing when I heard the telltale sound of steel drums and a male vocalist belting out Bob Marley lyrics. "Is this a good time to talk?"

"Yeah, just lying here by the pool. Nikki went down to be pampered at the spa, so I'm free to talk."

"How are things going with her?"

"Alright, I guess. I mean, we're having fun, but she's kind of high maintenance. Two weeks with her is way too long. Just this morning, she literally flipped out on our room attendant for forgetting the mints on her pillow yesterday. I'll say one thing, it was fucking embarrassing. I'll probably ditch her once I get back to the States."

"You always find something wrong with them," I laughed and shook my head.

"Hey, at least she got a vacation out of me."

"True."

"I'm sure you didn't call to talk about my trip. What's up?" he asked.

"When do you get back?"

"Sunday night. Why?"

"Just wondering so I can plan. My father's scheming and I want to run a few things by you."

"I can only imagine what the old kook is up to. What does he want you to do now? Cut off your left nut?" he laughed.

I frowned. Devon always thought it was funny when it was someone else's balls on the chopping block.

"No. He wants me to run for the Virginia Senate."

"Senator, huh? What do you think? Do you want to follow in the old man's footsteps?"

"I don't know. I'm thinking about it. I was supposed to have a meeting with the RNC last Saturday, but I didn't go. I don't know why, but I didn't take my father seriously when he first told me about it. It's since been rescheduled, but I need to make sure you're okay with my decision if I decide to run. You might need to pick up some of my clients."

Devon was quiet for a moment before he asked, "I don't get it. What's your father's angle?"

"Senate Majority Leader."

"Ah, now I see," he said, drawing out the recognition. Devon knew my father's ambitious tendencies almost as well as I did. "Hey, do what you need to do. You know I've always got your back. But I've got to say, a senator? For fuck's sake, Fitz. You hate politics."

"I know. I guess the only thing I can say is I've recently started thinking about my life. We still live in a world where there is still racism and inequality. Our country still denies minorities equal opportunity and children go uneducated. I've done nothing to help any of those things. I can't explain it, but I have this sudden urge to do something more."

"Wow. That's out of left field. You feeling alright?"

I released a long, drawn out sigh.

"I ran into Cadence, Devon."

He went silent for a heartbeat before responding.

"Cadence? As in *the* Cadence?"

"The one and only."

He let out a low whistle.

"It's been a long time since I heard that name. How did it go?"

I filled him in on all that transpired after our initial run in, including the subsequent coffee shop conversation and the research I'd done on her afterward. I finished up with the jog around the National Mall that morning but I left out the part about the kiss. I didn't know what had come over me but knew kissing her was a ballsy move. I didn't want to hear the shit he was bound to give me for it.

"So now she's planning on going to this gala thing with some lawyer. It pissed me off even though it shouldn't have. It was almost like she deliberately did it to spite me. Anyway, I've got Angie working on getting me a ticket for it."

"Hang on. Let me get this straight," Devon said with an incredulous laugh. "You see her, but you spied on her before actually talking to her. Then you go back to the office, look her up, and buy a bunch of her kids' books. Today, you go out looking for her again, then end up buying a ticket to her event but keep your name off the guest list so she doesn't know you're going to show up. I better come home soon, man. You're turning all stalker on me."

I knew he was only joking, but when he phrased it like that, I supposed it did look kind of bad. The only thing I could say was willpower was a bitch. And apparently, I still had none when it came to Cadence.

"I'm not going to let her go this time, Devon. I can't."

"What does she think about that? Does she know you want to rekindle the old flame?"

After today, I was pretty sure she knew where I stood, yet I didn't know how she felt about me. I'd always felt that Cadence was somehow out of my league, so beautiful and fierce in that soft and wistful way. She had an inherent goodness to her that was far better than me. She was grace. Beauty. My feelings for her had always been real, yet now they seemed to multiply tenfold. Every time I saw her, energy seemed to crash through the air with a torrent of emotion, resonating and pulsing through every vein in my body. I wasn't sure if it was just an echo of the past or if this was something new. Perhaps it was one and the same.

"She knows, but I think it's going to take time for me to bring her around."

"If I know you, you'll figure it out. You always were single minded when it came to her."

The light on the console of my office phone flashed, signaling an incoming call. Looking at the caller ID, I saw it was Austin's school.

"Devon, I'll have to call you back. Austin's school is calling."

"Oh, that reminds me. I've got tickets to the baseball game next week. I haven't seen the little punk in a while, so I thought I'd take him."

"Sure. I'll see if he's free."

"Cool. Catch ya later."

I hung up and clicked over to the incoming call.

"Fitzgerald Quinn speaking."

"Hello, Mr. Quinn. This is Principal Weaver calling from St. Aloysius Prep. I need you to come to the school today for a conference with me and the vice principal. Austin was in a fist fight."

A fight?

That sounded so unlike Austin.

"Is he okay?" I asked with concern.

"He's fine and sitting in the office with me. However, the other boy is in the nurse's office and will most likely be brought to the hospital after his parents arrive."

Dammit!

I shook my head, almost unable to believe it. Austin had been acting a little off lately, but I just attributed it to normal teenage mood swings. Never did I think his moodiness would lead to physical violence. I wanted to wring his neck for getting into a fight and he'd definitely have hell to pay. However, if he was having a hard time at school and I somehow missed it, this was also on me.

"I see, Ms. Weaver. I'll be there in twenty minutes."

Austin plopped down in a chair at the kitchen table of our home in Alexandria. His fists gripped handfuls of his shaggy dark brown hair in frustration. He'd be sixteen in a few months and was still all legs, yet he was starting to grow into his body. His arms were beginning to fill out, the wiry muscles finally showing some definition. When he looked up at me, gray eyes that matched mine flashed indignantly.

"This is total bullshit," he swore. I didn't reprimand him for using foul language like I probably should have. Instead, I leaned against the side of the table and crossed my arms. I tried to understand his frustration and knew he needed to vent.

"It doesn't matter if it's bullshit, Austin. Fighting isn't the way to solve things. You know better than that."

"What was I supposed to do? Just sit by and let the guy maul her?"

I hated to admit it, but I kind of agreed with the poor kid. When I got the phone call stating Austin had been in a fight, I assumed the worst. Then I got the full story. Apparently, he just started seeing a girl at school. He was kissing her goodbye before class. I remembered those days and didn't find it to be anything out of the ordinary for teenagers in high school. However, her ex-boyfriend saw them and didn't like it. When he started shoving her around, Austin stepped in and pummeled the guy.

"Look, I get why you hit the jerk," I began. "But breaking his nose? Come on, Austin. I saw the guys face. That wasn't just from one punch."

"Troy Adams is a dick. He deserved it," he spat out.

"Yeah, maybe he did. But still." I uncrossed my arms and began to pace, trying to decide on the best way to deal with this. I could be a hard ass, or I could go easy on him. I looked back at my son who was still scowling and staring at the ground. "I know I should probably punish you or something, but I think Principal Weaver already gave you more than your fair share."

"Yeah, she did! This blows! I mean, I get the in-school suspension part, but pulling me from the French trip? All my friends are going!"

"I know. I tried to argue with the principal about not pulling you, but you heard what she said. No extracurricular activities are allowed when you have in-school suspension. That includes the trip. If she made an exception for you, she'd have to do it for everyone." Austin just scowled some more, and I sighed. "Look, I know I've been working long hours lately. Uncle Devon is getting back from his trip next week and that should free up some time for me. I know hanging out with Dad probably won't be as much fun, but let's plan something."

He glanced up at me. I could tell that he stubbornly wanted to stay irate but saw when his expression slowly began to morph into one of resignation.

"Yeah, that could be cool I guess," he mumbled. "Maybe I can kick your butt at Madden again."

"Kick my butt! I think I'm the one who kicked yours the last time," I razzed, giving him a light jab to the shoulder.

"In your dreams," he scoffed. He stood and shook his head, shoulders still slumped in defeat. "I'm heading up to my room. I've got homework to do. What's the plan for dinner?"

It was barely two o'clock, yet the kid was already thinking about dinner.

Figures.

"I could probably run to the store and grab some steaks. Feel like grilling?"

"Sounds good to me. Get some of that garlic butter stuff when you're at the store too," he added. "That was good on the steak last time."

"Sure thing, kid," I said to his back as he slowly walked away from me.

After he was out of sight, I sat in the chair he had vacated and dropped my head in my hands. Sometimes, when things were going smoothly, I'd think I had the parenting gig all figured out. Then there were days like today, moments where I questioned everything I did with him, wondering if I knew anything at all. It was making me second guess whether I should continue to pursue Cadence. I knew what I wanted to happen with her—with us. I wanted to be together again. However, I worried if bringing a woman into my life was right for Austin at this stage in his life.

For the first time in a long while, I allowed myself to miss my mother. Somehow, I knew if she were here, she'd know what to do. At least I'd like to think she would. I'd been only ten years old when we shared our final memories. It was possible she wasn't the woman I'd envisioned her to be at all. Either way, I was alone now. I would just have to figure things out on my own.

11

CADENCE

Nine days flew by remarkably fast, one day blurring into the next. My daily jog around the Mall with Fitz continued. With each day, it felt as if one more brick in my wall broke free. It terrified me to know I was leaving myself vulnerable to heartbreak. There wasn't any more kissing, which I was thankful for and disappointed about at the same time. It was so confusing. Every time we talked, he'd eventually bring the conversation back to where we began over seventeen years ago. It was like he was trying, ever so subtly, to remind me of all the good we once shared. Little did he know, I had never forgotten. Nor did I forget all the pain that came with that good.

Still, his words always seemed laced with sexual undertones. The sound of his voice stayed with me long into the night. I couldn't get him out of my head. I wanted him in ways that made my body ache. Perhaps it was something to do with the change of hormones women experience in their thirties, but I still couldn't believe I had broken down and bought my very first vibrator. I told myself I had bought it just in case. It still sat in the package, burning an embarrassing hole in my nightstand drawer—I had yet to summon the courage to actually use the damn thing. Still, I knew a rubber toy, combined with the memories of what once was and the present day, would be a poor substitute for the real thing. I'd never fantasized being with someone the way that I was with Fitz. I was so distracted by my thoughts of him and constantly had to remind myself of the predicament I was in.

Before I knew it, Friday was here. Kallie was set to leave for her French class trip to Montreal in the morning and I was helping her pack. With all this confusing emotion surrounding Fitz, I didn't know which way was up. I no longer knew if I was trying to rediscover him for Kallie's sake or because of my own selfish need to take back what had once been mine.

As I listened to her debate between a green wool sweater and a blue one, my heart tightened from the swell of love that engulfed me. What I felt for her was so powerful. She was the center of my heart. My world. She was a gift given to me when I thought I couldn't go on, reminding me of the bigger purpose in my life. It wasn't about protecting my battered heart that had once been broken to pieces. It was about her. Everything I did was for her.

"I think the green one," I told her. "It will bring out your eyes."

"Yeah, but blue looks good on me. I think I'll pack both."

I laughed.

"Just remember to save enough room in your suitcase for souvenirs."

"I will. Austin made me promise to bring him something back."

My stomach sank. She hadn't mentioned his name since the prom, and I still wondered if he was going on the class trip. Perhaps this was my opportunity to tell her the truth. But then again, I wasn't sure if telling her and then sending her off to another country was the right move.

"Austin? Is he not going?" I pressed, taking advantage of the opening she left me.

"No, he can't anymore."

"Why not?" I asked, trying to sound as casual as possible.

"He got in trouble in school. He was kissing Jessica Bradford and Troy Adams saw them. Troy is Jessica's ex," she explained. "Troy and Austin got into this big old fight because Troy was pushing Jessica around. All the other kids circled around them and were chanting 'fight, fight.' It was childish in my opinion. They shouldn't have been egging Austin and Troy on, even if Austin was in the right. Anyway, they both got yanked down to the principal's office and now Austin can't go with us to Montreal."

She rattled off the high school gossip so quickly, I struggled to keep up. As her words began to compute, a feeling of relief washed over me.

Good. Kissing another girl. Not my daughter. I still have time.

"Oh, that's too bad," I said, but internally I was doing fist pumps.

"Yeah, it stinks. The whole group from prom was going to be there. Austin will be the only one missing," she said. She looked sad, but it only appeared to be a general disappointment and not the longing expression a girl would have if she were going to be missing her boyfriend. Although I didn't like to see her unhappy, her expression gave me another thing to be relieved about. I was finally beginning to believe Austin and Kallie really were only friends.

"I know what will cheer you up," I offered. "Aunt Joy and Marissa are going to stop by later to see you before your trip. I asked them to pick up a birthday cake on their way over. Since you'll be in Montreal when you turn seventeen, they wanted to do a little something for you before you go."

"That's so sweet of them! I haven't seen them in forever! How are they?" she asked excitedly.

I didn't point out she'd just seen them three weeks ago. In the eyes of a sixteen going on seventeen-year-old girl, I was fairly certain three weeks was equivalent to an eternity.

"They're good. They went away to Philadelphia a couple of weekends ago for an early anniversary celebration. When they were there, Marissa finally convinced Joy to adopt. They haven't started the process yet, but we may have a new baby to spoil before the end of the year."

"Ooh! A baby!"

"Yes, but mums the word. I don't know if I was supposed to share that with you. These things are complicated and not all adoptions go through as planned. They may want to keep it quiet until something is for sure."

"My lips are sealed," she promised, sliding her finger across her mouth as if there was an imaginary zipper.

I felt my phone vibrate in the back pocket of my jeans. Pulling it out, I saw a familiar number flash across the screen. It hadn't been programmed into my phone, but I'd listened to the voicemail that went along with it enough times to know who exactly was calling—it was Fitz.

Shit! Should I answer it?

Panic seized my chest and I glanced at Kallie. She was still rifling through drawers in search of the perfect articles of clothing to bring.

"Kallie, I've got to take this call. I'll be right back."

"No problem," she waved off over her shoulder.

Moving as fast as I could down the stairs, I practically hurdled over the banister in a rush to get out the back door. As soon as I stepped out into the early evening air, the vibrating in my hand stopped.

I stared at the motionless phone, watching the screen fall

dark. I didn't know if I should call him back. Before I could decide what to do, the phone lit up and began to vibrate again.

"Hello?" I answered tentatively.

"Hey, sweetheart."

"Hi...um, why are you calling me?"

"Shouldn't I be?"

"I don't know. We normally just chat during the morning jog. We aren't phone people."

He laughed.

"Maybe not yet, but that could change. I wanted to talk to you about something."

I glanced nervously behind me to make sure Kallie wasn't lurking anywhere, then moved further into the backyard.

"What is it?" I asked.

"I didn't tell you about this during any of our morning runs because I needed to think things out. Everything is fine now, but my son got in trouble at school last week. He was in a fight, trying to defend the honor of some girl. Teenagers," he scoffed.

I already knew this of course, but I couldn't let him know that.

"That's too bad," was my only reply.

"What I needed time to think about was you. I want to see more of you. The time we spend together in the morning is great, but I want more. I know you do too. I can feel it. However, we need to talk this out. It's not just me in the game. I have to consider Austin. Teenagers are so impressionable. I'd like him to meet you one day, but I need to do it right if you know what I mean."

Oh, I know what you mean alright. Especially since I've already met your son.

I didn't voice the words, but I was beginning to feel the walls closing in around me. My heart began to pound rapidly in my chest. I wasn't used to lying and knew I couldn't keep this up for much longer. He was going to have to know the truth sooner rather than later.

"I get it, Fitz. But let's not stress about it. I'm good with how things are for now. Keep it casual," I stated, working my hardest to sound as offhanded as humanly possible.

"I'm not okay with that, Cadence," he said in a low voice before he unexpectedly swore. "Dammit. I didn't want to do this over the phone."

"Do what?"

"I never expected to see you again. But now—after bumping into you, seeing you, spending time with you—I feel like I've been waiting my whole life for this moment. I'm ready to take the next step and see where it leads."

My breath caught in my throat.

"Fitz, don't..." I warned.

"Hear me out. I never got over you. I tried, but there wasn't a woman on the planet who could hold a flame to you. Even when I was married, I thought of you. She knew it too. She didn't know your name, but she always knew my heart belonged to someone else."

A wave of shock reverberated through me. The girl inside me wanted to leap through the phone and into his arms. But the woman in me didn't know if I should believe it. He said he loved me the day he took my virginity. Less than two weeks later, he left me broken, alone, and pregnant.

"We weren't together long enough for you to hang on to me all these years," I whispered. Tears stung the backs of my eyes. I couldn't let them fall.

"Yes, we were, and you know it."

I did, but I didn't want to admit it. There had been men over the years, casual dates that fizzled out to nothing. I'd always been afraid to go the final step, not allowing anyone to touch me. I told myself a sexual relationship with a man would spell trouble for me and Kallie. It would complicate the life I'd so carefully built. However, I always knew the true reason deep down. Opening up physically and mentally to another man would mean moving on from Fitz. It meant letting another man claim a place only Fitz had been.

"Fitz, I can't do this with you right now. I have to think about..." I trailed off.

"Think about what?"

Kallie! I wanted to scream, to finally come clean with everything. However, this wasn't a conversation that could be had over the phone. I gave myself a mental kick. This deserved a face to face. I needed to look into his eyes and physically see his reactions.

"I have to think about my responsibilities, but I agree. We need to talk about things."

"So, what do you say? How about having that dinner with me?"

"Yeah, I guess that could work," I conceded.

"When is good for you?"

The doorbell rang, interrupting my response. I heard a chorus of shrieks and looked back toward the house. Through the windows, I could see Kallie racing to greet Joy and Marissa in a huge group hug.

"Fitz, let's talk about this more on our next run together. Tomorrow morning," I told him in a rush. "Friends of mine just arrived so I have to go."

I didn't wait for him to respond and managed to end the call just in time before hearing Kallie call out to me.

"Mom! They're here!"

"I'll be right in!"

As I turned to head back toward the house, I paused to allow myself a moment to compose myself and looked around the yard. The lush green lawn was bathed in moonlight. The wooden fence I had installed when Kallie was a little girl cast long shadows over the grass, occasionally interrupted by the flicker of a firefly. Kallie and I had planted the small garden flourishing in the far-left corner. Along the fence line, we dug the dirt to make room for a long row of dahlias which were now just starting to bud. My eyes traveled the fence to where the flowers ended, marking the grave where I had buried Dahlia's ashes. The yard had been an oasis for Kallie and me as she grew up, often spending our evenings reading books or making up our own fairytales while swinging on the hammock hung between the two large oaks.

I sighed and continued on to the house. I tried to protect Kallie over the years, to shelter her from the monsters in the closet, both fictitious and real. It crippled me to know there was no way I could protect her from the firestorm of emotions she would feel learning who her father was. There was nothing I could do. My life with my daughter, as perfect and as precious as I tried to make it, was about to be blown apart.

12

CADENCE

I lugged Kallie's two-ton suitcase through the noisy and congested crowd toward the check in counter at Reagan National Airport. Well, it wasn't two tons, but it was heavy enough for me to worry about whether she'd be within the airline weight restriction guidelines. It also didn't help I was bone tired. Between thoughts of Fitz and worrying about Kallie's trip, I'd barely slept much at all the night before. I looked at my daughter who was weighed down with a carryon bookbag on one shoulder and a large duffel on the other.

"I swear, you did not have this much stuff packed last night, Kallie. What in the world did you add?"

"Sorry," she moaned. "I looked up the weather. The temps up there are all over the place this time of year. I didn't want to be too cold or too hot. I called Gabby this morning, and she said—"

"Never mind. Forget I asked," I sighed. I didn't have the patience to listen to a 'what Gabby said' rambling. Sweat was beginning to form on my brow and my patience was beginning to thin. Ever since Kallie was little, large crowds tended to make me jittery. I think it came from the fear I'd lose her. Either way, that anxious feeling never seemed to go away even as she grew older.

Thankfully, bag check went smoothly without any issues. As I walked Kallie to security, a new sort of anxiousness came over me. The longest Kallie and I had ever been separated was when she stayed overnight at a friend's house. Now I was letting her go for a full week. When I thought about it, just sending her to kindergarten practically sent me into cardiac arrest. I had to be out of my mind to allow her this trip.

"Here we are!" Kallie sang with cheerful excitement once we reached the back of the long line for security. This was the end of the road for me, and I couldn't stay with her any longer. My heart began to pound uneasily in my chest.

"Do you have your passport?"

"Yep. It's in my bag."

"And your cell phone and extra chargers?"

"All set."

"What about your toothbrush?"

She frowned.

"Come on, Mom. You double checked that yourself this morning. We can't stand here going through everything. My friends and teachers are probably already at the gate."

"You know your gate number, right?"

"Yes," she said in exasperation. "Can I go now?"

I smiled sadly, knowing I'd have to get used to this. She was almost grown up. Before long, we'd be sharing many more goodbyes.

"Come here, baby girl."

I swept Kallie into my arms, my devotion to her bubbling through me like the gentle flow of a stream. My heart no longer felt like it was going to fail because I had my reason for living in my arms. She was all that mattered. I pressed a tender kiss to her forehead, and she squeezed me tight. I felt her heart beat against mine, the thrumming in perfect sync to each other. I clung to her, knowing I was hanging on a little too tightly, as overwhelming emotion caused tears to sting my eyes. It wasn't every day a mother sent their only child off on a plane to Canada.

I pulled away and swallowed back the lump in my throat.

"Have fun and be good," I told her, knowing I didn't even need to mention the latter.

"Love you, Mom."

"I love you too, honey. Call me when you land."

"I will."

I stood there watching her for a while, making sure she got through security okay. She looked so grown up as she handed her passport to the TSA agent for approval, and once again I began to feel old. Time went by way too fast.

As I walked back to my car, my mind drifted to Fitz. For the first time, I began to feel guilty about all the time he'd missed with her. When the time came for me to tell him about her, I would need to do something to try to make up for it.

THIRTY MINUTES LATER, I ENTERED THE BUILDING THAT HOUSED Dahlia's Dreamers. For me, Saturday and I had a love-hate thing going on. While I didn't like working on what was supposed to be my day off, I loved it because I usually had the place to myself. That meant uninterrupted research, organizing, and strategy time. However, I knew someone else was in the office as soon as the elevator doors opened on my floor. I smelled coffee and heard the telltale gurgling of a fresh pot being brewed.

Joy sat at the reception desk looking at something on the computer.

"It's Saturday. What are you doing here?" I asked, making a beeline for the coffeemaker. Thankfully, I remembered to wash my favorite mug yesterday. The black ceramic cup with 'The Future is Female' in boldface type sat next to the brewing machine, just waiting to be put to good use.

"Marissa's working, as usual. I swear, the investment firm she works for is going to put her in an early grave. I'd wish she'd just quit and go back to teaching pre-school. I keep telling her money isn't everything."

"No, but it does make things easier."

"You sound just like her. Something's going to have to give if we get approved for this adoption. She knows it, but she's afraid to rip the bandage off. Anyway, I thought I'd pop in here and work on a few things since she wasn't home. We got a birthday invitation in the mail," she told me. I glanced over my shoulder to see her waving a pink card in the air.

"Oh? For who?" I asked as I stirred sugar into the coffee.

"It's for Emilia's daughter, Mayra. The two of them are staying in Fairfax with Andrés' parents while they wait to hear news about what's going on. It's closer to the holding center and more convenient. Mayra is turning five and they're throwing a little birthday party for her."

"That was nice of them to think of us."

"Yeah, I thought so too. I'll talk to Marissa to see if we're free. I'd like to go." She paused when I turned toward her, her face assessing me. "Geez, Cadence. You look exhausted."

"I haven't been sleeping well. I think I need a new pillow. Until then, a fifth cup of coffee will have to do," I joked, holding up the mug.

"A new pillow, huh? How did it go with Kallie this morning?"

"I didn't start balling like a baby if that's what you're asking."

"Well, it's a good thing you saved your tears. I'm sure they'll be falling fast the minute you step into your office."

My brow pulled together in confusion.

"Why is that?" I asked, glancing down the hall toward my office door.

"You'll see."

Curious, I stepped away and headed down the corridor. When I rounded the corner, I was shocked to find bouquets of dahlias everywhere. Vases of them literally covered almost every available surface, creating a sea of yellow, purple, blue, and pink. It wasn't unusual for us to get flower deliveries, dahlias in particular since it was the name of the organization. However, we never received so many at once.

"Who in the hell…" I began to ask, trailing off when I saw a note card sticking out from the bouquet in the middle of my desk. I crossed the short distance and plucked the card out from the petals.

You once told me all colors were your favorite, so I couldn't choose just one. Instead, I chose the ones that reminded me of a sunset. I missed you this morning. I hope that wasn't your way of telling me you weren't up for going to dinner. Call me.
Yours, Fitz

Without thinking, I had told Fitz last night over the phone we'd discuss dinner plans at our next morning run. However, I forgot about having to take Kallie to the airport when I said it. When I didn't show up this morning, it was only natural for him to think it was because of something he did or said. Now, as I stared at the hundreds of gorgeous dahlias that flooded my office, a million emotions swept over me—guilt for unintentionally standing him up, delight at his thoughtful gesture, and a kind of schoolgirl giddiness at his request for me to call him. As I processed it all, sadness also crept in. Tears blurred my vision as I tried rereading his words a second time. It was like he was trying to untie this string inside me. I was terrified if he pulled hard enough, I'd completely unravel. This man, the keeper of my heart, made me feel so much, and I didn't know what to do about it.

"Secret admirer?" Joy asked. Startled, I stuffed the card back into the envelope.

"I guess so," I replied, my voice hitching. I blinked, hoping to hide the tears.

She raised one very skeptical eyebrow and leaned against the door frame.

"You're a terrible liar."

I plopped down in the chair behind my desk. Shifting the bouquets to peer at Joy between the vases, I let out a shaky breath.

"Apparently, I'm a very good liar. I've been doing it for seventeen years!" I looked around at all the beautiful arrangements, fighting back the tears that wanted to spring into my eyes again.

"Honey..." Joy said softly. With just that one word, the floodgates burst open and every worry I experienced over the past two weeks came rushing forth.

"I don't know what to do, Joy!" I sobbed and began to ramble. "I don't know how to tell Fitz. I don't know how to tell Kallie. I'm still torn over selling the last part of my parent's land. I'm worried about our heavy caseload and the families who are at risk of separation. I'm stressed about our finances—or lack thereof, I should say. Then tonight, I have to go to this gala with Simon Reed, all because I stupidly asked him to go to keep Fitz at bay. Everything is a mess! I don't know anything anymore. All I know is I've been jogging with Fitz every day for nearly two weeks. I told myself it was because I was trying to get to know him again before I brought Kallie into things, but now everything is so

confusing. I'm feeling things I don't want to feel for him—
can't feel for him!"

Joy came over and squatted down next to my chair.
Grabbing the box of tissue that must have been hiding
somewhere within the gale of flowers, she handed it to me.

"You asked Simon Reed to the gala?"

"Of all the things I said, you picked up on that most?" I
asked incredulously, hiccupping through a sob.

"Forget about Simon. Although I really hope for your sake
he doesn't own an argyle tuxedo."

I laughed through the tears.

"Knowing my luck, he probably does!"

"Just breathe. Everything will be fine," she tried to reassure.
She held up a hand and began ticking things off on her fingers.
"Let's back it up one step at a time. Kallie is in Montreal for the
next week, so you don't have to worry about telling her right
away. The Austin thing seems to be sorted out, so no worries
there. Our caseload will get easier in a few weeks when Victoria
gets back from maternity leave. As for the families, that worry
will always be there as long as there are immigrants in this
country. You can't make yourself sick over it. Only focus on
what's within your power. The money situation is fine. I
literally just read an email from the publisher. *And I Smile* drops
on Tuesday, and presale numbers show it's on track to hit the
New York Times list. No need to sell your parents' land right
now."

I peeked at her over the tissue I held to my nose.

"It is?"

"Yes. So relax. The only thing you truly need to worry about
right now is Fitz. Telling him about Kallie is important, but I
think you need to sort out whatever these feelings are you're
having for him first. Tell me, what's going on in that big heart of
yours?"

"It's hard to explain, Joy. It's almost like we picked up where we left off, yet it's so very different. He makes me mixed up inside. He remembers things, little things that should have been insignificant, yet he remembers them all the same." I paused and handed her the note card for her to read. "He called me last night. It was right before you showed up at the house."

"Is that why you were out in the backyard?"

"Yes."

"I knew something was off when you came in. What did he say?"

"He wants to talk about things, about meeting his son in particular. I nearly laughed, having already met the kid! What kind of person does that make me? Then he tells me he never got over me, and thought about me even when he was married. I should have found it appalling, but I was thrilled!" I practically shrieked. "So you see? I'm a terrible monster!"

As a fresh wave of sobs wracked my body, Joy started to laugh.

"You're not a monster. You're human is all."

"He asked me out to dinner."

"You said yes, right?"

"No...ah, yes. Kind of, I guess. I don't remember now. See? I told you he was messing with my brain!"

"Oh, honey. You are one hot mess," she said with a chuckle. "Get yourself together. Go to dinner with the man. Allow yourself a minute to feel, explore this thing going on with you two, and see what happens."

"But don't you think that will make things worse? It's one thing for me to have feelings for him again, but I can't very well let him have the same for me while I'm holding onto such a big secret."

"I think it's too late for that. I mean, look at all these flowers, girl! The guy is obviously already head over heels for you. If Fitz is worth his salt, he'll understand once you explain why you did what you did. It probably won't be easy at first, but I'm confident if he meets Kallie, whatever hard feelings he might have will disappear."

"What about his father?" I asked, suddenly remembering a huge potential obstacle. "I'm worried about that too. Not only do I lack elite social status, I'm speaking tonight at a gala fundraiser where I'll be mingling with politicians who vote against his anti-immigration proposals."

Joy nodded, her expression somber.

"That could complicate things. However, that's politics. This is personal."

"Politics are personal, Joy. You know that. Your favorite President said it," I pointed out.

"I'm trying to say what's between you and Fitz has nothing to do with your beef with Washington. Cut the crap and stop looking for excuses. I think you're ready for more than you're willing to admit. I also think you're a lot stronger than you give yourself credit for. Go to dinner and enjoy yourself. I mean, look around you! These flowers had to cost a fortune. I highly doubt a man like Fitz will take you to the Capital Burger. Let yourself be wined and dined. You never know where it's going to lead."

I glanced around the room at the abundance of dahlias, overwhelmed by the sheer number of them.

"That's exactly what I'm afraid of," I whispered.

I knew where it would lead. I'd most likely get distracted from telling him the truth, too busy getting lost in the endless depths of his beautiful gray eyes. After the way he kissed me last week, with all that power and dominance, I learned exactly how weak I was when it came to him. However, my heart didn't have room for more breaking. I had barely recovered the first time. Joy was wrong about my strength. I didn't have it in me to withstand a second broken heart. My body wanted him something fierce—the physical attraction so strong, I ached—

but I wasn't emotionally ready to end up in his bed, assuming that's where things led to. Not to mention, I couldn't allow that to happen while he was still in the dark about Kallie. The problem was, I knew if faced with the choice, I wouldn't be able to stop it.

13

FITZ

I struggled to shake off the foul mood I was in as I walked into my father's house in Highland, Maryland. Cadence hadn't shown up for what was quickly becoming our routine morning run. I worried my call to her last night had scared her off and could only hope the flowers I sent would make up for anything I might have said wrong. However, as much as I wanted to track her down, I couldn't at the moment. I needed to focus on this meeting with the committee members from the RNC.

My father—in an attempt to make up for my absence at the last meeting—rescheduled it to be in his own home. It was rare for my father to host anything, he was usually too selfish to be bothered. However, when he did host something, no expense was spared. As I walked across the oriental rug in the foyer, I spotted my father's housekeeper coming down the stairs. Her hair was swept up into her usual tight bun, looking slightly grayer than I'd remembered. She was holding a feather duster in her hand, and she beamed when she saw me.

"Afternoon, Rhonda."

"Boy, where've you been? I haven't seen you in ages!"

Hurrying over, she wrapped her slender arms around me, her familiar scent filling my nose. It was a combination of lemon Pine-sol and cherry pie, reminiscent of my time growing up in this house. Rhonda had been the one to tuck me into bed and pack my school lunches. She'd bandaged my knees when I'd fallen off a skateboard and cried when I went away to college. She'd been my anchor and the only good thing about living here. I felt guilty not coming to see her more often. The truth was, in an attempt to avoid my father, I hadn't stepped foot in this house in nearly two years.

"I'm sorry I haven't been around, Rhonda. Work has kept me busy."

Her kind brown eyes were soft when she pulled away. She just smiled at me again, allowing me to have my lie.

"Well, it's good to see you again finally. All the men are already in the dining room. I trust you remember the way?"

"I do, thanks."

I didn't promise to visit more often. She knew I wouldn't and understood the reasons. However, I made a mental note to invite her over for dinner in the near future.

As I made my way to the dining room, I smelled the aroma of garlic and thyme wafting from the kitchen. I suspected a top D.C. chef had been hired for the occasion. Still, when I walked into the dining room, I barely noticed the silver plates and sparkling crystal goblets spread across the long mahogany dining table. I was too busy looking at the people who sat around it.

Thomas Hagel, Rick Thurmond, Fred Gramm, James Helms, and my father sat around the table. Despite the early hour of the afternoon, they'd already been into the scotch. However, I noticed their glasses were practically down to the rocks. I glanced at my watch. It was going on one o'clock, the exact time I was told to arrive. Clearly, they had started well before I got there. That fact rattled me a bit, but I shook off the apprehension.

"Gentlemen," I said with a slight nod, refusing to show an ounce of intimidation.

I did the formalities and went around the table to shake each man's hand.

"Fitzgerald, it's been a while. We're looking forward to this campaign. Your father has said great things about you," Hagel said.

Funny, he's never said them to me.

The words were on the tip of my tongue, but I just smiled and moved on to the next person. I recognized many of the men from various functions in support of my father. I was young at the time, and more often than not, I got a pat on the head as they showed obligatory tolerance for a child they knew was only there to help sway the voters. Now, I was a grown man, and they were all pushing seventy, some even older. No females were present, but that was typical. My father tended only to surround himself with the good ole boys club.

I sat down, and my father's staff began to bring out the food. The committee leaders began to talk about potential campaign strategies, and what *they* thought should be the most important things for my agenda.

I quietly listened, hardly enjoying the lobster frittata the chef had prepared for lunch. It wasn't that the food didn't taste good, but more because I was too engrossed in their convoluted ideas about how the country should be run. It was a joke. They were so far behind the times, it was actually sad. My youth might actually give me the upper hand in this charade. The Party needed a drastic change. And if it meant it had to start with me, so be it. When they brought up immigration reform, I finally spoke up.

"I understand your concerns about border security. What I

don't understand are the reasons you're all so eager to kick out the people already here—especially if they are contributing members of society. Every person in this country is more interlaced than ever before, yet we're still divided. Have you forgotten this country was founded on immigrants?" I asked pointedly, looking directly at my father. It was a bold move, but I didn't break my stare, almost daring him to challenge me in front of the other men. "The people you're going after came here as infants and children who didn't have a choice. I think uprooting them from everything they know is inhumane. I won't support that, nor will I agree to use it as a campaign talking point to get votes."

The room fell silent and my father's face turned red. Every person in the room supported my father's attempt at dismantling DACA. Thanks to Cadence, I knew all of this from the research I'd done. However, based on what I'd heard today, my father had only just gotten started.

It was Thurmond who broke the silence first by clearing his throat.

"Well, perhaps that's not the right campaign platform for you. We shouldn't have assumed that just because your father..." He trailed off with an awkward laugh, his bushy eyebrows giving him the appearance of constant annoyance. "There are plenty of other options to choose from. There's tax code reform, voting system standards..."

I tuned him out, zeroing in on my father's expression. The vein in his neck pulsed, and his gaze was piercing and cold, but I didn't back down. Through the remainder of the meal, the two of us seemed to have this silent power exchange—me telling him I wouldn't be his puppet while his eyes shot daggers coated with bloody threats.

After dessert was served, the conversation turned to the official campaign kickoff party and advertising strategies. I paid close attention to this part since not one person here seemed to realize I hadn't even said yes to running.

"We have the kickoff party already planned," Helms explained. "It'll be held two weeks from today on the rooftop of the Marine Gate Hotel. We'll start with your formal announcement. After that, cocktails and hors d'oeuvres. During this time, you'll need to connect with lobbyists, high ranking union officials, and private campaign donors. We'll be there to help of course, but all eyes will be on you. We've hired a couple of speechwriters who worked for the second Bush administration. Once we draft talking points for you, we're confident the cash will flow in. We don't have a lot of time to work with here, so we're going to need the funds for the aggressive television and radio campaign we have planned."

I held my hands up, signaling him to stop. This was all getting to be way too much.

"Alright, we need to slow down here. If I'm going to do this —and that's a really big if—I'm going to do it my way." Many eyes widened in surprise, but I continued. "TV ads and mailers will only go so far. I work in PR, remember? Image is everything. A flyer doesn't show personal investment. I'd want to give voters that in-person connection. I'd want people canvassing neighborhoods and not just for 'knock' count. I've been around my father's campaigns long enough to know the drill. Campaign operatives who rush through neighborhoods, hurrying to rack up an impressive number of knocks get nowhere. You won't reach voters that way. Real conversations will."

Gramm, who had been silent almost the entire meal, piped up.

"Sounds like a great concept, but your inexperience is showing. Do you know what that takes? First of all, there isn't time for a boots-on-the-ground style campaign. Secondly, there's a lot of strategy involved. We've got to come up with scripts to ensure the conversation isn't awkward. We'd need to facilitate training, hire supervisors. It's too monumental a task to put together in a short amount of time."

I shrugged.

"If you want me, you'll make it happen."

His laugh was almost condescending as he shook his head and continued.

"I don't think you understand how things work around here. If you do things our way, you'll find your opportunities can be quite lucrative."

"I'm not following you," I said cautiously.

They all looked at one another like they had a secret I wasn't privy to. Finally, my father spoke up.

"Tell him, Gramm," he said. Then he glanced at me with a smug expression, signaling he was getting ready to throw his ace on the table.

I looked back at Gramm who leaned back in his seat, running one hand over his round, overstuffed belly while the other fiddled with the end of his gray mustache. His eyes narrowed on me like he was assessing whether I was trustworthy. I wasn't intimidated, but I had to admit there was something sinister about him that made my skin crawl.

"The RNC has been hacked," he began. "It's not public knowledge yet. We're still investigating it and are looking to hire a PR firm to deal with the news once it breaks."

"What kind of hack?"

"Emails of top-ranking members. Cybersecurity was alerted to the breach four months ago as was the FBI."

"Four months ago? And nobody else knows about this yet?"

"We're trying to keep the hack quiet for as long as possible. We don't want public scrutiny to compromise the investigation and possibly sway the election," Gramm explained. "However, reporters have begun to sniff around. It will only be a matter of time before they draw some far-fetched conclusion that a foreign body is trying to influence the election."

I raised an eyebrow.

"Is that the case?"

Gramm just smiled, but there was something disturbing about it.

"The RNC is prepared to pay five hundred thousand dollars to the PR agency that takes on the mess," he told me, rather than answer my question. "If all goes well, another two hundred fifty thousand will be given as a bonus. So you see, Fitzgerald, cooperating with us can prove to be very beneficial to you."

I looked back at my father, disgusted by how little the man actually knew me. When he couldn't persuade me by threatening Austin and my reputation, he thought offering to buy me would secure the commitment he needed.

"Three quarters of a mil, you say? Well, I've got news for you. I won't be bought," I told them, ensuring I made eye contact with every man at the table. Standing, I tossed my napkin on the seat of my chair. "I get to choose my platform and campaign promises. I'll also want to be kept apprised of all advertising strategies. There won't be any smear campaigns on my watch. If you're good with all of that, I'll be at the kickoff party to make my formal announcement to run. If you're not good with it, you have until then to find a replacement. Gentlemen, I'd like to say it's been a pleasure, but I think illuminating is a better word to describe this meeting."

With that, I turned and walked out of the room, not stopping until I reached the Audi and was seated in the driver's seat. I gripped the wheel in an attempt to stop the angry tremors coursing through me. If I weren't in the room to hear what they had to say, I almost wouldn't have believed it myself. Every single suspicion I'd ever had about D.C. politicians had come to fruition in under two hours' time. Slamming my head back against the seat, I swore quietly to myself.

"Fuck! What the hell have I gotten myself into?"

I could only imagine their reaction once they found out I was in attendance at the Helping Lives Bloom fundraiser tonight. I supposed I could make up some bullshit excuse about trying to scope out the competition, but the explanation would be weak at best. They'd never buy it. At the end of the day, I knew I wasn't cut out to play their games. The whole thing was nothing but a goddammed circus orchestrated to get the votes they needed to push their agendas. They mercilessly exploited the working class while sleeping all fucking cozy in their beds purchased with inherited money. It was sickening.

If I truly wanted to make some sort of difference in the country, I'd never do it as long as I was saddled with this lot. Independent might be the only way to go, but there wasn't time to launch into a campaign like that now. I didn't have the power, nor did I have the political backing. Hell, I still wasn't even convinced this was how I wanted to go about things. If I wanted to make an impact, there were plenty of other ways I could do it. For now, I would just have to wait and see where the chips fell.

14

CADENCE

As I stepped off the stage at the Helping Lives Bloom fundraiser, the crowd was still applauding. I ducked my head to hide my blush, moved by their reaction to my speech. Public speaking was never part of my comfort zone. All I did was speak from the heart, recapping stories of the families who Dahlia's Dreamers had helped. I didn't deserve their applause as much as the families who survived devastating heartbreak did.

"You killed it, girl!" Joy said as I approached her and Simon Reed. She wrapped her arms around my shoulders in a congratulatory hug.

"I agree. If donors don't open up their wallets after that, I'll be surprised," Simon said.

As I was about to offer my thanks, Simon leaned in for his own hug. I stiffened, feeling unnecessarily uncomfortable with the quick embrace. I had hugged Simon many times in the past, more often after we scored a big win in court. But today, it felt different. Perhaps it was the flowers he'd given me when he picked me up before the gala. Roses. I hated roses. It had been an awkward moment, and I hoped to hell he didn't view our being here together as an actual date.

"Thanks, Simon," I said, taking a compromising step back when it seemed like he wanted to hang on a little too long. I glanced over at the computerized flower filling the large projector screen on the wall. The stem was lit green to the bottom leaf. The goal was to raise enough money throughout the night so the flower's head would bloom. "Ann Marie from Families United is supposed to speak next. Hopefully, she'll get us to the next leaf. The sooner that flower blossoms into color, the sooner I can relax."

"The really hard part is over. At least now you can grab a drink and mingle," Joy said, holding up her apple martini. "You've got catching up to do!"

"Good idea. I'll go grab us something," Simon offered as he pushed up the wire rimmed eyeglasses that always seemed to be slipping down his nose. "What would you like?"

I contemplated what I wanted to drink and glanced down at my dress. I supposed I wouldn't look very classy holding a beer bottle while wearing a black evening gown. Spaghetti straps and rhinestones just didn't seem to jive all that well with Budweiser.

"I'll have what Joy's having," I told him.

"One apple martini coming right up!"

As Simon walked away, I turned to Joy.

"You need to save me," I pleaded. "I think Simon thinks we're here as more than friends."

"Paisley bowtie isn't doing it for you, huh?" Joy laughed. "He'd have to be dead not to want something more. Have you looked in a mirror today? You look amazing!"

"Right," I said and rolled my eyes. "With the expense of Kallie's French trip and the tuition bill due, I couldn't spring for a new dress. This was the only suitable thing I had. My closet mostly consists of power suits and yoga pants."

"Either way, I don't think Simon cares if your dress is old or new. But I think you're right about him, he's been standing a little too close to you. If you want saving, I have an idea." She turned and pointed to the left corner of the room. "Marissa is over there talking to John Hasting from McGann and Hasting's Law Firm. Simon's been trying to get in there for years. If I have her make introductions, I guarantee he'll be out of your hair for the rest of the night."

"You're a life saver!"

I glanced around the ballroom and thought about the guest list, looking for potential donors who I had to try to connect with throughout the night. While I looked, I couldn't help taking in the elegance of both the crowd and the room. Chandeliers sparkled in the dim lighting of the room. Round tables were spaced across the floor, with ivory tablecloths and centerpieces of glittering flowers and scrolling vines. This event, hosted by Dahlia's Dreamers and four other non-profits, was the first of its kind. We split the cost of hiring an event planner as none of us had the experience to put on a gala. The hope was to raise money for our organizations as all of us had taken a big hit when our Federal funding was slashed. A lot of time went into the planning—and a lot of money too. I worried we wouldn't get people to buy the expensive tickets, but the event planner assured me our ticket prices were in line with other similar fundraisers. From the size of the crowd alone, it was obvious the planner knew what they were doing.

As I scanned the large space, the hired band began to warm up, preparing to entertain guests between the planned speeches. I noticed a few members of Congress in attendance who were on our side. That made me happy to see. We needed their support now more than ever. I made a mental note to thank them at some point during the night.

My eyes continued to roam until I was suddenly overcome with the feeling of being watched. I could feel it blazing from somewhere on the other side of the room. It was like a pulsing energy that was all too familiar. I should have known better than to look, but there was nothing I could have done to stop myself. For some reason, I knew who I'd discover standing there. I turned to face the blistering heat, and my mouth dropped open in a sharp gasp. All that energy crashed like the flares of the sun, searing as the flames licked my skin.

What was he doing here?

My legs seemed to wobble on my four-inch heels. My hand shot out to clutch Joy's arm, bracing myself so I didn't fall. Joy grabbed my hand and searched my face.

"Honey, what's wrong?"

The words seemed to lodge in my throat and I felt starved for oxygen as my gaze locked on the man who stood across the room. I cleared my throat and turned my back to him.

"He's here," I whispered.

"Who?" she asked, scanning the crowd of people.

"Fitz."

"Are you freaking kidding me?" she hissed. Her stylish braided updo bobbed when she turned back to me. "Where is he?"

I pointed in a general direction over my right shoulder. She looked behind me for a few moments before recognition flashed across her face. I wanted the floor to reach up and swallow me whole. It wasn't because I didn't want to see him— it was because I *couldn't* see him. Not here. I had a job to do. Networking with donors needed to be my focus, and I knew his presence would be a distraction I might not be able to keep at bay.

"God, Joy. I can't have this right now. Not tonight."

"What do you need me to do? Do you want me to tell him to leave?"

"No. Just let it be. I'll... I'll figure something out."

"Good. Because girl, if I were batting for the same team as you, I'd be hightailing it right over there. That's one fine specimen of a man. He makes Chris Evans look like a troll."

I turned around to look at Fitz again, but Simon stepped in front of me, blocking my view. He held up a martini glass filled with pretty green liquid and a flower topped stir stick.

"Oh, um..." I faltered, having already forgotten he'd gone to get a drink for me. "Thanks."

"Simon," Joy said, linking her arm through his. "My wife is over there talking to someone who I'm sure you'd like to meet." She pointed toward Marissa and Simon followed the line of her finger. When he spotted John Hasting, his face lit up. Joy winked at me.

"Oh, you definitely need to talk to him," I gushed, hoping I didn't sound too obvious.

"Aren't you going to come with us?" Simon asked.

"Oh, no. You go on with Joy. I have some people I need to catch up with."

He seemed conflicted, but only for the briefest of moments before he and Joy walked off. Breathing a sigh of relief, I looked back to the place I'd seen Fitz. Deciding to confront the situation head on, I moved in his direction. I didn't think he had spotted me yet. If he did, he was making a good show of pretending otherwise. He didn't appear to be here with anyone and looked like he was trying to find someone. The young girl in me wanted to believe he was looking for me, but the grown woman in me knew better than to get my hopes up.

I was used to seeing Fitz dressed casually in a t-shirt and shorts. Today, he had traded the look for a fitted, expensive black tuxedo over a crisp white shirt and platinum tie. He looked so different wearing it, appearing even more broad shouldered than usual. His casual hair was styled in a sophisticated way around his gorgeous face, accentuating his strong jaw and prominent cheekbones. A shiver ran down my spine at the sight of him.

When he turned his head, I knew the moment he saw me. His eyes locked on mine. I felt pinned beneath them and had to remember to put one foot in front of the other. His lips curved into a smile so gorgeous and plush and made for kissing. I suddenly found it hard to swallow. A flash of the old love I once felt for him ricocheted in the depths of my heart. It was a love I convinced myself I had given up on, knowing that waiting for him to come back to me would cause me to lose myself completely. Yet here he stood, appearing taller, broader, older. It made my heart flutter. He watched me as if he knew what I was thinking, his expression full of something dangerous, possessive, and alive.

All of those things combined with a young girl's emotions only made him that much more appealing. I wondered if that appeal was messing with my brain, or if what was quickly building between us was so much bigger.

15

FITZ

Since the moment I met her, she always had the power to drop me straight to my knees. Time hadn't altered that. She was so stunning, I went stupid, a reaction I seemed to have whenever she was around.

Tonight, her golden hair was styled in loose curls, allowing it to cascade down her back in silky waves. Even from where I stood, I would swear I could feel the warmth emitting from her very essence. She moved with devastating graciousness combined with a body wrapped in a silky black dress meant for sin. Those tempting curves had been my sin once upon a time. Taking her, then leaving her had been the biggest mistake of my life. Nevertheless, here I was again, feeling that same intense lust overtake me. It was so forceful, it made me dizzy.

I sucked down a breath and took a few steps toward her, closing the remaining distance between us.

"Small world," I remarked with an impish smile. I took her hand and brought it up to softly brush my lips over her delicate fingers.

"Small world indeed. It's funny, I didn't see your name on the guest list," she noted, eyeing me suspiciously. My hand migrated to her wrist, giving it a subtle squeeze before releasing her.

"That's because I wanted to surprise you. Did it work?"

"Oh, it worked alright. Thank you for the flowers by the way."

"You're very welcome."

"They're beautiful, but next time, I think just one bouquet will get your point across," she noted, her perfect lips slightly tilting up in a demure smile. Turning her head, she surveyed the room. "I didn't think this was your kind of crowd."

"Maybe it is, maybe it isn't. God knows, I'm going to be in a world of trouble for being here tonight," I admitted with a light laugh.

She cocked her head to the side, emerald eyes sparkling with curiosity.

"Why is that?"

"I had a meeting with the RNC today about taking a shot at the Senate seat. I'm not sure if I'm going to do it yet. Their agenda leaves a lot to be desired and I told them as much. I'm sure my being here tonight will only add to the uphill battle I could potentially have," I added warily.

"So, then why come?"

"I wanted to see you," I answered matter-of-factly before glancing up at the stage. The band had finished their warm up and struck up their first song. I took the glass Cadence was holding and placed it on an empty tray that passed by. With an exaggerated bow and a teasing wink, I said, "Please allow me the honor of the first dance, my lady."

She giggled—like actually fucking giggled. The sound reminded me of our days at Camp Riley when she'd been so carefree and innocent—when she'd been mine.

"I'm sorry, Fitz. I can't. While the band is playing, I need to be on the floor talking to donors. They'll play for thirty minutes, then we'll break for our next speaker. Do you see that big flower over there?" she asked, pointing to a wall-sized flat screen television. "I need to make it bloom. I can't do that if I spend all night dancing with you."

"Just one dance," I insisted, wrapping my arm around her waist and leading her to the dance floor anyway.

"Fitz..." she warned. I chuckled and pulled her against me just as the band's female vocalist began to sing. Splaying my palm firmly against her lower back, I guided her into a slow dance.

"You look beautiful tonight, sweetheart."

She blushed but tried to conceal it with a roll of her eyes.

"Stop that," she scolded.

"So, where's your date?" I asked, not bothering to hide the hint of jealousy that crept into my voice.

"Simon? Oh, he's off with Joy talking to some fancy law firm," she waved off.

That was good to know. Her date was a fool as far as I was concerned. If I had brought her here, I wouldn't have let her out of my sight. But that was okay. His loss turned into my good fortune.

"So, tell me, what's Simon to you? Colonel Brandon or John Willoughby?"

She jerked her head back in surprise.

"Oh, well...neither I guess," she faltered, blinking in confusion. "He's just a friend. He does a lot of pro-bono work for us. Why?"

"I was only wondering. I have to know my competition, that's all. You used to say I was like a little of both, Brandon and Willoughby that is. Is that how you still see me?"

"Fitz, those are just characters in a story. It's not real life. Besides, what I said back then was nonsense and nothing more than ramblings from a teenager girl."

Her body moved with mine to the music as I led her around the dance floor. Our feet shuffled in time effortlessly as if she were made to be dancing in my arms.

"I don't agree. You see, I've thought about the characters and I think I've gotten to know them pretty well. I think if we crossed storylines, say *Wuthering Heights* with *Sense and Sensibility*, the two of us are more like Heathcliff and Elizabeth Bennet."

"What? You can't cross stories like that! It's preposterous. And don't you dare mess with Colonel Brandon. He's good and steady, and—" She stopped short when I started to laugh.

"I love when you get all literary. It's good to know that hasn't changed."

She started to say something, but then a look of incredulity suddenly crossed her face.

"Wait a minute. Are you telling me you actually read those books?"

I chuckled again and pulled her tighter against me, not caring about who was watching—including the asshole named Simon. I leaned in close to whisper in her ear.

"I've read every single one."

I felt the shiver run down her body and grinned in satisfaction, knowing I was getting to her and breaking down those walls she tried so hard to hold up.

"Why did you read them?" she asked, a hint of disbelief still in her tone.

"Honestly? I read them because they reminded me of you during the lowest time in my life. Not to bring up ancient history but being married to Bethany wasn't a walk in the park." I saw her flinch but continued, needing her to know exactly how much I thought of her over the years. "She was a raging alcoholic, always out partying. She was a terrible mother, choosing to get completely annihilated with booze or pills instead of taking care of her own son. When she was out trying to find the next good time, I was home with Austin. His colic was bad. Rocking him was the only thing that seemed to calm him, so that's what I did for hours on end every evening. I took to reading to pass the time. Those stories you always talked about weren't necessarily my preference in genre, but they brought me solace when I needed it most. They always brought me back to you."

I watched her as we moved ever so slowly across the dance floor, the beat of the music somehow matching the beat of my heart. Her expression went from astonishment, to hopeful, to sadness all in a split second, but then I saw regret.

"Why did your wife die, Fitz?"

"Car accident. She was wasted, drunk and high on whatever poison she decided to put into her body that night. She hit a telephone pole head on. Died instantly."

Shock registered on her face.

"Oh my gosh, I'm so sorry."

"Don't be. As bad as it sounds, her death was the best thing that could have happened to me and Austin," I shrugged off, speaking words that couldn't have been truer.

"Did you ever love her?" she asked hesitantly.

I paused at that, afraid of her judgment if she knew the truth. I wondered if she'd think I was a monster if I said I never loved my wife, the woman who gave birth to my son. I'd never felt anything for Bethany other than disgust.

"Would you think I was a bad person if I said no?"

"I think you were put into an impossible situation. I don't think you'd be a bad person for not loving her."

"Well, I didn't. Not even a little bit," I admitted. I hesitated, not sure how she would take my next statement. "It was always you, Cadence. Just you."

As if on a cue, the band changed songs and a male vocalist took the mic. I instantly recognized the steady drumbeat and synthesizer as it rippled across the room. A high, sustained guitar was soon followed by the lyrics to *With or Without You* by U2.

I looked down at Cadence, studying her face. Her eyes were wide and glassy. She blinked rapidly, almost as if she were fighting back tears.

"That was one dance, Fitz. Thank you, but I have to go now," she all but whispered and pulled away.

"Wait," I said, reaching out to her. She didn't pull away again but let me guide her slowly back into my arms.

"Just one more," she whispered the warning like she didn't really mean it. She knew what I was feeling—she felt it too.

The moment, the song, it was all too real. It brought me back to another time and another place. It was reminiscent of all we once shared together—the sunsets, the slow and tender touches, the mixed tapes we listened to for hours on end. Even the smell of her was the same— that vanilla scent I'd never forget. A lump formed in my throat, and I swallowed it back, wanting to beat myself for wasting so much time. Too many years had passed.

"Do you know how many times I thought about finding you? I went to your parents' house once. It was right after Bethany died. Your father answered the door. I begged him to tell me where you were, but he said I'd had my shot. He told me you were happy and had moved on with your life."

She sucked in a sharp breath.

"I never knew."

"I left the house thinking it was for the best. I was trying to deal with the mess Bethany left behind, my business, and Austin. I wasn't in the right frame of mind. Years passed and I tried to forget you. It didn't work. I never should have left you in the first place. I've spent my whole life regretting that decision, but you have to know I'm not the same man I was then. I was twenty-two years old with more baggage than I knew how to carry."

"Shhh...please don't. I can't. Don't ruin this moment by talking about the past."

We fell silent and moved to the music, her body moving with ease against mine. The song began to come to a close all too soon, and I didn't want to let her go. When she began to pull away for a second time, I didn't hold her back. She had a job to do and it was wrong of me to get in her way.

"U2 revived the *Joshua Tree* tour," I said offhandedly, trying to break the intensity in the air. "They're playing FedEx Field. I should see about getting tickets for us."

"Yeah, maybe," she said so quietly, I barely heard her over the final guitar riff from the song. She took another step back. "That was two dances, Fitz. I really need to go work on lighting up that flower."

She stared at me for a beat, her expression unreadable. Then without another word, she turned and walked away.

I must have stood there like a fool for another three minutes at least, stunned by the connection I still had to this woman. I shouldn't have been surprised. It had always been there, but now it was burning brighter than the sun. I shook my head, forced myself to leave the dance floor, and made my way over to the bar. I needed a fucking drink.

After ordering a Jamison's neat, I scanned the crowd until I spotted Cadence. I watched her work the crowd for a while, completely in awe of her ability to move efficiently around the expansive ballroom, never lingering too long with one guest before moving on to the next. She was beautiful—the whole package—and not just in appearance. It was her whole persona and the way she presented herself. There was so much goodness in her, and I wondered if she even knew it. I always saw greatness in her, and tonight was proof.

The music stopped, and another speaker took the stage, but I barely heard a word of the speech. I was too focused on watching Cadence. I never wanted her more than I did right then, to feel her pressed against me in another dance. I recalled the feeling of her tight little body, the way she moved with me in time to the music, and I began to envision more. Being with her again. Inside her. Hearing her scream my name. I could almost picture her just as she was that summer, eyes wide with startled desire. I wanted to see that look on her face now, but this time as a grown woman.

I looked up at the flower on the flat screen. The stem was completely lit, the lights just barely grazing the petals. The sooner the flower bloomed, the sooner I could have Cadence all to myself.

On impulse, I headed over to the area where workers were accepting donations.

"How much more do you need to make that thing light up?" I asked the young girl behind the table. She looked down at her computer screen, then back up at me.

"Only thirty-eight thousand more to go!" she announced cheerfully. "Would you like to make a donation? You can do it right here or we have a website set up where you can donate anonymously right through your smartphone."

"Does the website take credit cards?"

16

CADENCE

The entire ballroom erupted into cheers, causing me to pause the conversation I was having with Tyler Mansfield, the hopeful candidate for Maryland's second district. I turned around to see what the commotion was all about and saw the donation flower had bloomed. Bright pink, blue, and yellow petals lit up the flat screen to illuminate the entire room.

"Congratulations, Ms. Riley!" Tyler said. I looked back at him, my mouth turning up in an ear-splitting grin.

"Thank you!"

"I guess you don't need my donation after all."

"It's funny you should say that. You see, I was just speaking with Erin Brooks from the California Teachers Association. Word is, national support will go to all candidates who step up to protect students who are impacted by the recent DACA changes. You do realize that Learn to Dream is one of the non-profits to benefit from tonight, right?" I hinted.

He offered me a wry smile.

"Alright. You've made your point," he chuckled. "I'm going over to the donation table right now."

I laughed as he walked away but startled when I heard a loud shriek from behind me.

"Ah! You did it!" Joy exclaimed. I turned toward the sound of her voice. She and Marissa were coming up to me with glasses of champagne. I looked behind them. To my relief, Simon was still talking to the associates from McGann and Hasting's.

"No, *we* did it," I laughed. "Can you believe it? It's barely eight o'clock!"

"I was just over at the donation table," Marissa chimed in. "Apparently, an anonymous donor came through and brought the team to the final goal."

"You've got to be kidding me! Wow! And here I was worried about the expense of tonight!" I shook my head in disbelief and accepted the offered glass, holding it out in a toast. "Cheers to a successful event and many more after!"

The three of us clinked glasses. After taking a sip, I scanned the room for the heads of my partner organizations in this endeavor. They were gathered with their staff in celebration as well. I smiled to myself, thinking of all the people and families we'd now be able to help.

Today is a good day.

The band took the stage for another set, this time starting out with an upbeat tune to match the excitement of the crowd.

"Now that your work is complete, I believe you have more time for dancing," said a low voice from behind me. I slowly turned to meet the intense gray eyes I'd felt on me all night.

I glanced at Joy. Both she and Marissa were watching me with knowing looks.

"What are you waiting for, girl? You earned it. Go dance!" Marissa told me as she pulled Joy by the hand toward the dancefloor.

I looked back at Fitz and smiled, feeling overcome with excitement from the jubilation that emitted throughout the room.

"You heard the lady. Apparently, I earned it!"

Not needing further encouragement, he grabbed me by the arm and twirled me out onto the floor with the other dancers.

Another hour passed in what only seemed like five minutes. We danced and talked, our conversation jumping from one topic to the next. Some dances were fast while others were slow, but the slow dances were different from the first two we shared. There was this buzz in the air that made it seem like everything had a sexual undertone. Fitz hadn't lost his playful side. His flirtations were deliberate as were his hands which shamelessly roamed over my back and hips. He made all the little hairs on my body stand on end, and my nipples went painfully hard every time I pressed against him. With only a single look from him, my body seemed to hum to life.

After a while, we both needed a break and decided to head over to the bar. Once our drinks came, Fitz turned to me and leaned in close to my ear.

"Room twelve-ten. Fifteen minutes," he whispered. Then he pressed a plastic card to my palm before leaving me alone and slack-jawed with a keycard to a hotel room in my hand.

As I stared down at the black plastic, my heart thudded loudly in my ears. I wasn't naïve. I knew what the invitation meant without him even saying it.

Oh God. No. I can't do this.

I still had too many secrets. While I managed to bury them for a little while tonight, I couldn't take that next step with Fitz. He had no idea. He probably thought we were rekindling an old flame. Little did he know it was so much more. If I went to his room, if I slept with him before he knew the truth, he'd hate me and think I was nothing but a liar. In a way, I was.

Overwhelming panic consumed me. I searched the room

for Joy. I needed my friend, my sounding board to help me work through this and hold me up in the way she always had. I spotted her with Marissa, the two of them line dancing to a cover song of Shakira's.

Shit!

I didn't want to interrupt their fun for my self-imposed drama. I took a long swig of apple martini number two. I wasn't a big drinker, so having already consumed a martini and a couple of glasses of champagne, this one was going straight to my head. I set the glass down on the bar, knowing I needed a clear head to work through this.

Tonight had been fun with Fitz, but I was flirting with danger and couldn't shake the overwhelming feeling of dread. Things had shifted so fast with us, and I had to put it in perspective. I needed to stop this before I got to a point of no return—I feared I already had. A part of my soul told me no attempt on my part would be able to stop the avalanche of emotions sure to ensue. There was no easy way to tell him about Kallie. I was terrified I wouldn't tell him the right way, or I'd say the wrong thing and risk losing him forever. My heart broke at the thought.

After ten minutes of indecision, I knew what I had to do. I couldn't hide from the truth anymore. Stepping onto the dancefloor, I made my way over to Joy and tapped her on the shoulder. Turning toward me, she leaned in so she could hear me over the music.

"Can you cover for me?" I asked. "Tell Simon something came up and I had to leave."

"Sure, but where are you going?"

"To talk to Fitz."

"Good, I'm glad. The two of you left so much unfinished, Cadence."

"Yeah, we did," I admitted sadly and looked down to stare

absently at the way the strobe lights glinted off the toes of my silver heels.

"Hey, look at me," she said, lifting my chin to meet her gaze. "I've been your friend for a long time. Trust me when I say he needs to know how you feel. This is bigger than just your secret about Kallie. After watching you dance with him tonight, you owe it to yourself to find out what's going on between you two."

"No, Joy. I'm not going to talk about my feelings," I told her sadly. "It's time for me to come clean. About everything."

MY HANDS TREMBLED AS I FUMBLED TO INSERT THE KEYCARD INTO the slot of the hotel room door. My chest ached with a heavy feeling I couldn't shake, knowing I was about to do the hardest thing I'd ever done in my life. Nerves gripped me as I pushed the door open, the shaking in my hands taking over my entire being.

When I entered, I found more than just the average hotel room. He had reserved a suite, complete with a sitting area, dining room, and separate bedroom. Music played softly in the background. Fitz stood near the couch, filling the space with everything him. He'd removed his tuxedo jacket, leaving it tossed haphazardly on the back of a settee. His tie was loosened at the neck, and one hand rested in the pocket of his pants while the other ran anxiously through his gorgeous dark hair. His presence pummeled me, so powerful and raw, and energy seemed to crawl the walls.

Hesitation was evident in his eyes as he took me in, but there was also desire.

"I'm glad you came," he said huskily.

Memories—flashes of another time—ricocheted through the depths of my being, causing a shiver to race down my spine. I could see the lake, candles and dahlias on the dock, a young

Fitz looking nervous and apologetic. I forced myself to blink it all away and took a step forward. Struggling to gather myself, I tried to find the courage for what I needed to do.

"Fitz, we need to talk about some things."

"And we can. Over strawberries and cream."

My brow creased in confusion until I looked down at the coffee table in front of the sofa. An entire platter of strawberries had been set out, each one artfully arranged to surround a bowl of whipped cream. Champagne had been poured, the little bubbles slowly rising to the surface of two crystal glasses.

Oh, no...what is he doing?

I didn't expect this. This had disaster written all over it, and I couldn't let us get any deeper than we already were. It just wouldn't be right. I needed to remember the reason I came to this room in the first place. It was about the truth. His seduction was not supposed to be in the cards. I'd never be able to withstand him.

"I, um..." I faltered, words just seeming to ramble from my mouth. "I don't know...Fitz. I can't, I'm not..."

I felt rooted to the spot, undecided whether I should stay or flee from the room. As it turned out, I didn't have to make the decision because Fitz made it for me. He was already moving closer, possession in each measured stride. He leaned in and pressed the gentlest kiss to the curve of my neck. His spicy and masculine scent clouded my senses. I trembled when he reached up, his fingers softly brushing along the side of my cheek. I dared to look into his eyes, gray pools that swirled with something fierce.

"You wanted to talk?" he asked huskily. When it was clear I'd been rendered speechless, he laughed. "Come on, sweetheart. Let's sit down."

He led me over to the couch, and we sat. I stared at the plate of strawberries, my mind in a daze. I blinked once, then twice, in an attempt to push away the fog. I should have known this was coming the minute I decided to come to his hotel room. We could never ignore what was between us. Joy was right. Fitz and I had left too much unfinished. There were parts of me I tucked away, hid from and ignored, but they would always belong to him. Acknowledging those parts only made the guilt I felt for lying that much worse.

"Fitz," I began, attempting to find the strength to say the words on the tip of my tongue. But anything I might have said was silenced by the strawberry he brought to my lips.

"Taste," he demanded.

Oh God...

So much more was laced in that one little command. My already pounding heart began to race faster and faster, knowing I was already losing the battle after only being in his presence for a mere few minutes. Every single dirty fantasy I'd ever had about Fitz wanted to come to life right here in this room. I thought I might combust just from the images conjuring in my head. I needed to rein it in—to try harder.

"When you left, I didn't know—"

"It killed me to walk away from you," he interrupted. Stark vulnerability oozed from his truth. My throat tightened from his expression, filling my head with an onslaught of emotions I wasn't ready to admit to him, yet I couldn't stop the words from tumbling from my mouth.

"You took a piece of my heart when you left."

"And I left my whole heart with you," he confessed, grief written in his expression. I nearly broke from his words as his head dropped to rub his nose against the side of my face.

"Fitz, I'm terrified of you hurting me all over again. There's too much at stake this time," I began again, ready to lay it all out on the table. My mouth felt dry. I unconsciously ran my tongue over my lips to moisten them so I could speak. Fitz's eyes dropped and followed the path of my tongue, before finally making their way back up to mine. Just as I was about to speak, his lips crashed down on mine.

I didn't even attempt to protest, surrendering to a merciless kiss that set me on fire. Our tongues quickly found each other, his more aggressive than mine. This was not the kiss of a college boy I once knew nor was it like the kiss we shared near the Lincoln Memorial. This was so much more. It had the ferocity of a hot-blooded male taking complete and utter control.

"I never meant to hurt you. I'm so sorry, sweetheart. So sorry," he murmured against my lips. Tears sprang to my eyes, confusion winding through the very depths of my soul. Layer by layer, he was stripping me bare, peeling away the hurt to expose all the love.

"I would have waited for you," I whispered in between kisses.

"I couldn't let that happen, Cadence. You deserved more. So much more."

His hard contours pressed against the softness of my body and I found myself reaching up to thread my hands through the hair that skimmed along the edges of his collar. Fitz groaned when I tugged, and he pulled me tighter against him. I'm not sure when or how it happened so quickly, but we went from kissing to feverishly groping each other in a matter of minutes.

My fingers found the buttons of his shirt and I worked my way down, a desperate need to feel his bare flesh under my palms all consuming. He caressed a hand down my back, along the zipper of my dress, and settled at my waist. Shivers raced down my spine, wishing he'd just tug the zipper down.

Why did he get to me like no one else ever could?

I was too far gone to answer that question. I'd worry about tomorrow when tomorrow came. Every time he was near, I felt an unexplainable connection between us like an invisible line that remained unchanged over time. I wanted to be with him more than anything else.

No. I need to tell him about Kallie. I'm not supposed to be doing this.

I pulled away quickly, leaving us both panting.

"Wait," I breathlessly told him, the one syllable word coming out pained. I leaned back and adjusted the strap of my dress that was slipping down my shoulder. Fitz was a disheveled mess, his hair sticking up wildly. His shirt twisted up, only having been partially removed. His chiseled abdomen rippled as he shrugged impatiently out of the rest.

Once it was off, he reached for me again, but I froze when I caught sight of a tattoo. It was high on his right arm, a thorny vine that wrapped around his bicep up to his shoulder. In the center was a light blue dahlia, so similar to the one I had inked on my own shoulder. Except with his, the words *Fade Into You* were scripted underneath.

I felt like I'd been punched in the gut. It was the name of the Mazzy Star song that had been playing when I gave myself to Fitz for the very first time. I brought my eyes up to meet his, terrified of what I'd find but still desperate to see his expression. He pressed his forehead to mine. I almost couldn't breathe.

"When did you get that?" I whispered, fearful of what his answer might be.

"Six years ago. I told you, Cadence. I've never stopped thinking about you. I've never stopped loving you," he said, his voice low and throaty with emotion.

I clutched a hand over my drumming heart. All the oxygen seemed to suck completely from the room, replaced by him— only him. If he'd said that to me a few weeks ago, I would have accused him of lying. I would have assumed it was some fairytale designed to dupe me into dropping my panties. I pulled back a few inches to study his face. I saw the torment in his eyes, but there was also devotion and love. I couldn't doubt his words. He was speaking the truth.

I choked back a sob.

"Fitz, I..."

"I don't want to live in the past anymore, Cadence. I want what I have here. Right now. I want to be with you."

Elation raced through my veins like a potent drug. He was all around me, his presence thick and consuming in a way only he could be. It had been so long since I'd wanted—and I mean, really wanted. It was too much. It would be so easy to give in. I'd fantasized so many times about what it would be like to make love to Fitz again, but never in my wildest dreams did I think I'd have the opportunity. I closed my eyes as he pressed soft kisses down the line of my neck. He exuded testosterone, drugging my senses until I was high on him. I soared, my blood heating, my flesh on fire. My brain tried to tell me I should push him away, but I was no longer in control. My body had completely taken over.

When he brought his lips to mine, he hovered over them, barely touching. My lips parted and we breathed together, slowly inhaling each other's need. I'd never loved anyone the way I had loved him. At that moment, I realized I never stopped. It was still there even after all this time.

Everything was so wrong, yet oh so right. I knew I should end this madness—I should tell him about Kallie first—but I couldn't bring myself to do it. I feared his anger and was afraid to lose him again. Perhaps if I allowed myself to have tonight, if I gave into this burning need I had for him, I'd find the courage I needed to do the right thing. But for now, I only wanted him. My body, the shell that had lain dormant for seventeen years, had finally awakened because of Fitz. My Fitz. Only he could make me feel this alive.

I gave in and felt my body melt into him, burying the fear and surrendering every ounce of resistance.

17

FITZ

I sensed the moment she surrendered. Her cheeks flushed and her eyes darkened, the color turning a deep green and brimming with possibilities.

There it is. There's my sweetheart.

It was wrong for me to take things so fast with her again. I knew I should be taking my time despite the electric heat burning through my system. I had planned to take her out to dinner first, then maybe to see a show at the Kennedy Center. I had wanted to give her romance like I never did all those years ago. But then tonight happened. After feeling her warm body pressed against mine and her hips gyrating against me on the dance floor, I threw all thoughts of taking things slow right out the window.

Now, I could barely believe she was here in my arms. We had left so much undone and so much unsaid. It had taken me years to figure out, but I knew what I had with Cadence was nothing but pure and good. It was real. My biggest mistake was I'd allowed too much time to pass. I missed her. I missed this.

The other women I'd held over the years had always felt awkward because Cadence was the only person I'd ever truly wanted there. Nobody had ever felt the way she did.

"It's been too long. Just too damn long," I whispered against her mouth before running my tongue over her heart-shaped lips, demanding she open to me. I kissed her. Tenderly. Passionately. Desperately. I wanted her to feel everything I felt, to feel the relief from finally having something we'd denied ourselves for so long, and to breach the distance time had left between us.

My arms banded tightly around her, and I hauled her to my chest, lifting her petite body to carry her to the bedroom. I never took my lips from hers, guiding her as I plundered her mouth. Once there, I carefully set her back on her feet and turned her around to press her back against my chest. I held her close, palm splayed across her abdomen as I leaned in to graze her ear. My breath was hot on her neck as she tilted her head so I could nibble down to her shoulder. I felt a shiver rock her body and she moaned.

"Fitz..." she sighed and tried to turn to face me. I stopped her, keeping her back firmly against me. I wasn't in a hurry. I wanted to savor every moment with her.

"I don't want to be rushed. I want to take my time. To make you feel good."

"I need to touch you," she persisted.

"We'll get there. First, I want to relearn your body. I want to feel every curve of you, to memorize you with my hands. With my tongue. I want to taste every inch of you."

She shuttered again as I moved my hand up her back to the zipper of her dress. Slowly, I tugged it down to expose the delicate curve of her spine. Looping a finger under each strap at her shoulder, I slid them down until the silk pooled at her feet.

I pressed my lips to her shoulder, trailing soft kisses along the hollow at the side of her throat as I reached around to cup her breasts through the black strapless bra. The material was rough against my palms and felt nothing like the basic cotton she had worn all those years ago.

This was mother fucking lace.

Sexy.

Intimate.

And all woman.

My cock strained in my pants and I thought I might come on the spot. I wanted nothing more than to toss her on the bed and fuck her senseless. Reining in the mad desire I had for her, I forced myself to do exactly as I'd promised, memorizing every delicious inch of her body. My mouth moved across her shoulders, working my way down her back and over her hips.

More lace. And a thong no less.

I groaned.

"You're unbelievable. You don't know what you do to me," I uttered as I raked my tongue over the curve of one cheek, then the other, before moving down and up each of her legs. "I've missed this so much. Your taste. Your scent. Your goodness. You've always been my light even when all I could see was the dark. I'm going to take care of you now. Show you how sorry I am. It's just me and you, sweetheart. That's all it ever was."

Working back up her body, I finally turned her to face me. Pure lust thrummed through my veins, and I felt my jaw tighten, desperate to see everything that was underneath the few scraps of black, sexy lace. I reached around to her back with slow, purposeful grace and unclasped her bra. Those perfect mounds and dark pink nipples spilled free.

I cupped her neck and ran my tongue down the base of her throat until I captured one hardened peak in my teeth, relishing in her startled cry as I rolled the other nipple between my thumb and finger. I lured her back toward the bed until the backs of her knees hit the mattress. Legs buckling beneath her, she sat down.

"Lie back," I told her. She hesitated, her eyes fraught with worry, and my stomach sank. I nearly swore, hoping like hell she wasn't having second thoughts now. "Cadence, don't look at me like that. Don't tell me to stop."

"Then don't talk. When you apologize..." she trailed off. Her expression was pained before a flash of determination sparked. "I don't want to be confused about the past. I want this, Fitz. I need it. I need you. No more talking. Just touch me, please."

"No talking? I'm sure I can think of something to keep my mouth occupied," I teased as I coaxed her back, eager to remove that final barrier of clothing so I could taste her like I never had the chance to all those years ago. If she didn't want to remember the past, that was okay. I didn't want the chains of history to hold us down any more than she did. I would give her this moment and show her all the pleasure we could share. Seventeen years ago, we had been a mess of fumbling limbs. Now I wanted to teach her all the things we could become.

Sliding down the lace, inch by beautiful inch, I tossed them aside and dropped to my knees between her legs. Grabbing her ankles, I pushed her legs apart, careful to gauge her expression as I did. Desire pooled deep in her emerald eyes, the delicate blush moving from her cheeks to her breasts, and I knew she wanted this.

Tearing my gaze from her face, I allowed myself finally to look down at her now exposed sex.

So fucking gorgeous.

I slid the pad of one finger gently over her clit. Her back immediately arched and an elicited gasp wrenched from her throat.

"Oh!"

I parted her folds and slowly sank one finger inside her heated well, a sharp hiss escaping me.

"God, you're exquisite. So wet. So ready. So dammed tight." I slid another finger in, stroking her inner walls while my thumb traced slow, leisurely circles over that pulsing bundle of nerves. She gasped again, and I sank down to her, unable to go another minute without tasting her. "Tell me you want me, sweetheart. Tell me you want this."

"Yes, yes! I want it," she shamelessly begged.

Wedging my shoulders between her legs, I rested my face against her inner thigh and inhaled her scent. Dipping down, I swiped my tongue over her entrance in one long lick. She tasted as sweet as she smelled. Her hands reached down and grasped the ends of my hair, searching for something to hang onto as I explored every nook and crevice of her most intimate parts. I dipped into her core before laving her oh-so-sweet spot, making her writhe beneath me. I pressed my tongue flat against her, rolling until that beautiful nub began to pulse. It was only a matter of time before she came apart.

"That's it. Let go, baby. Let me taste you on my tongue. I want you to feel it. I want you to feel all the things I was meant to make you feel."

"Oh God. Please!"

She pushed up against my mouth. I glanced up to find her head lolling from side to side, golden hair splayed out on the bed, desperate for the release that was so near. Cadence without inhibition was intoxicating. I could drown in her. Her hips bucked, but I held her still and brought her to new heights.

I felt her body stiffen and heard her sharp inhale. When she came, she screamed out my name, and it was the most glorious fucking thing I'd ever heard. The way she responded so readily to me was one of the things I remembered most about her. I loved her carefree trust and the way she allowed me to take her to places she'd never been. Before long, she'd realize I'd only taken her for a stroll around the block. I had a trip around the world planned for her tonight.

I toed off my shoes and shed my pants, leaving only my

boxer briefs in place. I eased her body up the bed and blanketed her with my weight, sinking us deeper into the mattress. My throbbing cock pressed against her abdomen as I worked my hand up her thigh, peppering light kisses along her collarbone.

"Do you feel how hard you make me?" I whispered.

"Fitz, I...I," she panted through glazed eyes. I lifted my head to look at her. A mix of embarrassment and longing stretched across her features. "It's been so long. There's only been..."

She trailed off, hesitating as she traced a finger over my arm tattoo. I trembled from the contact, remembering the yearning I'd felt for her on the day I'd gotten it.

"There's only been what, sweetheart?" I prompted.

"You, Fitz. I don't know how to do this with you now," she told me, her voice just a husky whisper. "I've only ever been with you, but I'm sure there were all kinds of women for you between then and now. It's crazy. I didn't seem to care about my sexual inexperience when I was eighteen, but I care now for some strange reason. Go easy on me, okay?"

I froze at her words, seeing the raw vulnerability in her eyes.

There's only been me?

Fuck.

There was something caveman-ish about the way that fact thrilled me. She was mine. Just mine. I was the teacher of everything. But it was also scary to know how easily I could hurt her. I desperately didn't want that to happen. If things didn't work out with us for some insane reason, it would be so, so bad. It could be even worse than seventeen years ago.

She knew this, yet she was here, trusting me once again with her body. We had so much history and so much hurt we were up against. That didn't make our situation ideal, but there was just something about her. Something about the way she curved into me, the way she smelled like vanilla and sunshine that made none of the what-ifs matter. She was the only woman I could ever remember wanting to hold on to for more than a fleeting moment of time. I knew, without a shadow of a doubt, I still loved her. We belonged together. As bad as things could potentially be, I also knew there'd be so much good.

"Cadence, I love you. I've never stopped loving you. All other women were nothing but a temporary high. Every time I closed my eyes for the past seventeen years, I was with you. It's always been you. I'll stop now if you want me to, but sweetheart, I've never wanted anything more than I want you right now."

She reached up to cup my face.

"Then what are you waiting for?" she asked, echoing the words she had spoken to me so many years before.

Not wanting to spend another moment hesitating, I got up from the bed and opened the nightstand drawer to remove the box of condoms I had placed there earlier.

"Were you planning this all along, Mr. Quinn?" she teased, but there was a hint of suspicion in her question as well.

I chuckled.

"I know how it looks, but no. I shot over to the corner store while you were schmoozing donors. After dancing with you, I figured I should grab them just in case."

I shed my boxers and made quick work of the condom. Before climbing back onto the bed, I took a moment to appreciate her naked form spread out before me. Cadence was always beautiful, but a naked, luminous Cadence was something poets could write sonnets about.

I crawled up her body and she bent her legs, cradling me between. Positioning myself at her entrance, I pushed forward, barely sliding through the arousal between her lips. Her slender arms clung to my neck encouragingly and I pushed all the way in. I sucked in a gasp so hard it made my lungs hurt. The effect she had on me hit me like an earthquake. Lacing my fingers through her hair, I captured her mouth with mine.

"Fitz," she whimpered as my forehead rocked against hers.

"Do you remember what I told you the first time you gave yourself to me?"

When she responded, her voice was thick with emotion.

"You said I was beautiful, and you loved me."

"I meant what I said then, just as much as I mean it now. I love you, Cadence. Nobody has ever fit me the way you do. You've haunted my dreams for seventeen years. I've wanted to touch you. To feel you. To kiss you. To fuck you. I let go of you once. I won't ever do it again," I declared, the words a breath of a whisper against her lips.

She moved her hips, matching my thrusts as she gripped my shoulders. The girl I once knew was innocent—untouched. But this... this was Cadence defined. It was like she couldn't get close enough, and it was a feeling I understood all too well. I felt it too. I had to remind myself to go slow when every fiber of my being wanted to fuck her hard and claim her as mine once and for all.

Her nails raked down my back to my ass. I felt the bite of them against my skin as she made those little gasping noises that made me impossibly hard. Nothing had ever felt or sounded so damn good. She was perfect—my treasure. There was just the right amount of give-and-take as I drove into her deep and hard. The air in the room seemed to come alive—the energy and the connection the truest thing I'd ever felt. I could worship her all night long.

I tried to keep some modicum of control, but it was to no purpose. I could feel her body building, the pleasure mingling with my own as she moaned my name. Our bodies were slick with sweat, pleasure bound, and full of need. When I felt her start to come apart again, I pinned her arms above her head. I plunged into her, possessing her, the tightening of her perfect body making me feel like I could live forever.

My body raced, my dick pulsing with need, hard and

desperate. Hunger ravaged through my veins and every muscle in my body tightened, rippling with an unbearable force. I slammed home and my world flashed white. So bright. A blinding light that left me quaking in her arms.

We lay there panting for what seemed like hours, but it was probably only minutes. After a time, I rolled off of her and she snuggled into the crook of my arm. Her arm draped across my torso, so warm and familiar. It was where she was meant to be.

She looked up at me, her eyes searching for something. What it was, I didn't know. I reached out and brushed my thumb across the bottom of her swollen lip. Old hopes mingled with new ones filled my mind, thoughts of what once was and what could be.

"You're beautiful," I said softly. She reached out and pinched my arm. It wasn't a hard pinch, but it surprised me nonetheless. "What was that for?"

"Just making sure you're really here. Is this real? Are you really with me?"

"I was a fool to walk away from you, but I'm here now. This is as real as it gets."

"I need you, Fitz. I've always needed you," she whispered into the quiet room. "No matter what happens, don't ever forget that."

18

CADENCE

Sunlight streamed through the sheer white curtains on my bedroom window. I looked at the red neon numbers on the clock and saw it was after eight. I rarely slept in that late. But, then again, I had quite the workout last night. I gave in to a good stretch and all but purred as I recollected the memories.

I'd heard tales from female friends about how the best part of sex was oral, but I'd always had my doubts because it seemed a little too intimate for my tastes. However, last night I learned how wrong it was to assume. Fitz had taken me to new and impossible heights. I didn't think it was possible to orgasm so many times in one night. He'd taken me on the bed, then again on the sofa in the sitting area where he licked strawberries and cream from my body as if I were a feast he wanted to savor.

My experience with him had shaken the foundation of my very soul. Nothing could have prepared me for it. It was more than just sex. The way we moved together and the way he demanded I yield everything to him had caused sensations to take over so much more than just my body. He'd taken over my heart as well. The young man who stole my heart when I was a teenager had done it once more. I had, without a doubt, fallen in love with Fitzgerald Quinn all over again. Only this time, it was stronger.

The hours had passed much too quickly. I could have stayed wrapped in his arms all night long, but around midnight, I reminded Fitz why we should leave. His son would probably do more than just raise an eyebrow if he found out his father had been out all night.

I crawled from my bed and headed to take a shower. As I allowed the hot stream to flow over my head and shoulders, I recalled the conversation from the night before. Fitz had insisted on taking me home while I insisted on handling it myself.

"Let me take you home," he said.

"I'll just grab an Uber."

"No, Cadence. It's late. You're a beautiful woman. You shouldn't be all alone at midnight. What did you tell me about creepers? My car is already here. I'm taking you home."

"Still trying to save me, Mr. Quinn?"

My teasing jest ended up delaying us for another hour as Fitz felt the need to take me again right there on the floor. As a result, I didn't get home until well after one in the morning. Allowing him to bring me home had been a mistake. I'd been too drunk on him to actually think it through. While I currently didn't have the risk of him running into Kallie, his knowing my address made me vulnerable. It meant I truly only had a little less than a week to tell him the truth. I couldn't risk him coming here unannounced and possibly finding out about her before I was ready.

After I finished the shower, I put on a t-shirt and yoga pants before pulling my hair back into a French braid. I didn't bother with makeup, having no plans to leave the house. Today was for catching up on house chores—especially laundry, which was piled a mile high in the first-floor laundry room off the kitchen.

I flipped on the stereo and began to separate the mountain into piles of colors and whites. After tossing the first load into the washer, I went to the closet in the front hall and pulled out the vacuum. Just as I was about the start it, a knock at the door sounded behind me. Turning, I peered out the sidelight. My stomach sank when I saw Fitz smiling at me through the narrow window.

Shit! What is he doing here?

It was exactly what I'd been afraid of happening. For a moment, I debated not opening the door, but he already knew I was inside. I glanced around the room. Framed pictures of Kallie were literally everywhere. Panic jarred my bones. There was no way he could come in.

Slowly, I stepped up to the door and unlocked the deadbolt. Opening the door just a few inches, I smiled and tried to hide my apprehension over his being there.

"Fitz, what a surprise!"

"I brought breakfast," he said with a crooked grin, holding up a bag with the logo of a popular bagel joint stamped across the front.

"Um, actually. I was just cleaning. The house is kind of a mess. Can I get a raincheck?"

"Don't be ridiculous. I don't care if the house is messy," he insisted and moved to push open the door. I braced my foot firmly at the bottom so he couldn't push it open without a lot of force. I scrambled to think of an alternative plan—one that didn't include Fitz stepping foot inside my house—all while ignoring the little voice in my head screaming at me to tell him the truth.

"No, really. How about we take it over to Arlington Ridge Park instead? It's a nice day out," I suggested, hoping like hell I sounded convincing.

He cocked a puzzled brow but nodded.

"Alright, I guess that could work too."

"Perfect. Let me just go change, and I'll be right out." Quickly, I shut the door in his face. Locking the deadbolt again, I pressed my forehead against the back of the door. I said a silent prayer to anyone who would listen, begging for some kind of guidance. It was clear I had no idea what I was doing.

LESS THAN TEN MINUTES LATER, I SAT IN THE PASSENGER SEAT OF Fitz's sleek black Audi as we headed toward Arlington Ridge Park. Tension filled the space due to my refusal to let him in the house and it made for awkward conversation. When we didn't turn off George Washington Memorial Parkway when we should have, I turned to him in confusion.

"Where are we going?"

"To my house in Alexandria."

My eyes widened in fear, the earlier panic I'd felt coming back in full force.

Shit! Austin.

I couldn't let him see me.

"I'm not ready to meet Austin yet, Fitz," I rushed out, unable to cover up the high-pitched sound of anxiety.

"He's not home. He's out shooting hoops with a few friends and will be gone for most of the day." He reached across the middle console to give my hand a light squeeze of reassurance. "I won't push you until you're ready. It'll be okay."

I leaned my head against the car window and exhaled a sigh of relief. Still, I couldn't help but worry about the possibility of him returning home early. It would be disastrous. Fitz pulled his hand away, but his touch lingered on my skin long after and his words remained in my head.

It'll be okay.

"Just give me a heads-up next time, okay?"

We stopped at a red light, and Fitz turned to me. I could feel the heat of his gaze, and I slowly looked his way. Gray, stormy eyes met mine.

"What are you so afraid of, sweetheart?"

"Who said I'm afraid?"

"After last night, I thought..." he trailed off, and the light turned green. Turning his attention back to the road, he hit the accelerator. Reaching toward the dash, he fiddled with the dial of the radio. "I think we could use a little music. Current or throwback?"

Oh God. No throwback.

I couldn't handle being catapulted back in time any more than I already had.

"Current is good."

He settled on a station, and I listened to Imagine Dragons sing apologies about everything they'd done as we drove the rest of the way in silence.

Jesus Christ...I should have picked throwback.

When we pulled into his long driveway, I nearly gasped at the size of his house. When I compared his home to the modest house I shared with Kallie, we might as well have lived in a cardboard box. White pillars flanked the front door of the stone and stucco, two-story home. Meticulous landscape lined the walkway and steps leading to the main entrance, following the front of the house and disappearing around a stone wall that ran the length of the property. I barely had a minute to take it all in before he pulled the Audi into a large three-car garage.

Fitz killed the engine, then walked around to my side of the car to open the door for me. I took a moment to compose myself, not wanting to appear like I was gawking. It was only a house after all—albeit, a very big house—but still just a house. He'd told me he ran a successful business. I guess I just hadn't realized exactly how successful it truly was.

When we entered the house, I wasn't surprised to see the stunning interior. The kitchen was a modern design with brushed stainless-steel appliances, black granite countertops, and tall white cabinets. Light fixtures hung from the ceiling at various heights. They appeared to be there more for ambiance than light, softly illuminating the six bar stools wrapped around the kitchen's center island. Through the door to the kitchen, I could see a large family room leading to a sun porch and the backyard. I couldn't see beyond the porch but could somehow envision Fitz playing with a young Austin on the lush, green lawn surrounding the house.

"You have a beautiful home, Fitz."

"Thanks. I'll give you the tour after we eat," he replied as he placed the bag of bagels on the counter. Moving to the refrigerator, he peered inside. "Looks like Austin polished off the apple juice. Is orange juice okay?"

"That's fine," I murmured, feeling relatively uncomfortable in this posh space.

Fitz came back over to where I stood, pulled out a barstool, and motioned for me to sit. After retrieving a couple of plates, he sliced the bagels apart and spread cream cheese over the halves of each one. I took a tentative bite and stared out into space, unsure of what to say.

He watched me curiously and seemed to sense my uneasiness because after we finished eating, he took my hand and led me through the living room toward the sunporch. As we walked, I couldn't help noticing the many photos dotting the surfaces of end tables and walls. Most were pictures of Austin throughout the years, growing from a boy to a young man. It wasn't all that different from what was in my house. A family lived here—Fitz and Austin, father and son. My heart ached, feeling I'd been robbed of something precious, wishing pictures of Kallie were among his collection.

Once we stepped out into the warm morning air, Fitz

turned to pull me into his arms. The raw strength of him enveloped me. A calm stillness held fast to the air as the sun rose closer to its peak in the sky. He pressed his forehead against mine and softly ran his hand up and down the curve of my spine.

"What's wrong, Cadence? You've been acting strange since I showed up at your house this morning. And please, don't tell me it's because you didn't want me to see a mess."

There was an acute worry in his voice, a kind of brokenness that seeped into my reply.

"Why did you bring me here?"

"Because I wanted you to see another part of me and to tell you more about Austin before you meet him. I also wanted to talk about us—where things stand and our future together."

Our future together.

My knees nearly buckled, struggling to find balance as my throat thickened. This man was making me wish for things I had no business wanting. A heavy ache began to build in my chest.

"What about our future?"

"I've decided I want to make a go for the Senate seat, but I want to make sure you and Austin are okay with it before I tell my father. I haven't spoken to Austin about it yet. I figured I'd talk to you first."

I shook my head, unable to comprehend how things progressed so fast. He was speaking to me as if we were in this together—like I had a say in his life choices.

"You don't need my permission, Fitz."

He shifted back a step and stared out at the horizon. Raising a hand, he ran it through his dark hair and inhaled a deep breath. When he looked at me again, uncertainty clouded his features.

"Actually, I do. I want to be with you. If you're a part of me, people will want to know about you."

"What do you mean? What people?" I asked cautiously.

"The RNC will dig into your background to make sure there isn't any kind of embarrassing scandal that could potentially hurt my campaign. It's for my protection and I won't be able to stop them from doing it. I can try to shield you from the press, but your photo will inevitably be taken by journalists whenever you're around me. This is why I need your permission. I want you by my side, but you're more important to me than a Senate seat. If you're not on board, I won't do this."

His words caused fear to rake over me in a rough caress. I stared at him in shock, unable to believe he was thinking so long-term about our future. But more, realizing what would be uncovered when they began to dig into my past terrified me. I had allowed Fitz to crawl back into my heart, and clearly, he'd allowed me to do the same. That was the problem when someone affected you. It caused you to entertain all kinds of foolish ideas about what could be. Now we were at a crossroad.

Telling Fitz about Kallie was now irrelevant. I would still have to come clean of course, but everything he said put a new spin on things. This campaign—the scrutiny that came with what he wanted to do—would throw us into a spotlight I didn't want. Kallie would be the subject of only God knew what. Plus, I had to consider Dahlia's Dreamers. My organization was built on years of sweat and blood. It was my heart and soul. Joy wasn't far from the mark when she spoke about Fitz's father. He had already made it his mission to make life miserable for organizations such as mine. The minute he found out I was the cause of scandal for his son, I knew he'd destroy everything I worked so hard to build. I might be able to handle whatever was thrown at me, but I would never allow Kallie or the good people at Dahlia's Dreamers get caught up in this.

My shoulders fell as I processed the implications, never feeling more defeated than I did at that moment. I should have thought this through better. Just as he had seventeen years ago,

Fitz's father would once again stand in our way. My head shook back and forth in denial, unwilling to accept the idea of having my world picked apart by the very man who went against everything I believed in. I slowly backed away from Fitz, bringing one hand to my heart, the other to cover my mouth. Angry tears began to well in my eyes as I processed the terrible twist of fate life had thrown at us.

"Cadence, what's wrong?" Fitz reached for me, but I pulled away.

"I'm sorry, but I can't be a part of this."

"I understand why you might have reservations. We can talk about it. But, sweetheart, there's no reason for you to get so upset."

"There's nothing to talk about. I can already see how things will play out." I turned to go back into the house, but he grabbed my arm to stop me, forcing me to face him. "Please, Fitz. Don't make this any harder. I need to go home and think about things. I can't do that here—with you."

"There's something you aren't telling me. I can feel it. What's really going on?"

I could only stare at him, overcome with confused emotion as I grappled to put what I was feeling into words. I wanted to scream and yell about all the injustices in the world. I wanted to hate Fitz for leaving me and marrying another. I wanted to hate myself for not running away like I should have all those years ago. Perhaps if I had, Kallie wouldn't have met Austin, and none of this would be happening. I wanted to meet Fitz's father, so I could rip into him for the way he'd destroyed his son's life, my life, and for his daily attempts to crush the opportunities for so many hardworking immigrant families. Too many tears were shed because of him. He was the epitome of everything I tried to shield Kallie from. My daughter represented everything good in the world. I'd die before giving Fitz's father the chance to manipulate her like he had so many others. I didn't want him anywhere near her.

"It's your father, Fitz. He wants to destroy everything I stand for!"

His eyes widened in surprise, disbelief clouding every inch of his beautiful face.

"That's why you're upset? Because of him?"

"He's gotten in the way of us before. Mark my words—he'll do it again. I don't know how, but he will. Once he finds out who I am, it'll be gloves off. He'll dig into my past and manipulate the situation until you want nothing to do with me. I allowed the man to dictate my future seventeen years ago. I can't sit by and watch him do it again. I need to protect myself and everything else I hold dear."

His fists balled in frustration.

"Dammit, Cadence! I'm not my father, and I won't lose you because of him. Not again—not when I've waited this long to find you. I won't let him stand in the way of us."

"Please, just bring me home," I pleaded again.

"You don't need to run from me. I won't let him manipulate anything. Things are different from what they once were."

He was right. Things were different—so much different. We were no longer kids who could pass our nights away making love as the sun dropped low behind the trees. We were adults with real-life responsibilities that couldn't be ignored. For every action, there was an equal and opposite reaction. And while I was acutely aware of Newton's Third Law, there was one force that had remained unchanged over time—the connection between Fitz and me. I half wondered if I was focusing on all the wrong things. Perhaps, if our connection had defied the laws for this long, I could dare to hope.

"Why do you want to run for Senate, Fitz?"

He released his hold on me and let his arms fall to his sides. Pinching the bridge of his nose, he moved to sit down on a white wicker loveseat and motioned for me to join him. After I sat, he put his arm around my shoulders and pulled me close.

"I feel like I've been coasting. Sure, I have a good life. I got through all the bullshit from the past. I have a successful business, a beautiful home, and an amazing son. But I always felt like something was missing—like I'd yet to find my true purpose. When I ran into you, something shifted in me. I can't explain it, but I found myself needing to do something more. After that, everything strangely began to align. When my father proposed the Senate seat, my initial response was a firm no. But then, because of you, I've spent my evenings reading about the DREAM Act, border security, and everything else in between. In the process, I learned how far the Party has fallen off the moral compass. I feel like I can change all that, but I can't do it alone."

I couldn't help smiling at his words.

"Moral compass, huh? You sound like a liberal."

He shrugged.

"Perhaps it's not liberal at all, but common sense. I know all the ugliness that can come with politics and can handle swimming with the sharks, but I'm not well-versed on the interworkings of the government. Proposals are one thing, but actually enacting good policy is completely different. I worry I'm making the move too soon and I'll be in over my head. I'm not naïve. I know I have a lot to learn." He paused and twisted in his seat so he could look down at me. "I want you to help me, Cadence. You've been in the thick of this for years and I could use your guidance and wisdom."

"Fitz, you're shooting for a Republican seat," I said, shaking my head. "I appreciate your enthusiasm about making a change, but I hope you're not taking this on to try to impress me. You have no idea what you're up against."

"I know better than you think. I may need you to help me to navigate the ins and outs, but I can handle the rest."

I shook my head again.

"If you're really hell-bent on doing this, you should get to know the people you're planning to fight for."

"That's part of my campaign strategy. Knocking on doors—"

"No, it's more than that," I interrupted. "I mean *really* get to know them. Do you remember me telling you about Andrés Mendez? The man who's facing deportation for a traffic ticket?"

"Yeah, why?"

I hesitated, not sure if I should extend an invitation that could put Emilia's future in-laws at risk. They were still considered undocumented after all and it was rare for people in their situation to extend invitations to outsiders. They trusted me to keep their secret safe, but they didn't know Fitz. However, if Fitz truly wanted to help, he'd have to embrace the passion that would inevitably fuel his fight. To me, the best way he could attain that was to make a personal connection to the people he was fighting for.

"Emilia, his fiancée, invited me to their daughter's birthday party on Thursday night. Her name is Mayra and she's turning five. You should come with me and learn the human side of things."

He cocked his head to the side curiously before slowly nodding in agreement.

"That's a good idea. I'd like that."

"After the party, I'll be curious to hear your thoughts. If you come out of it with a fire in your belly that's even remotely close to mine, I'll help you."

I bit my lower lip, feeling nervous about the promise I'd made. While it was a promise I intended to keep, I wasn't sure he'd still want my help after all was said and done. I crossed my fingers superstitiously, hoping I didn't make an already precarious situation so much worse.

19

FITZ

I pulled in the driveway to a little Cape Cod-style house in Fairfax with Cadence at six o'clock on Thursday evening. Through the large front window, I could see people milling about and hear their jovial chatter carrying through to the outside.

"You ready for this?" Cadence asked, giving my hand a slight squeeze as we walked up to the front door.

I grinned and looked down at the box wrapped in pink unicorn paper tucked under my arm. That morning, Cadence and I had met for our routine run. When she mentioned the present she bought for Mayra, I realized I probably shouldn't show up to the party empty handed and went out during my lunch hour to get a present for the birthday girl. Clueless on what to buy, I scanned the shelves of purple and pink frill for what seemed like an hour before Google ultimately saved the day.

"Yeah. Thanks for the invite, sweetheart. I'm excited to meet them."

"Don't thank me yet," she laughed. "Kid birthday parties can get a little rowdy."

Cadence knocked on the door and a short woman with dark brown eyes opened it a moment later.

"Ah, Miss Riley! I am so glad you came!" the woman exclaimed, her subtle Spanish accent coming through in the way she added importance to her vowels.

"Please, Emilia. I've told you before to call me Cadence," she laughed and embraced the woman in a brief hug before we were ushered inside. "Emilia, this is Fitz. I hope you don't mind I brought him along."

"Not at all!"

"It's nice to meet you," I said and extended my hand. After we exchanged pleasantries, Emilia stepped in between Cadence and me and looped her arms through ours.

"Please, come with me to the kitchen so I can introduce you to the family."

Swarms of kids ran past my legs as we walked through the living room toward the kitchen. Balloons drifted around aimlessly on the floor and happy birthday banners draped the walls. A stack of unopened presents piled high in the corner of the room. I didn't think I'd ever seen so much pink in my life.

When we got to the kitchen, loud conversation and laughter assaulted me. In a mix of Spanish and English, everyone seemed in competition to be heard, each person practically shouting over the next. I half wondered how any of them knew what the other was saying.

Emilia clapped her hands loudly.

"*Atención!* Everyone, this is Cadence Riley, the wonderful woman who is helping to bring Andrés back to us. This is her friend, Fitz."

I nodded to the crowd of men and women who simultaneously called out "thank you for coming" and "*bienvenido*" before returning to their previous shouty conversations. I couldn't help but smile. I never had big, loud family gatherings growing up and had only witnessed them on TV. However, being in the thick of it was something else entirely.

"Oh, good! I'm glad you made it," I heard Cadence say. I turned to see who she was speaking to and recognized Joy and the woman I'd seen briefly at the fundraiser gala. "Fitz, you already know Joy. This is her wife, Marissa."

As more hand-shakes where exchanged, a strange look passed between Joy and Cadence. Joy looked almost wary while Cadence's eyes widened with an unspoken message.

"Uh-oh. I saw that. Is there anything I need to know?" I joked.

"Nothing at all!" Joy's dubious expression evaporated, and she laughed. "Unless you don't know about Mrs. Mendez's specialty."

"Ah, yes! It's delicious!" Emilia said with an excited nod. She pointed to a platter of what looked like green leafy packages wrapped in twine on the center of the kitchen table.

My brow furrowed, trying to figure out what it was, and Cadence began to laugh.

"Your expression is priceless, Fitz. Those are tamales."

"They only get made on special occasions because they take so much time to prepare," Emilia explained. "Would you like to try one?"

I shrugged.

"Sure. Why not?"

She scooped up one of the green bundles, removed the twine and outside leafy part, and set what was inside a plate for me.

"The plantain leaves are only meant to preserve the flavor. What's inside is the good part. Think of an enchilada but less saucy," Cadence suggested.

I took a hesitant forkful only to find myself pleasantly

surprised by an odd combination of chicken, cheese, tomatoes, and some other kind of meat. Slowly, I nodded my appreciation.

"This is really good!"

"I'm glad you like it," Emilia beamed. "Please, make yourselves at home. Now that everyone is here, I'm going to round up the children. Mayra is very excited to open her presents."

As if she had ears in the walls, the most adorable little girl with wide brown eyes came whizzing into the kitchen. She was sporting pigtails with bows and a pink animal print dress. This had to be Mayra.

"Present time?" she asked excitedly.

"Yes, *princesa*. Now go get your cousins and sit nicely in the living room."

After we finished our tamales—which was probably one of the most delicious things I'd ever tasted—Cadence and I followed the other guests into the living room. Joy and Marissa were already there chatting it up with an older woman on the sofa. Kids circled, seeming to materialize out of nowhere, vying to get the best seat next to the birthday girl.

Mayra opened each present one by one, stopping in between to politely thank the person who'd given it to her. After all of her gifts were opened, everyone piled back into the kitchen to sing happy birthday. And again, there was more pink. The platter of tamales had been replaced by a huge cake decorated with pink icing and rainbow hearts.

"*Feliz cumpleaños*, Mayra," the group began to sing. I didn't know the Spanish words, so I just hummed the birthday tune along with them.

Cadence stood on her tiptoes to whisper in my ear.

"I love how they've hung on to their culture and traditions, yet still embrace the American way. That's what makes this country so great. This is what I wanted you to see."

"What are you two whispering about?" Joy asked. I turned, not realizing she had been standing behind me in the doorway.

"I was just telling Fitz how I liked that they haven't completely abandoned their heritage to fit a mold." An indecipherable look passed between them before Cadence said, "I'm sorry, Joy. That wasn't directed at you."

"I didn't think it was. You're right though. It's nice to see them staying true to who they are."

"What did I miss?" I asked, feeling completely confused.

Cadence glanced at Joy but fell silent.

"It's okay," Joy said with a nod. "He can know."

Cadence turned to me, placed her hand on my arm, and leaned in closer so as not to be overheard.

"Joy's family is originally from Colombia. In the late seventies, before Joy was born, they fled to find sanctuary in the United States to escape the Colombian conflict. All of them, including her older brother, were undocumented. Joy's parents are still undocumented, which is why I was hesitant to speak. Undocumented people don't generally like to have their status broadcasted."

My brow furrowed, still relatively perplexed.

"Okay... so what does that have to do with traditions?"

Both Joy and Cadence glanced around with worried looks as they scanned the room.

"Why don't the four of us go back to the living room while everyone else enjoys their cake? It's quieter in there," Joy suggested. Unsure what the big secret was, I followed the three women into the living room. Once we were seated comfortably on the overstuffed sofa, Joy turned back to me. "My family name is actually Martínez, not Martin. It's a name my parents stopped using once they came to the U.S. They wanted nothing to do with where they came from—including the language. To this day, I've never heard them speak a word of Spanish. Cadence knows it has always bothered me to think about the customs my family chose to wipe out. That's why she apologized even though I knew she didn't mean anything by her comment."

"I gotcha now. Why did your parents do it? Was it to fit in?" I asked.

"Partly. Being a black family in America in the seventies already had its challenges. Add a language barrier to the mix and it would have been even worse. However, with my parents, it was more about forgetting all the bad things they left behind. They wanted to start anew, but everything came to the forefront after my brother's arrest."

I raised my eyebrows in surprise.

"His arrest?"

"Yes. That's the reason I wanted to come in here where it was private. I didn't want to scare Emilia or the family any more than they already are," Joy explained and looked sadly toward the kitchen door. "My brother was arrested when he was twenty-five years old. He was still undocumented. My parents didn't want him to apply for Deferred Action. They were afraid the application would be denied, and he'd be sent back Colombia. So, he never filed. As a result, he didn't have the same opportunities I did. It's amazing what having a social security number can do for a person. People don't realize how those little nine digits define their rights, freedoms, and opportunities."

"So I'm beginning to see," I murmured, thinking about all the conspiracy theories I'd read about undocumented immigrants. They weren't eligible for the same benefits afforded to legal citizens. That was a fact, yet, so many believed otherwise.

"Anyway, he wasn't a bad kid, but he had his struggles. One night, he got caught up in a bar fight over something stupid. He and four others were arrested and charged with assault. Within in a matter of weeks, my brother was sent back to Colombia."

Her voice cracked, and she paused to take a deep breath. A single tear slid down her cheek and Marissa squeezed her hand encouragingly. A look of understanding and sympathy passed between them before Joy continued. "We tried to speak to him over the phone, all while trying to find a way to get him back. He managed to find a place to live and we sent him money until he could find a job. Then one day, we couldn't reach him. One month later, we found out he'd been killed. He was shot dead while sitting outside a local store, an innocent bystander caught in the crossfire between the store owner and one of the drug cartels. That's when my parents finally decided to open up about the place they'd escaped. The things they saw and lived through were terrible. It was no wonder they wanted to bury it all."

I had no words as I tried to wrap my head around the horrific story. Other than the momentary tear, Joy told the tale with little emotion. She spoke matter-of-factly as if she were numb to recounting a story she knew all too well. I'd read similar stories in recent months, but somehow it was different hearing it from someone I knew.

"That's why Joy really came to work at Dahlia's Dreamers," Cadence added. "It wasn't because she couldn't find a job. She had a great job teaching high school music in Baltimore. She gave it up in order to help others from meeting the same fate as her brother."

I wanted to ask more questions, but the crowd from the kitchen began to gravitate back into the living room, effectively ending the conversation. I looked around the room at Andrés Mendez's family members, feeling as if I were seeing them in a whole new light. They'd welcomed me graciously with open arms and treated me like one of their own.

However, as the night wore on, I was able to see past their display of happiness as they celebrated little Mayra's birthday. When I looked closer, I could see sadness and worry about

Andrés in their eyes. I saw the sorrow when Mayra asked if her daddy would be there soon. I saw the concerned glances they gave Emilia when they thought she wasn't looking. I wondered how she was holding up through all of this. They were a family who felt the same love, devotion, and worries as anyone. That simple fact was overlooked by so many, the human side easily cast aside and overruled by fear of the unknown.

I draped an arm over Cadence's shoulders and fiddled with the end of her braid. For the first time, I truly began to understand what drove her to help these people. I didn't think it was possible, but my love for her—for this remarkable, unselfish woman—seemed to grow even stronger. I didn't know what I did to deserve this second chance with her. She'd been the one who got away, but there was no chance I would let her go again. I pulled her tight to my side and vowed right then and there to do something to try to help this family and the poor little girl who didn't know where her father was.

I sat quietly, listening to the warm chatter between family and friends and attempted to think of ways I could help. I knew my asshole father would be of no use, but he wasn't the only one with political connections. Leaning in closer to Cadence, I whispered in her ear.

"What's the name of the judge?"

She angled her head up to look at me.

"What judge?"

"The one handling the Garcia-Mendez case."

Her face screwed up in disgust as if just the thought of the judge turned her stomach.

"Judge Perkins."

My head snapped back in surprise.

"Perkins? As in Jonathan Perkins?"

"Yeah, I think so. Why? Do you know him?"

I knew him alright. That shady bastards backdoor deal stole years of my life. He and my father schemed to throw every possible criminal charge at me, deliberately scaring me to accept the nuclear option. Because yeah—my fake marriage had been nothing but fucking nuclear. My hatred for Jonathan Perkins surged. His crooked ways bound me to his daughter and to a life I never wanted. The only good thing to come out of it was Austin, the grandson who Perkins had little to do with over the years. Considering all the man had put me through, I'd say he owed me more than just a few favors. Perhaps it was time I played his own game and called one of them in.

I looked down at Cadence and met her curious emerald eyes. If I told her my thoughts, she'd get her hopes up. I didn't want to do that until I knew whether Perkins would even hear me out. I hadn't spoken to the man in years.

"Yeah, I know him. Let me see what I can do," was all I said.

My phone buzzed in my pocket signaling an incoming text. I pulled it out and glanced at the screen, frowning.

"What is it?" Cadence asked.

"It's Austin. Devon took him to a Nationals game tonight. Traffic is a bitch going over the bridge, so they decided to stay in the city at Devon's condo. Austin's going to crash there for the night and Devon will just drive him to school in the morning."

"Oh. Is that a bad thing?"

"No, I'd just planned on spending some time with Austin after I left here. I wanted to talk to him about the campaign and get his thoughts on it. It's no biggie. I can just talk to him tomorrow night." My gaze dropped to her pink, heart-shaped lips. I took in the subtle sheen of gloss coating them as I thought about the possibilities of being kid free for the night. "Come home with me."

Her eyes widened in surprise.

"What?"

I leaned in close to her ear and breathed her in. She smelled like vanilla and desire—it was intoxicating. The seriousness of the past thirty minutes seemed to melt away.

"You heard me. Austin's gone for the night, and I have the house to myself. It's fate, who are we to argue with it? Stay the night with me."

"Fitz," she hissed in a low whisper. "I can't stay the night with you!"

"Yes, you can, sweetheart. Come home with me," I repeated before lowering my voice to a breath below a whisper. "I want you naked. I want to taste you. I want you screaming."

Her eyes darted about the room nervously as she looked for anyone who may have overheard our private conversation. I knew my words were highly inappropriate for a kid's birthday party, but I didn't give a shit. Nobody could hear me, but they would eventually see the tent threatening to pitch in my pants if I didn't get out of here soon. Just thinking about a naked Cadence did all sorts of things to me.

Her demeanor shifted, and her eyes glimmered with a barrage of conflicted emotions—desire, longing, apprehension. She squirmed slightly but didn't say yes or no to my request. Instead, she stood up and walked over to Emilia.

"Emilia, it's been a pleasure. Fitz and I are going to take off."

Hell, yeah.

I smiled to myself and followed her lead. After we exchanged farewells with everyone, we headed for the door. Cadence turned to me as soon as we stepped outside.

"I'm not going to stay the whole night, but I will come for a few hours."

"I can do a lot in a few hours, sweetheart."

"I'm sure you can, Mr. Quinn, I'm sure you can."

20

CADENCE

During the car ride to Fitz's house, the air crackled with inexplicable sexual tension, and we barely managed small talk. Once we got into the house, we stumbled up the stairs to his bedroom like a couple of teenagers in a hurried frenzy.

When we reached the upstairs hallway, his arm snaked around my back and he lifted me effortlessly. It was as if I weighed nothing more than a feather in his arms as he carried me to his room. Setting me down on the center of his bed, he cradled my face in his hands and pulled back. We both stared into each other's eyes.

"I love you so much it hurts," he whispered.

I wanted to repeat his words more than anything. I'd loved this man my whole life, but I couldn't voice the words while I was still looking for excuses to hide the truth. I stared into his deep gray eyes and my chest ached. I wanted him. I loved him. I *needed* him. My throat thickened with overwhelming emotion.

"Fitz, I..." I paused when I felt a lonely tear slide down my cheek. Fitz leaned down and kissed it away.

"God, Cadence. Don't cry, sweetheart."

"They're happy tears," I explained. "I'm just so happy here with you. This moment. I... kiss me, Fitz."

He grabbed my head and yanked my mouth to meet his. My heart felt like it would explode. Everything in my body tensed. I breathed him in and felt his heat. He made me feel so much all at once. I felt frightened, happy, desperate, and hopeful. My tongue danced with his and I poured every single thing I'd ever felt for him into the kiss. This was where I belonged. I'd found my place again—and it was in his arms. It was home and there was no place I'd rather be.

We kissed frantically—nothing had ever felt so good. His tongue collided with mine and my back arched. I moaned into his mouth. I had no sense of time as we began to claw at each other's clothing. In a matter of seconds, I was down to my bra and panties feeling breathless as I tried to recover from his merciless kisses.

"Holy shit," he panted.

"Yeah, I'll say," I replied as I tried to slow my racing heart. My body was buzzing as I stared at the pulse beating at the base of his throat. I kissed it, needing to taste his skin with my tongue. When I pulled back, his gray eyes were burning with desire as they raked over my face.

"I want to taste you."

"As much as I'd love that, not yet. Roll onto your back," I told him.

He did as I asked without question. I climbed over him and straddled his hips. His hands came around to cup my ass as I leaned down. I pressed my lips to his chest, slowly moving my hand down his torso to push down his box briefs and wrap my fingers around his length. Working my way down, I trailed kisses over his abs. The last time we were together, Fitz had gone down on me. It was an experience I'd never forget. Tonight, I wanted to return the favor.

When I reached his thick member, I hesitated and licked my lips. I'd never done this before and hoped like hell I wouldn't screw it up. I only knew everything in the past seventeen years had brought me to this moment. He was the person who had walked me home because he was worried about my safety, the one who planned a picnic on the floor of a stockroom so I wouldn't be disappointed, and the man who had shown gentle tenderness when I gave myself to him for the first time. He'd always lived in my heart. His touch reminded me of the girl I once was and made me believe in the woman I was today.

"You don't have to, sweetheart."

"Shhh... don't make me lose my nerve."

I tentatively swiped the head of his cock with my tongue.

"Jesus fucking Christ," he hissed as he gripped my head. His fingers tangled in my hair and I felt a heady rush of power. Growing bolder, I sucked the head into my mouth.

I'd never felt such an intense need to pleasure someone, but with him, everything was different. Skills I never knew I had came to the forefront as I took in more of him. I ran my tongue around the smooth crown. He groaned and it gave me the courage to lower my head further. He was thick and soft on my tongue as I sucked, his ridges sliding back and forth over my lips.

He thrust himself deeper and forced a steady rhythm. I opened my throat to accept him, sucking and twisting my tongue around his thick shaft, using my hand to pump faster. I felt desperate and unable to get my fill of him. I swallowed and opened my throat even more to take in every inch I could. I pushed my head forward, taking him deep with my swallow and held steady.

He inhaled sharply.

"Cadence, stop," he panted. "I'll never last if you keep that up. I don't want to come in your mouth. I want to be inside you when I do."

I flipped back onto my elbows and watched as he stood up to slide his boxer briefs the rest of the way down his muscular thighs. He was way too attractive for his own good. When his cock sprang free, I took in his length and girth as he sheathed his hard shaft with a condom. There was nothing I liked more than looking at him. We might have been well into our thirties, but Fitz's chest was just as broad and ripped as it had been when he was twenty-two.

Suddenly, I became self-conscious of my own body. I'd been so wrapped up in the moment the last time we were together, I never paused to consider my breasts weren't as perky as they'd once been. I'd tried to stay in relatively good shape by religiously jogging every morning. My legs and ass were decent, but my belly was definitely a lot softer than it used to be. Fortunately, I'd escaped horrible stretch marks during my pregnancy with Kallie and only had a few faint lines which had mostly faded over the years. Still, my body wasn't nearly as tight, and I couldn't help but wonder if Fitz found the looser version of me to be just as beautiful as he once did.

Without thinking, I closed my eyes and pulled the bed comforter over to cover myself.

"Cadence, what's wrong?"

"Nothing," I responded quickly.

Climbing back onto the bed, he blanketed me with his body.

"Sweetheart, look at me." My eyes fluttered open. "You're beautiful. I don't ever want you to hide your body from me. It's flawless."

"How did you know what I was thinking?"

"I can read it on your face. I can see it in the way you tensed up and tried to hide. There's no reason to hide from me. All I see is how perfect you are."

My heart swelled as I brought my legs up to surround his waist. I felt his erection grow impossibly bigger as it pressed against my core. Shamelessly, I rocked my hips up, relishing the friction from his iron hard length against the lacey material of my panties. My sex clenched, and I buried my insecurities, imagining his length thrusting inside me.

Reaching beneath me, he wound his hands behind my back and unclasped my bra. My breasts spilled free and he cupped them instantly, rolling the peaks between his thumb and forefinger until I thought I might buck right off the bed. I struggled to find coherent thoughts. Moans and pants took their place. The air smelled of sex mixed with his cologne, making an all-encompassing vapor designed to intoxicate. Heat flooded my core, needing to feel him inside my body more than I needed to breathe.

I allowed my fingers to explore the ripples of his abdomen —touching him, needing to feel the heat of his skin. Our lips danced, and our hearts beat wildly against each other's. He led, then I led, each of us giving and taking. My insides tightened, and I whimpered.

He prowled down my torso, his mouth moving over my belly and kissing the inside of my knee. Fire shot right through me when he pushed aside the crotch of my panties. He slipped a long, thick finger deep inside and every part of me came alive.

"God, sweetheart. You're so fucking wet."

His finger worked through my folds, lightly grazing over my clit. Electricity flowed through me causing every nerve ending in my body to stand at attention. He teased me for a minute or so before pushing another finger inside of me. Every part of my body sizzled. Fire burned through my bloodstream. I panted toward the ceiling and closed my eyes. My hands fisted in the sheets as a feeling of ecstasy began to build. Time seemed to stand still. My muscles tightened, and heartbeat quickened. It beat so hard I could feel it in my ears. I was already close. So close.

All at once, he removed his fingers from my body. I gasped from the sudden stop of pleasure and snapped my eyes open. He was looking at me with intense arousal as he brought his fingers to his mouth. I watched as he licked my juices from his fingers and something inside me quickened.

"Please, Fitz! Don't... I need to feel you!"

He didn't listen to my unashamed begging but instead, brought his fingers to my lips. Without question, I opened my mouth and tasted the tanginess of my own essence. Leaning in, he pressed his mouth to mine in a blind assault of lips and tongue, moving in perfect harmony.

His hands slid down to my waist, and he looped his thumbs through the sides of my panties. He slithered down my body and ripped them down my legs with a ferocity that made my head spin. I gasped from the heat that blazed across my skin.

"Say it again," he growled. "Tell me what you need."

"You, Fitz! I need to feel you inside me."

A groan rumbled from somewhere deep in his chest as I guided him to my willing, wet sex, bringing him to the place only he had been. He plunged inside.

"Fuck," he growled. "Your body. The way you feel. It's like you were made for me."

He pushed harder and faster, riding me in a way he never had before. I thought I might combust from the pleasure of it.

"God, you feel so good!" I gasped.

Something in him seemed to snap, releasing whatever measure of control he had been trying to hang onto. A scream escaped me as he plunged forward. Each thrust was deeper than the last, filling me completely and bringing me to new heights of ecstasy. I was lost, floating weightlessly and I didn't care if I ever came down.

His fingers laced through my hair and he tugged, causing my scalp to tingle in the most delicious way. He was everywhere —inside me, touching me, kissing me. I couldn't feel anything except him. He was a part of me, and I was a part of him. It was an overload of sensations, consuming me with inexplicable, mind-altering need.

Rolling our bodies, Fitz pulled out and flipped me onto my stomach to take me from behind. Strong hands gripped my hips as he pulled me to meet him thrust after thrust. He molded my ass with his palms and pleasure wound fast. When his thumb raked across the most sensitive part of my behind, I sucked in a sharp breath. I jumped, unable to process he would touch me in such an intimate spot. More shocking was my disappointment when he moved his hand away. Alarm gripped me as I realized how deep I'd fallen. I was ready to submit every last part of me to him.

I didn't know what it was with him. Whatever it was made me forget about everything—the past, my responsibilities, the lingering unspoken truths. It was as if we were destined to be together, bound in the most fundamental ways—like nothing could have stopped our reunion from happening.

Holding fast to my hip with one hand, he reached around with the other to circle my clit with his finger. Tremors rolled through my limbs as he pounded into me. My arms wrapped around a pillow, trying to find something to hang onto as he drove me higher and higher. Shockingly, he pulled out and flipped me onto my back once more.

"I want to see your face when you come, baby," he said huskily, his lips curving up in a way that read pure sex.

In an instant, he was back inside me, plunging with a ferociousness that took my breath away. Pulling all the way out, he pushed in again all the way to the hilt. He wasn't gentle in any sense of the word. I raked my hands down his chest, then back up to grip his shoulders. Drenched with sweat, he fucked me and fucked me, over and over again. Dizzying shimmers of color began to dot my vision and I cried out.

"Fitz! Oh, oh!"

"Look at me. Keep your eyes on me."

Noises I'd never made before ripped from my soul. I moaned and drowned in the waves of ecstasy. My legs started to quake, and the earth stilled. Energy spiked, my core clenching in a blissful state of euphoria as the orgasm rocketed through my body.

"Let go, Fitz. Let me feel you come," I rasped.

Dropping his head to mine, his hips brutally continued to snap in and out. The intensity billowed, making us one. I'd never felt more connected to him as I did the moment his body began to tremble. He jerked and shook as he swelled and pulsed inside me, crying out my name over and over again. I felt him shudder before he finished, his body going still.

I didn't want to move and break our connection. I think he felt the same because he groaned in disappointment when his softening cock slipped from my body. Rolling onto his back, he shed the condom and tossed it into the wastebasket next to the bed. He slid his arm under my head, pulling me tight to his side, and I curved into him. We laid there for what seemed like the longest time with my hand resting on his pounding heart.

As I listened to his breathing slow to a steady rhythm, I forced myself to separate the euphoria of the present moment and think about the reality I was faced with. I'd allowed myself to get lost in him once again, but things had gone on for far too long. I should never have come here tonight. At the rate our rekindled relationship was moving, no time had seemed like a good time to tell him about Kallie and she was due home on Sunday. I only had a few days left and I couldn't put off the truth any longer. However, now wasn't the right time. I needed a concrete plan before I brought the avalanche of passionate emotions surging between us to a screeching halt.

An idea about how to tell Fitz began to form in my mind as he traced slow circles with his index finger over my tattoo.

"Fitz," I said into the quiet room.

"Yeah, sweetheart."

"There are a lot of things we need to talk about. I know you said you wanted to hang out with Devon tomorrow night, but I was wondering if you'd want to stop by on Saturday morning? Maybe do breakfast?" I suggested.

"That sounds like a great idea," he murmured against my head. "I have a lot of questions after meeting the Mendez family tonight. We can go through them, then maybe go over my speech. I was emailed the drafts for the kickoff party this morning."

"Yeah, maybe," I replied weakly.

Assuming he still wanted me to attend the party after he learned the truth.

I had to believe he would. The connection we shared wasn't something years could sever. When two people loved each other the way we once had, there was no chance of ever being the same again. It was too strong. My heart had finally found its way back to him, but I had to tuck it away again—even if it was only for a little while. It didn't matter what was present in every look, touch, and kiss. It was time he learned everything.

———

WHEN I GOT HOME LATER THAT NIGHT, I WENT STRAIGHT TO MY bedroom and pulled out the box of letters I had written to Fitz all those years ago. Carrying the box down to my tiny home office on the first floor, I set it on the old maple desk and bent to open the safe situated underneath. I rummaged through the contents, pulling out any document related to Kallie—her birth certificate, hand and feet prints taken at the hospital where she was born, old report cards. One by one, I placed each paper on the scanner and printed out a copy. After collecting various pictures of Kallie taken over the years, I put everything I'd gathered inside the box.

Replacing the lid, I brought it back to my room and set it on the dresser before changing for bed. After turning off the lights and climbing into the comfort of my cotton bedsheets, I stared up at the shadowed blades of the ceiling fan swirling round and round. I thought about all that had happened tonight, the past few weeks, and all the way back to a young love that had blossomed under a setting sun.

Whenever I was with Fitz, I saw flashes of the young man I once knew coming out in the older version of him. There were so many memories between us, and I could recall all of them. It reminded me of a time when life was easy. I was so carefree, spending my days with Fitz as if nothing could touch us. Now, things weren't so simple. There were no guarantees my plan to tell him about Kallie would work, but I couldn't spend the rest of my life wondering. I could only hope he'd come to understand.

21

FITZ

I left the office an hour early on Friday afternoon. End of the week rush hour traffic in D.C always brought out a special brand of crazy. When combined with the thunderstorm that rolled in thirty minutes earlier, the commute was a nightmare.

On the way home, I stopped by the grocery store to grab a four-pack of Guinness for me and a two-liter of soda for Austin, then hit the local pizza joint to pick up dinner. I was looking forward to getting home and spending some long, overdue quality time with my son.

"Austin, I'm home," I called when I came in. "I've got pizza and those parmesan breadsticks you love."

"Sweet! I'm starving!" he yelled back.

I shook my head. The kid always thought he was starving. I headed down the hallway off the garage and rounded the corner into the kitchen. Austin was standing at the kitchen table riffling through the contents of a large box.

"Get some plates from the cabinet, will you?" I asked and set down the pizza so I could grab two clean glasses from the dishwasher. Cracking open a can of Guinness, I poured the dark liquid until a nice, creamy head formed, then filled Austin's glass with Pepsi. "I'm just going upstairs to change out of my suit. I'll be right back."

After shedding my sports coat, tie, and dress pants, I threw on a pair of jeans and headed back down to the kitchen. Austin was still standing over the box at the kitchen table and hadn't gotten the plates.

"Dad, why did you order all of this?"

"All of what?"

"These kid's books. I know the lady who wrote them. She's my friend's mom."

Somewhat annoyed he hadn't followed my direction about the plates, I went to the cabinet to grab them myself.

"No, it can't be your friend's mom. I know the person who wrote them. She's a friend from a long time ago. She doesn't have any kids," I replied absently. With the pizza box and plates balanced in one hand and my glass of beer in the other, I motioned my head toward the soda. "Come on. Grab your glass and the two-liter. Let's head down to the basement."

"You're wrong, Dad. I'm telling you it's the same lady," he insisted. Sighing, I walked over to where he stood. Opening one of the books, he pointed to the author photo in the back. "The girl who I went to the prom with, that's her mom. I've met her."

He pulled out his wallet, removed a picture from a plastic sleeve, and held it out to me. Setting my load down on the table, I took the photo from him.

"What's this from?" I asked impatiently. My stomach began to rumble. Apparently, I was just as hungry as Austin was.

"It's a group shot of all of us at prom," he told me. He pointed at a pretty blond in the middle of the group standing next to him. "That was my prom date, Kallie."

The smiling girl in the photo was practically a spitting image of Cadence. If she wasn't Cadence's daughter, I'd be a monkey's uncle. I frowned. If this was, in fact, her daughter, I didn't understand why she hadn't mentioned her before.

Suddenly, a thought hit me—one so blinding it was as if I'd been sucker punched. As a sophomore in high school, Austin wasn't old enough to go to the Junior prom on his own, and his date had to have *been a Junior.*

One year older than Austin.

She looks just like Cadence.

All the air deflated from my lungs and my hand began to shake. I allowed the picture to fall free from my grasp and jammed my hands into my pockets, not wanting Austin to see how rattled I was.

"Austin, how old is Kallie?" I tried to ask as casually as possible.

"She's a year older than me. Why?"

I looked dow*n at the photo* again.

Could it be?

I shook my head. No, Cadence would have told me. There was no fucking way she would have *hid my daught*er from me.

My daughter.

For some reason, just thinking those two words made the possibility all too real.

"No reason," I lied and plastered on a fake smile. "Ready for me to kick your butt at Madden?"

Austin grinned.

"Yeah right! You won't be kicking anything, old man! It's on!"

We made our way to the lounge area in the secluded basement which was basically set up as a man-cave with couches, a large flat screen television and a pool table. I was a good place to unwind or for Austin and me to take turns kicking each other's asses in a video game. Normally I enjoyed the time we spent here together, but I couldn't find the usual appreciation today. I was too busy trying not to be sick from the realization seeping in.

Cadence lied, and she'd been lying for seventeen fucking years.

Austin turned on the TV and the PlayStation. The Madden intro music began to play as we both grabbed a slice of pizza and settled into the gaming chairs in front of the TV. The food tasted like ash in my mouth. The shock I'd felt in the kitchen had begun to subside, slowly being replaced by the worst feeling of betrayal.

I stared at the TV, absently selecting my team and players, but when it came time for the opening kick-off, I barely registered what was on the screen. Conversations rushed in as I considered all the things Cadence had said *to me over the past few weeks.*

"I can't shirk my responsibilities."

"I'm terrified of you hurting me all over again. There's too much at stake this time."

"I need you, Fitz. I've always needed you. No matter what happens, don't ever forget that."

I recalled the phone conversation I overheard her having with Joy on that first day *I ran into Cadence jogging the Mall.*

"The stars seem to be aligning in a really weird way. It doesn't matter how long it's been. You need to tell him."

I remembered the strange, panicked behavior in the car when she told me she wasn't ready to meet Austin. I didn't understand it then, but I now realized it was because she'd already met him. If he saw her, her secret would be out. Then there was the way she seemed to want to push me away and the refusals to let me into her house. All the signs she was hiding something had been there, but I didn't see them. Now, it was blatantly clear, and it all made perfect sense. I felt like an idiot. Her words and push back weren't meant to put me off. They were meant to conceal the truth.

Looking at my son, another thought struck. I racked my brain, trying to remember the name of the girl Austin had been kissing at school when he got into the fight.

"Austin, the girl you got into a fight over—the one you just started seeing—what's her name?"

"Jessica. Why?" he asked through a mouthful of food.

I exhaled in relief, but that still didn't mean his teenage hormones weren't active on prom night. I'd already had sex with a few girls by the time I was his age, and it occurred to me I'd never had the talk with him.

"You didn't do anything with Kallie *on prom night, did you?*"

"What do you mean?"

Christ, was he really going to make me spell it out?

The referee in the game whistled and the ball snapped. I tried to defend against Austin's three-man route combination, but my brain was too damn distracted. I cleared my throat, hoping I didn't sound as awkward as I felt.

"You know, fool around. Did you make out or anything like that?"

His face pinched up as if he found the mere idea completely disgusting.

"Hell, no! Trust me, Dad. We're only friends. That would be like kissing my sister or something," he assured as he maneuvered his players down the field. "Touchdown! Yeah, baby!"

I glanced back at the screen, the cheering *from the* virtual crowd a dull buzz in my ears.

His sister.

His words made me want to vomit and I had to swallow the bile forming in the base of my throat.

"Nice play," I weakly congratulated.

"Dad, what's up with you tonight? It's never that easy. I basically just wiped the field with you. You let me hold your safeties, leaving a huge opening."

I closed my eyes and pinched the bridge of my nose. I didn't know how to respond to him. Anger at what Cadence had done leached into the marrow of my bones. Blinding, white-hot rage flashed. My brain scrambled to organize every feeling and thought I ever had about her, trying to make sense of it all.

"Sorry, kid. Just distracted tonight. Can we pick this back up in a few hours? There's something I need to do."

"Ah, yeah, sure," he slowly agreed, his expression perplexed. "I'll text my friend, Jace. Maybe he'll want to play a game online or something."

I gave his shoulder a light squeeze before standing to walk back up the stairs to the kitchen.

I looked around the kitchen. The children's books Austin had pulled from the box were strewn all over the kitchen table, the mess symbolic to the shambles my life had become in the blink of an eye. Once again, my life had been sucked into a violent twister, barreling down an uncharted path. Where it would spit me out was anyone's guess.

22

CADENCE

After I got home from work, I called Kallie to wish her a happy birthday, then went through the pile of bills that needed to be paid. Once I was through, I set out to clean the house top to bottom. I wanted everything to be perfect for Fitz when he came by the next day. It was strange, but I felt if I showed him a neat and tidy environment, it might somehow show I was a good mother and ease the blow about Kallie. I thought I did a good job with raising her and wanted him to feel confident about that.

The air was thick with humidity, the crisp spring air beginning to change over to summer heat, and rain showers had moved in a few hours earlier. The weather, combined with my mad dash to make everything in the house sparkling clean, made my skin sticky with sweat. I needed to shower before I could relax and unwind. Tomorrow would most likely be the most emotionally draining day of my life and I needed to be well rested if I had any hopes of getting through it.

After a quick shower, I felt more refreshed as I combed

through my tresses. Slipping into a pair of cotton shorts and a tank top, I went down to the kitchen, happy I had remembered to grab wine at the grocery store on my way home. I uncorked the bottle, poured myself half of a glass of red, and went to the living room to see what old movies might be showing on the TV.

Deciding on *Casablanca*, I settled back into the plush couch pillows. Lightning flashed outside, and thunder boomed. Rain pelted loudly against the windows and I had to turn up the volume on the television to hear it better. Just as Humphrey Bogart discovered his old flame was in town, a loud bang caused me to jump. The booming continued, and it took me a minute to realize it wasn't thunder, but someone repeatedly knocking on the front door.

"Who in the hell..." I muttered.

I walked to the door and peered out the side window. My heart stopped when I saw Fitz standing on my doorstep in jeans and a crisp, white button-down shirt with the sleeves rolled up to the elbows. His eyes flashed angrily as he ran a hand through his already messy hair.

"Open up!" he barked.

Startled by his uncharacteristic behavior, I cautiously cracked the door a few inches.

"Fitz, I thought you weren't coming by until tomorrow."

"We need to talk, Cadence. Now!" he stated gruffly without any sort of greeting. Not waiting for me to invite him inside, he pushed past me. I barely had a minute to react. He looked around the house, almost as if he were searching for something.

Or someone.

My stomach plummeted to the floor and my palms began to sweat. I was going to tell him about Kallie in the morning anyway, so I didn't attempt to hide the pictures of her. Perhaps I'd end up telling him tonight instead. Still, I'd never seen him this angry and couldn't help but think he might already know. Not wanting to contemplate what this unexpected visit could mean, I nervously moved to the end table and picked up the bottle of wine.

"Drink?" I asked.

His head snapped around to look at me.

"No. I prefer not to drink when I'm fucking pissed off," he spat out.

My stomach twisted and turned into a million knots. I drew in a shaky breath.

"Fitz, what's wrong?"

"Where is she? Is she here?" he demanded in a gruff voice.

"Who?" I feigned, hoping like hell this wasn't what I feared.

He moved toward me with purpose, closing the distance between us in just a few short strides. Once we were toe-to-toe, he grabbed me by the shoulders and startled me. He didn't hurt me, just held me still.

"You know who I mean, damn it! Kallie!"

I felt all the blood drain from my face. My worse fear had come to fruition. He was so angry and I could tell he didn't even want to look at me. His eyes flitted back and forth between pictures on the walls seeing them for the first time, his expression guarded and hurt. Sadness washed over me in waves. I didn't know how he found out, but I should have been the one to tell him. He deserved to hear it from me first. Regret nearly stole my breath.

"Fitz..."

"Why?" he demanded. The single word was forced, laced with pain and disbelief. I could see the war waging inside him.

"I'm so sorry. I know I should have told you sooner."

"You're damn right you should have! You lied to me. I've spent all these years believing you were perfect, good, and honest. I loved you...I love you so fucking much but you didn't even have the decency to tell me the truth! What else are you keeping from me?"

He squeezed my shoulders hard and I winced. A look of mortification crossed his face as soon as he realized what he was doing. Almost immediately, he dropped his hands to his sides. Taking a step back, he slammed frustrated hands through his hair and began to pace.

"I'm not hiding anything else. I swear it. I was planning to tell you," I whispered.

"When?" he bellowed. "Exactly when were you going to tell me we had a child together?"

"I was...I was going to tell you tomorrow when you came over."

"Why? It didn't fit into your schedule seventeen years ago?"

I flinched and tried to think of a way to explain it all.

"It was a long time ago, Fitz. I was barely eighteen years old —scared, broken, and alone. How did you find out?"

His eyes continued to dart around the room, and he didn't look at me when he answered.

"Austin. I ordered your kids' books. When they arrived in the mail, he found them. He saw your picture and it didn't take long for me to put the pieces together. When I finally did... fuck, Cadence! I felt as if my entire life had been snatched away from me. All that time..." He trailed off, his voice breaking, unable to find the words to express more. "Where is she now?"

"On the French class trip."

A look of recognition came over his features and he nodded.

"The French trip...Austin was supposed to go on it." He paused his pacing and looked pointedly at me. His eyes flashed angrily. "But you already knew that, didn't you?"

I looked away guiltily. Slowly, he walked over to the end table to pick up a framed picture of Kallie. It had been taken her sophomore year in high school. He stared at it for a long while, neither one of us speaking. An impenetrable expression hardened his beautiful face. Finally, unable to take the silence any longer, I sucked in a steeling breath and spoke up.

"She has your smile."

His head snapped up and regretful eyes raked over me. It was as if he were processing a million thoughts. In them, I saw all of his pain and heartache.

"I know what it's like to be a parent, Cadence. I've practically raised Austin on my own. I watched him play and grow. I taught him the rules of basketball and helped him with algebra. We've argued and fought, laughed and cried. We've shared birthdays and Christmases together. We established traditions—lots of fucking traditions! But, with Kallie—my daughter—I'll never have any of those things. You stole that from me."

I knew full well how important all of those things were. I covered my mouth and tried to choke back a sob, but there was no stopping the tears that began to fall freely down my cheeks. I never meant to steal those opportunities from him. I just did what I thought was right.

"Fitz, you don't understand. Like I said, I was eighteen and scared. The day I found out I was pregnant with Kallie was the day you got married. What was I supposed to do?"

"Tell me the truth, dammit! That's what you should have done! If I had known, I would have..." he trailed off.

"You would have what? Come back? You left, and we both know you wouldn't have come back to me. I had to accept that."

"I don't know what I would have done, and you can't assume!" he snapped. "You didn't tell me. You didn't think I deserved to know—to have that chance. How could you look at me again after all these years and not tell me right away? I can't believe you'd betray me like this!"

Memories of all those days I'd waited for him rushed to the

surface. It forced all the anger, heartbreak, and frustration that had been buried deep for seventeen years to come to a head.

"Betray you? How dare you sit there on your high horse and make accusations? I went back and forth about whether I should tell you during my entire pregnancy. There were days when I was sure I'd contact you and days when I hated you for leaving. I understood your hands were tied, but it didn't make the reality hurt any less. I cried almost every night, knowing I wasn't enough for you—that I wasn't enough to make you stay. If I told you I was knocked up, and you came back, it wouldn't have been for me. It would have been because of a baby. That would have made me no different from your father."

"How so?"

"It would have been another part of your life where you had little choice. Was I wrong for not telling you? Maybe, but I was so scared! I wasn't perfect. I was practically a child myself, being forced to make impossible decisions. No answer was the right answer, so I made the choice for both of us to protect Kallie. I had the sense to realize a baby wouldn't have made a damn bit of difference. You would have stayed married and nothing about the situation would be any different. If I'd found out I was pregnant before you got married, maybe things would have played out differently. But like I already said, I didn't know until it was too late. I was so mad, upset, and lost. I loved you, and you broke me. You have no idea what it was like for me. You don't know how bad I hurt!"

"Don't I?"

His eyes bore into me, flashing with accusation. I was swiftly filled with unexplainable resentment. Spine stiffening hard and straight, I glared right back at him and snapped.

"No, you don't! You can be angry at me for not telling you a few weeks ago, but you don't get to be pissed off at me for not telling you years ago. You made the choice to leave. You put everything else ahead of me. I used to be the girl who believed in fairytales and happily-ever-after. When you walked away, all of those grand ideas about Prince Charming were destroyed. There were options, and you didn't take any of them! While you were reciting wedding vows, I was left home to cry and worry about my future. Do you know how hard it was to give birth to Kallie—to our daughter—knowing I'd be reminded of the only man I'd ever loved every day for the rest of my life? I could have given her up, but I didn't. Instead, I worked to bury the bitterness and regrets. I promised you no regrets, and I was determined to keep that promise. I persevered through all the challenges and raised a remarkable young woman. I built my own damn castle and raised Kallie to believe she can breathe fire—and I did it all by myself!"

Something regretful flashed in his stormy gray eyes.

"You didn't give me much of a choice, now did you?"

"Just as you didn't give me one," I bit out.

Running his hands through his hair again, he violently tugged at the ends and swore.

"Fuck, Cadence! I can't do this with you!" he thundered and shook his head. "I need to get out of here. I shouldn't have come here unannounced like this. God, if she'd been here... I should have considered the possibility before banging down your door."

"Yeah, you definitely could have handled this differently," I sardonically stated.

"Wait—you think *I* handled this wrong? You're unfucking believable."

I took a deep breath and hastily wiped the tears from my face. This bickering was pointless.

"Look, I'm sorry. We both screwed up. I'm just trying to explain why I did what I did all those years ago. Fighting about it now isn't going to change anything," I tried to reason.

His eyes locked on mine.

"No, arguing won't help. But I can't ignore the fact you lied to me for more than seventeen years. I need to think."

He quickly moved passed me toward the front door, but I couldn't let him leave—not like this. I needed to make him understand. Rushing to him, I grabbed his arm to stop him.

"Fitz, wait a minute! Wait right here." Not waiting for a response, I dashed up the stairs to retrieve the box I had put together the night before. When I came back down, he was already walking down the porch steps, into the rain. "Here. Take this. It might help you understand."

He turned around, pain crashing over his features and lancing at my heart.

"Understand what?"

"Understand I've loved you since I was eighteen years old. When you left, a huge, aching hole was punched through my heart. A part of me died. You were the first man to really kiss me. To touch me. To make love to me. For me, there's never been anyone but you. I still love you. It was always you, Fitz. I just hope the contents of this box will make you see that. If not, then walk away. That's what you do best after all."

It was a cheap shot, but I couldn't hold it back. Taking a hesitant step forward, I shoved the box in his direction. Ever so slowly, he took it from my hands.

"It's you who doesn't understand, Cadence. I've carried guilt over leaving you for half my life. I've struggled to forgive myself. I loved you more than anything. For me, loving you is like breathing. But this betrayal... I don't know if I can survive this."

My stomach dropped, and I nearly sank to my knees. The finality in his words was more than I could bear, knowing once he left this time, it may be forever.

He stared at me for a moment longer before turning away once more. He walked slowly down the driveway, seeming oblivious to the pouring rain, and climbed into his black Audi. Then he was gone.

23

FITZ

I had spent most of the week in a full-blown rage, not knowing if I was coming or going. I was agitated, pissed off, and confused. I ignored calls from everyone, barely making it through the workday only to have to come home and pretend everything was normal in front of Austin. Devon had been giving me strange looks all week, but I didn't give a flying fuck. I'd basically operated on two frequencies all week—pissed off and really pissed off. Even now, I was supposed to be going over my speech for the kick-off party. It was already Thursday, and I had less than two days to make it satisfactory, but I couldn't focus on the words. As hard as I tried, there was no caging the blinding fury racing through my veins. I couldn't stop wondering what my life would have been like if Cadence had told me about our daughter. Yes—our daughter. It was just too much to wrap my head around.

When I finally felt calm enough to analyze the situation, I sat down at the desk in my study and opened the lid of the box Cadence had given me. I hadn't wanted to look inside it before now. For some reason, hanging onto the anger had just been easier.

On top of the pile, I found everything to do with Cadence and me from seventeen years ago. There was the origami I'd given her on the last day at Camp Riley, the mixed tape which included the song *Fade Into You*, and the playbill for *Singin' In The Rain*. I pushed it to the side irritably, not wanting to be distracted by what was once between us.

Underneath the old memorabilia, I located everything I could ever want to know about Kallie. There was a copy of her birth certificate, listing her full name as Kalliope Benton Riley. I liked the way Cadence had incorporated her mother's maiden name. It had a nice flow to it—almost whimsical.

Kalliope was born on the twenty-first of May, seventeen years ago. I looked at the calendar on my desk. Her seventeenth birthday had been the day I discovered her existence.

Another birthday I missed.

The father was marked as "unknown." Seeing the word caused a pain in my chest, but I pushed on, only stopping when I got to the school pictures. Over and over again, I flipped through the photos of Kallie taken over the years. The transition as she grew from year to year was inconceivable, and I couldn't help but be angry over all that lost time.

More regrets.

Austin taught me what it was like to be a parent—to have that unconditional bond—knowing I would sacrifice anything for his well-being. Raising him hadn't been easy. Between building my company and dealing with his drunk mother, he and I had definitely gotten off to a rocky start. However, things got better over time, growing easier as we settled into our groove. He was a good kid who I was proud to call my son—but 'son' was the keyword. I could relate to Austin man to man. I didn't have the faintest idea about what to do with a girl.

Would I have been a good father to her?

I flipped through the pictures again. My heart swelled every time I looked at her adorable little face, then filled with pride to see how she'd grown into a beautiful young woman.

I set the pictures down and moved on to the next thing in the box—a stack of envelopes that had aged yellow over time with my name written in flowing script across the front of them. Removing the paper inside the first one, I began to read.

To the keeper of my heart,

It's only been a few days, but already I miss you so much. My heart is broken. I know why you had to leave, but I don't know if I'll ever accept it. I'll always love you, and you'll always be the person I gave myself to so openly and freely. Despite your words, I'll never stop seeing the good in you. Now that you're gone, all I feel is a hollow emptiness. I don't know how I came to feel like this in just a few short months. Every time I close my eyes, I see you. In the silence, I hear your voice. In the darkness, I see your face. I don't know if I'll ever escape it. I wish you'd come back to me. I wish you had picked me over your father's demands. I'll try to accept things for what they are, but until then, I'll keep writing to you with the hope one day we'll be together again.

All my love,
Cadence

I poured through letter after letter. She had written to me almost every single day since the moment I left Camp Riley. I read about the day she found out she was pregnant and about the support her parents gave her. Sometimes, her letters were sad. Sometimes they were angry and bitter. But then there were the happy letters—like the day she felt Kallie kick in her belly for the first time. A pain of grief hit me, wishing I'd been there to place my hand over her stomach and experience the moment with her.

Although the letters were written to me, they were more

like a dear diary of sorts. In between the letters were newspaper clippings mainly about my father but had my name thrown into the text for some reason or another. As I continued to read, I began to understand her struggles and fears. I could feel the way she battled with herself to seek me out but worried about the fallout I'd suffer. That's what it always came back to—me. She'd denied her wants and desires in order to protect me. Until the end. In the end, she did it to protect Kallie.

When I began to read the letter dated one week after Kallie was born—when Cadence finally decided to say goodbye—I felt my throat tighten.

I wish things could have been different for us, but I accept the choice I've made. I will never regret the time I had with you...

I'd left her isolated and scared. I could only imagine what seeing a picture of me and my pregnant wife did to her. Based on the transition of her letters, it was obvious Cadence had gone into survival mode and it was all because I'd left her alone. What she had gone through was not all that dissimilar to what my own mother lived through. The irony of it all wasn't lost on me. My mother made a choice to keep me hidden to protect me. Cadence had done the same for Kallie a generation later. I couldn't fault Cadence for that. She did what she had to do. Yes, I could be angry, but my anger had been misguided. I was the one who was truly to blame. I was the one who had left.

I still loved her so much—that fact would never change. I just didn't know how to handle what I was feeling. I couldn't articulate the pain and loss, and I certainly couldn't make any decisions about my future in this state of mind. I had no idea where to go from here, but one thing was certain. I couldn't waste any more time. I had to meet Kallie. Her mother and I had a lot to work out, but while that happened, I didn't want another day to go by where I didn't know my daughter.

My daughter. What would it be like to meet her? To know her?

A knock on the door jarred me from my thoughts. I scrambled to shove everything back inside the box, shoved it under my desk, and hastily wiped away the moisture in my eyes.

"Come in," I called, assuming it was Austin. I was surprised to see Devon poke his head in.

"Hey, man. How's it going?" I closed my eyes and dropped my head into my hands. "That bad, huh?"

"Devon, you don't even know the half of it."

"I could tell something was up this week. At first I thought you were just all keyed up about the kick-off party coming up on Saturday, but when you went ballistic on Angie today I knew it was more than that. I figured I should come by your place to run interference."

"Yeah, I owe her an apology," I guiltily admitted.

"No, dude. You need to give your secretary a goddamn raise. I didn't think the poor thing would make it until five o'clock when you finally decided to drag your miserable ass out the door. What's going on?"

I sighed and reached back under my desk to pull out the box. Opening the lid, I handed Devon Kallie's birth certificate. He gave it a quick glance, then looked at me in confusion.

"That's a birth certificate for Kalliope Benton Riley— Cadence's daughter," I explained.

"Her daughter?" He paused and looked at it more closely. He raised a hand and began to do mental math on his fingers. "Wait a minute. She would have gotten pregnant the year we... the summer..."

"The summer we were at Camp Riley," I finished for him.

"Are you telling me you have another kid? A daughter?"

"Yeah, but keep your voice down. I don't know how in the actual fuck I'm going to tell Austin. I've barely processed it myself."

"Shit, man. Lady luck just doesn't want to blow your way, does she?" I didn't answer. Instead I slid the last letter Cadence had written to me across the desk for him to read. When he was through, he shook his head. "This is nuts. I'm pretty sure Steve Holy sang a country song about this."

"Great," I scoffed. "As if I didn't already despise country music enough. I guess I'll need to buy myself a pickup truck and a dog."

"Hey, now. Remember what they say—play the song backward, and the guy gets everything back," Devon chuckled. "So now what are you going to do?"

"I don't know. I've been asking myself that all week."

"Well, what do you say I go to the fridge and grab us a couple of beers? We can figure this out. God knows, we've been in more than our fair share of jams. This should be a piece of cake, right?"

I laughed, but the situation was far from amusing.

"Sure. I think I've got a Guinness or two left and a bunch of those IPAs you like."

After Devon left the room in search of beer, I took a deep breath. I felt as if my entire life had been a current—every time I tried to swim against it, it just swept me away. I refused to be dragged down any longer. The problem was, I was currently drowning, and I didn't know how to fight this kind of undertow.

24

CADENCE

I dragged myself through the work week, fighting to keep it together. It had been the fight of my life, trying to hide the quiver in my voice and the tears constantly threatening to break free. Despite the fact I didn't think the situation could get any worse, it had. I hadn't heard from Fitz all week long. I knew I'd messed up and figured it would be best to give him time to think things through, but it had been seven long days. I didn't know how much more time he needed.

I fretted over whether I should tell Kallie, but I was terrified Fitz might be gone for good. I didn't know how to give her the truth if it meant I'd have to turn around and say he wanted nothing to do with her. I never wanted her to think she was unwanted or unloved by anyone.

Then there was this ache. It was an ache I knew I'd feel but never imagined it would be this bad. I missed Fitz so much, the pain just as present as it was one week ago when he'd left my house in anger. It clawed at me as I pulled the car into my driveway.

Throwing the car in park, I glanced in the rearview mirror. The makeup I'd slapped on that morning was still somewhat intact, but no amount of concealer could hide the dark circles under my eyes. I'd barely slept a wink all week, but at least it was Friday. If I really wanted to, I could stay in bed all day tomorrow.

Climbing from the car, I slowly walked toward the front door. I glanced at the flower planters flanking the porch steps. The dahlia blooms were wilted and in need of water. I usually watered them as soon as I got home from work, but all motivation to do much of anything had completely disappeared. A pint of Ben and Jerry's and comfy pajamas just seemed so much more appealing. As a result, the poor flowers hadn't had water for days.

I focused on putting on a happy face and stepped through the front door. I called out to Kallie.

"Kallie, I'm home!"

I shook my head as I took in the evidence everything was back to normal since she'd arrived home from her trip. She'd been back for only a handful of days, but I may as well kiss my clean house goodbye.

Her bookbag laid open on the couch, spilling papers out over the cushions. Her shoes, as usual, were left where they landed, and the maroon cardigan embroidered with the St. Aloysius logo was strewn haphazardly over the back of the recliner. Her suitcase still sat near the foot of the stairs by the front door, unzipped and clearly rifled through. I kicked her shoes to the side so I didn't trip over them and walked toward the kitchen. Kallie was a good kid but getting her to pick up anything around the house was like pulling teeth.

I found her sitting at the kitchen table pouring over college brochures.

"Anything pique your interest?" I asked. When she didn't respond, I walked over to her, plopped my purse on the table, and plucked an earbud from her ear. She looked up in surprise.

"Sorry, Mom, I didn't hear you come in."

"Perhaps, you would have heard me if the music wasn't so loud. You're going to damage your ears," I gently chided.

God, I sound like my mother.

"Check this out," she said, holding a brochure for some school in Colorado.

"Later. Right now, I want you to clean up this mess. I love you, girl, but you're a slob. I asked you to put that suitcase away the night you came home." I pointed toward the front door. She flashed me a guilty look but got up to do as I asked without argument. Before she left the kitchen, she paused and turned to me.

"Mom, are you okay?"

I didn't know how to answer that. I should tell her I was fine, but the truth was, I didn't think I'd ever be okay again.

"I'm good, sweetie. Why?"

"You've been looking like a sad-faced emoji all week."

Had I been that obvious?

Kallie inherited my mother's intuitive traits and easily spotted when something was amiss. It was no surprise she'd picked up on my melancholy mood, but I didn't think I'd been that transparent. Still, she didn't need to be burdened with my problems—at least not yet. Since it was now my turn to look guilty, I turned away from her and busied myself with getting a glass of water.

"A sad-faced emoji, huh?" I tried to laugh off.

"Yeah. I'm kind of worried."

"I'm fine—really. I just have a lot on my plate right now."

I leaned back against the counter and took a long drink water. I wasn't all that thirsty, but rather wanted to use the glass to hide my expression. My mother always said people could read me like a book.

"Do you know what I think? I think you've been alone for too long. You need to find a hot guy and go out on a date," she announced.

I nearly choked on the liquid pouring down my throat.

"A date?" I squeaked.

"Yeah, you remember how to do that, right? I mean, I'm probably going away to school in a year. I don't want you to be here alone after I'm gone. Aunt Joy and I were talking about it. She agrees with..." she trailed off and narrowed her gaze. "Oh my gosh! You have been on a date, haven't you? You're blushing, Mom! Do you have a boyfriend?"

There was no mistaking the excitement in her voice over the possibility. I needed to shut this down immediately. Knowing Kallie, it would be less than five seconds before the next question came pouring out. I set the glass down on the counter and brought my hands to hips.

"I'm not blushing. It's just warm in here," I tried to deny. However, from the suspicious look on her face, it was obvious she wasn't buying it. "I think Aunt Joy needs to mind her own business, and I think you have a suitcase to unpack."

I donned a stern expression and pointed toward the living room again. She continued to look skeptically at me for a moment longer, then smiled this small, knowing grin before turning to head out of the room.

I tilted my head toward the ceiling and closed my eyes. Taking a few deep breaths, I forced myself to try to relax. I needed to get out of the funk I'd been in. Life went on and I'd have to figure out a way to deal with it sooner rather than later.

While Kallie was cleaning up her belongings, I opened the freezer to pull out chicken breasts for dinner. I was deciding what to do with said chicken when my cell phone began to ring in the purse I'd set down on the kitchen table. Digging it out, I looked at the caller I.D. It was my real estate agent. She was probably calling about the buyer for the land in Abingdon. I had yet to give her an answer about whether I was going to sell it.

"Hello?"

"Cadence, it's Savannah Sterling."

"Hey, Savannah. What's up?"

"I'm calling about an offer made on the property in Virginia."

"I assumed that was why you were calling. I've actually thought about it. I think I'm going to hold off for now."

"No, there was another offer—one that might make you change your mind. It came in just this morning from a completely different buyer. It's a corporation called TDP and they're willing to pay three times the market value. I really think you should consider."

Three times?

I thought about all the things the money could buy. I could give the long overdue raises to the people at Dahlia's Dreamers, pay off my mortgage, and the last few installments of Kallie's school tuition. I might even be able to take her on a little vacation before she started college. Still, despite the generous offer, I wasn't sure if I could emotionally part with my childhood summer home. With everything currently happening with Fitz, I wasn't in the best frame of mind to make permanent decisions and I didn't want to do anything rash I might regret later.

"Email me the offer and I'll look it over Monday morning when I'm back in the office. No promises though, Savannah."

"I know, I know. I get it. Some things have sentimental value that no money can replace."

I didn't think truer words had ever been spoken. After thanking Savannah for the call, I pressed the end button on my phone and went back to preparing the chicken. Peeling off the cellophane wrapper, I popped it in the microwave to defrost. My cell phone rang again.

"Oh, for crying out loud! Can't a woman cook dinner in peace?" I shouted to no one who was listening. This time, it was Simon Reed. Inwardly, I cringed. I hadn't spoken to him since the gala, and I was nervous he might be upset about the way I'd abruptly left him that night. I debated whether I should answer the call, but ultimately decided I should in case it was work related.

"Cadence, I've got great news!" he said excitedly after I picked up.

"What is it?"

"It's the Andrés Mendez case. The judge dropped the charges against him. ICE is processing his paperwork now. His status is safe. Emilia can pick him up at the holding center within the hour."

Happy relief washed over me, excited to hear the first good news I'd had all week.

"Oh my God! Are you kidding me? That's great! What happened? Why did he change his mind?"

"I don't know the all details. The judicial assistant called my office fifteen minutes ago. I know the guy pretty well, which is probably the only reason I was able to get a few tidbits. You know how judges are normally super tight-lipped about their decision-making process. Anyway, all he said was Judge Perkins got a phone call from some guy named Quinn. A few minutes later, the judge came out of his chambers and announced he was dismissing the case."

I heard everything he said, but I could only focus on one word.

Quinn.

Did Fitz do this?

"You said Quinn, right? Do you have a first name?"

"No, it wasn't mentioned. Why?" he asked. I stared absently into space as I tried to wrap my head around what this might mean for Fitz and me. "Cadence, are you still there?"

"Yeah, Simon. I'm here. Thanks for the update and all your work on the case. I'm going to call Emilia now—she'll be absolutely thrilled!"

After I ended the call, I took a moment to process the information. I recalled the faraway look Fitz had when I'd told him the name of the judge. Then I remembered how upset he was when he left my house last week. I didn't know if he called the judge before or after our argument.

I made the call to Emilia, then to Joy. Both were just as ecstatic as I was over getting to add the Mendez file to the drawer with the smiley face sticker. However, I couldn't help but feel my excitement glow with a little something extra. The possibility Fitz had called the judge *after* we had our fight might mean there was a sliver of hope for us.

As I went about preparing dinner for the third time, I tossed the chicken in a marinade and sliced and diced the vegetables for our side dish. Except now, I felt a bit lighter on my feet.

I CRAWLED INTO BED AROUND ELEVEN. JUST AS IT HAD ALL WEEK, sleep eluded me. I tossed and turned for forty-five minutes before turning on my bedroom television. As I flipped through the channels in search of old sitcom re-runs, my cell phone chimed on my nightstand. I ignored it, assuming it was an email coming through. When it chimed again a few minutes later, I glanced over at it curiously and picked it up.

My heart began to race when I saw it wasn't an email at all. It was an incoming text from Fitz. Quickly, I typed in my password to unlock the screen and pulled up my messages.

11:56 P.M.
FITZ: WE NEED TO TALK.

11:59 P.M.

FITZ: I KNOW YOU'RE AWAKE. I CAN SEE THE LIGHT FROM THE TV COMING THROUGH YOUR BEDROOM WINDOW.

What? He can see...

Scrambling from the bed, I ran to the window and drew up the blinds. Across the street, Fitz was leaning against his parked car. When he saw me, he looked back down at his phone. Glancing down at mine, I saw the three little dots signaling he was typing.

12:01 A.M.

FITZ: GLAD I GUESSED RIGHT ABOUT THAT BEING YOUR ROOM. I DON'T THINK OUR DAUGHTER WOULD TAKE KINDLY TO A STRANGE MAN STARING UP AT HER BEDROOM WINDOW.

Our daughter. He said our daughter.

My heart ached, and hope bloomed deep within me. I didn't know what his words could mean, but I had to find out. Standing here staring out the window and texting wasn't going to get me the answers I needed. Acting on impulse, I dashed from the room, into the hallway.

I came to a screeching halt in front of Kallie's bedroom door, needing to make sure she was asleep. As quietly as I could, I slowly inched the door open to peek inside. The lights were off, and she seemed to be fast asleep. Relieved, I silently closed the door once more and continued my mad dash down the stairs.

When I got outside, I slowed to a more reasonable pace and walked across the street to where he stood. When I reached him, the day-old stubble covering his jaw and his expressive gray eyes took my breath away. I had to fight every bone in my body to stop myself from touching him. Whenever he was around, I was unable to resist being close to him. But with everything happening between us, I hesitated. For some reason, he seemed so far out of reach. We stared at each other in silence. I knew I had to say something one way or the other, but fear of getting the words wrong rendered me speechless.

"Hey," he said, shifting his weight, one foot to the other. He appeared as nervous as I felt. The air was wrought with tension. His being here could mean so many things, but I was afraid to hope.

"Simon Reed called me today. Andrés Mendez is free to go," I told him, attempting to break the ice with small talk. When he only nodded, I added, "Thank you, Fitz. I don't know what you did but thank you."

"The judge was Bethany's father. He owed me a favor or two." My eyes widened in shock at the coincidence. He laughed bitterly. "Yeah. It's funny how things work out sometimes."

"Yeah, I'll say." I studied his face, desperately trying to read the conflicting emotions. I couldn't tell if he was mad, unhappy, or relieved to be standing outside my house. "Fitz, look. Kallie... she doesn't know about you yet or else I'd invite you inside. Do you want to go sit in the backyard and talk instead?"

"No. It's late. I just wanted to see you for a minute." He paused and reached up to tuck a stay lock of hair behind my ear. The action seemed automatic before he seemed to catch himself. Shoving his hands into the pockets of his jeans, he rocked back on his heels.

"Why are you here, Fitz?" I whispered.

25

FITZ

I stared at her, completely forgetting my reason for coming by. She looked hot as hell in her little tank and cotton shorts. Her golden hair was woven into the braid she always liked to wear, and I could tell she was braless, reminding me so much of that first night I'd spent at Camp Riley.

But then I remembered nearly two decades had passed. The sky was now dark and there wasn't a sunset at her back. There was no lake. There was no dock. This was the present and things were so much different.

"I'm here because I couldn't stay away," I began, my words coming out hoarse. Her mouth opened to form a delectable little O, but I cleared my throat and continued. She deserved the humble pie I was about to dish up. "I went through the box you gave me."

"And?" she asked nervously. Looking down, she began to fiddle with the hem of her shirt.

Moving closer, I stepped toe-to-toe with her and placed my

hands on her slender waist. Stormy, emerald green eyes moved up to meet mine.

"I feel like every turn I've made in my life has sent me the wrong way down a one-way highway. I try to dodge the oncoming traffic, yet I know a crash is inevitable. It's time for me to get off that stretch of the road and travel the right one."

"What's the right road, Fitz?"

"You are. I'm so sorry, Cadence. I understand now. When I came here last week and flipped out, I didn't have a fucking clue. I never stopped to think about what you went through all those years ago. As much as I'd like to, I can't turn back time. You have the right to say you don't want anything to do with me —I deserve as much after leaving you alone all those years ago. All I know is I've never looked at another woman the way I do you. When I closed my eyes, it was you I saw. Even when I was angry with you for keeping Kallie from me, I still saw you. If I have to walk away knowing we don't have a chance in hell, I'll wait for you because there has never been anyone else *but* you."

Her lips parted, and my stomach squeezed. I leaned down and kissed the top of her forehead.

"Fitz, I…"

"There are a lot of things I have to come to terms with and I know we have a lot to work through. It won't be easy, but I want to give it a shot. Tomorrow night is the campaign kick-off party. The invitation is still open if you'd like to go. It should wrap up by nine, and I thought we could go for a drink afterward and talk. But you should know, Austin will be at the party. As far as he knows, you're an old friend. He doesn't know Kallie is his half-sister."

She stepped back, wrapped her arms around herself, and shook her head.

"I don't know if me being there is a very good idea. We always seem to rush into things and think later. We can't do that anymore. Austin aside, I assume your father will be there.

What will he say? Or what about the scandal in the press when they find out about Kallie? Aren't you worried? I mean, I don't know if I want Kallie to be dragged through the mud because of what you're doing politically. It's my job to protect her."

I felt the corners of my mouth turn up, appreciating the mother lion presence in her tone.

"I've thought about that too, but I think I can avoid a PR mess. It's what I do for a living, remember?" I reminded her with a wry smile. "I went over things with Devon last night and brought him up to speed on what's going on. I'll handle my father. Don't worry about him. As for the press, we can spin this a few different ways so there's minimal to no damage."

She curiously cocked her head to the side.

"How so?"

I paused for a moment, unsure of how she'd take to the ideas Devon and I came up with.

"We could just say you're my girlfriend, and Kallie is your daughter. Her birth certificate says as much. Nobody has to know she's mine." I tried to keep my expression blank, needing to hide the pain I felt over option one.

She shook her head again.

"No, I don't like that. I can't handle any more lies, Fitz. It wouldn't be fair to us or to Kallie and Austin."

Not realizing I'd been holding my breath, I exhaled in relief. God knows, I didn't want to deny my daughter any more than I already had.

"Good. I'm glad you said that, but I thought I owed it to you to give you the choice. Since we both agree burying it is out, it leaves two other ways to play it. We can say we were together years ago, you got pregnant, we had a falling out, but ended up reconnecting years later. That's as close to the truth as we can get without getting into the shady details about my father and Judge Perkins."

She squeezed her eyes closed as if she were trying to

visualize how everything would play out. When she opened them again, her expression was pained.

"Why do you still feel the need to protect them?"

"It's not about them, sweetheart. It never has been. It's about Austin. I don't want him ever to know he was the result of blackmail. I never want him to feel like he was unwanted."

She nodded her head slowly.

"I can understand that. I had similar sentiments this past week. I didn't tell Kallie about you because I wasn't sure if you were coming back. No child should feel unwanted or unloved." She sighed and rubbed her arms as if warding off a chill, despite the fact the night was warm and humid. "What's the third option?"

"I back out of running for Senate."

"Back out? But why?"

"After talking with Devon, it seemed like the most obvious choice. It will give us time to sort through this openly and honestly without putting the kids through a possible media circus."

"Fitz, I don't want our children to suffer embarrassment, but I also don't want to stand in the way of your aspirations. You have the chance to do something good. You shouldn't give that up."

"So, what if we go with option two then? I campaign as planned while we work through the rest. What's the worst that could happen?"

"People could get hurt—me, Kallie, Austin. You don't know what the future holds."

I took a hesitant step closer and brought her to my chest. Thankfully, she didn't pull away as I feared she might, but placed her hands on my shoulders and stared at me with those wide, emerald eyes.

"You're right, sweetheart. I don't know what the future will bring. But I do think it's worth taking a chance to find out.

When I ran into you after so many years apart, it was like my world settled. Everything finally began to make sense, but then I found out about Kallie and it completely flipped upside down. Now—just seeing you tonight—I feel it beginning to calm again. People say everything happens for a reason. Maybe things didn't happen seventeen years ago because they weren't meant to be. Maybe we wouldn't have been able to make it work back then. I may not know what will happen down the road, but I know I see you in every part of the journey. You were always supposed to be in my life."

Her eyes brimmed with tears and she shook her head. I couldn't tell if she was happy or sad.

"Fitz, I...I don't know if..."

She stared off, appearing lost in thought. I waited a beat before pressing her to finish.

"Tell me what you're thinking. I need to know where your head's at, Cadence. Can we make a go at this one more time?"

"I don't know. I want to say yes, but I'm confused about what the right choice is. I want to be with you with all my heart, but maybe we should think about this more. Plus, I need to find a way to tell Kallie, and you Austin."

"Tomorrow then—after the party. We can figure out the best way to do it, but I don't want to do it alone. I think we should tell them together."

She rested her head against my chest.

"I'm scared, Fitz," she whispered.

"About what? Talking to the kids?"

"No. I'm afraid of you. You left once before. I accepted it, but now... when you stormed out last week, it was as if you ripped my heart out all over again. But this time, it was so much worse. I've fallen completely in love with you all over again and you can hurt me worse than you know. If you leave again, it will destroy me."

She'd always been so open and honest about her feelings.

Tonight was no different and her words tore at my chest. I'd fucked up way too many times with this girl. It didn't matter what I did—I always seemed to mess it up.

"I won't hurt you, Cadence."

"You can't promise that."

I leaned back and tilted her chin up to look at me.

"No, I can't. But I can promise you I won't walk away easily. I love you, Cadence. I'll earn that place in your heart again and remind you that, despite all the time apart, sometimes the reward is worth the wait."

26

CADENCE

I checked my reflection in the full-length mirror behind my bathroom door one final time. Slowly, I spun in a circle.

"I don't know. Are you sure I look okay?" I asked Joy. She was currently propped up on the counter on FaceTime. I turned back toward her, allowing her full view of the cream-colored pantsuit I'd chosen.

"Honey, you look great. If you don't believe me, ask Kallie."

"I would if I could. She's at a friend's house until eight. I left her a note telling her I'll be at Marine Gate for the evening and would be back late." I paused to fiddle with the chunky gold necklace at my neck. I frowned and looked at Joy through the phone screen. "Too much?"

"A little bit. Maybe wear your silver necklace with the tiny pearls. It's dainty and feminine, not too ostentatious."

"Great idea."

After swapping out the necklace, I began fussing with my hair, even though I'd already spent close to an hour styling it.

"Stop messing with it. It looks good," Joy scolded. "Your hair is perfect, your makeup is perfect, and you're dressed to kill. Your nerves are what's going to ruin it all."

"Am I that obvious?"

"Just a little," Joy laughed. "Try to relax. I know you're worried about Fitz's father, but you have to remember—you know who he is, but *he* doesn't know who *you* are. Just take a deep breath. Your biggest concern should be about the afterparty."

"I'd hardly call drinks with Fitz to discuss how we should tell our kids a 'Once Upon a Time at Camp Riley' story an afterparty," I stated dryly.

"You know what I mean. Either way, you're going to be late if you don't get a move on."

"You're right. Thank you, Joy. I'll text you later."

After ending the video chat, I took off down the stairs, slipped into my nude pumps, and headed out the door.

Traffic was surprisingly light, and I made decent time. It was a good thing too because finding parking was a bitch. After twenty minutes of circling the block, I ended up having to park in one of the expensive ramps. I checked my reflection in the review mirror one final time and took a few calming breaths.

Time to get this show on the road.

I walked up to the Marine Gate Hotel and entered through the glass turnstile doors. Almost instantly, I spotted a sign that read 'RNC Event, Rooftop Patio, Elevator C' and followed the direction to where it pointed.

I walked past the hotel check-in desk and down the corridor leading to a bank of elevators. There were two security guards positioned outside the elevator I needed to take. One was checking off the names of the guests who were waiting to go up. The other loomed ominously over the line of guests as he discernibly looked each person over. When I got to the front of the line, I gave my name.

"Cadence Riley."

Security guard number one scanned his finger down the list.

"I'm sorry, ma'am, but I can't allow you to go up."

"What do you mean?" I asked in surprise and pinched my brows in confusion.

"It means you can't go up," he reiterated.

"That can't be right. Mr. Quinn is expecting me."

He pursed his lips in annoyance—as if he'd rather be doing anything other than dealing with me. He made a shooing motion with his hand.

"Please step aside so I can check in the other guests."

Ignoring his request, I crossed my arms stubbornly and dug in my heels.

"Check the list again," I demanded.

He sighed, huffing out a long and exaggerated breath as he absently glanced down the list again.

"There. I checked again, and you can't go up. Don't make this harder than it needs to be. I'm just doing my job—and it includes keeping out unruly protesters. So again, please step aside so I can check in the other guests."

I blinked and angled my head to the side feeling somewhat taken aback.

"I'm not a protester. I'm..." I trailed off, not sure how to describe what I was to Fitz. "It's like I said. Mr. Quinn is expecting me."

Another impatient sigh.

"If you must know, Mr. Quinn specifically has you down as someone who's not allowed to enter."

I shook my head.

"No, that can't be right," I repeated. The second security guard leaned over to look at the list, then whispered something to the guard who wouldn't let me pass.

"My apologies ma'am. I misspoke. Mr. Fitzgerald Quinn had your name on the approved list. However, we work for

Senator Michael Quinn. He's the Mr. Quinn who said you're not allowed to enter. I'm sorry, but we can't let you up."

There were murmurs from the people in line behind me, and I felt my face flush in embarrassment. Apparently, Senator Quinn knew who I was after all.

"He did, huh? Well, we'll see about that." Stalking away, I took my cell phone from my purse and dialed Fitz. There was no answer. "Dammit!"

I walked back toward the hotel lobby and tried him again. When it went straight to voicemail, I sat down on a cushioned bench, pressed against the wall, and took a moment to think. I didn't want Fitz to assume the worst if I didn't show up. There had to be another way to get up to the roof.

"Excuse me, Miss," said a voice to my left. I looked up just as a luggage cart ran over my foot.

"Ouch!"

"Oh, I'm so sorry!" said the bellman who ran me over.

I pinched my eyes closed, leaned down to remove my pump, and rubbed my smarting toes.

"It's fine," I waved off.

Just add this to the list of things that had to go wrong this week.

The bellman apologized again and continued on his way without another word. I watched him push the cart down the corridor and swipe a key card to open a set of large double doors. When the doors opened, I spotted a service elevator just inside.

Service elevator. That's it!

Moving as quickly as I could, I slipped my shoe back on and managed to wedge my hand between the doors to stop them from closing. The bellman never looked back but continued down a corridor leading to who knew where, completely unaware of the doors that failed to shut behind him. Once he was out of sight, I slipped inside and hurried to the service elevator.

I hit the button for the highest floor. When the elevator stopped, I stepped out and glanced up and down a long hallway. From the look of things, I'd been dumped off on the twelfth floor and not the roof. There was a window to my left and a long hall to my right. There had to be a staircase somewhere that would lead up to where the party was being held.

I walked down the hallway, peering in door after door, hoping to find a stairwell. The floor was obviously not meant for the public. Instead of hotel guestrooms, I found office space and supply rooms. The place was a maze of corridors branching off in various directions. Finally, I noticed a little sign on the wall with a picture of stairs, a stick figure person, and an arrow pointing up. Hoping this would lead me to my destination, I began to climb the steps.

27

FITZ

White satin sashes, peppered with silver and red glitter, hung from the glass guardrails of the rooftop patio. Spherical oil lanterns were strung between the metal poles dividing the glass panes, their flames flickering in the subtle breeze. I stood next to Devon by the podium that had been set out for me, the two of us taking in the crowd beginning to gather.

"Are you sure about this?" he asked.

"Nope, but I'm here now," I laughed. "Keep an eye on Austin for me tonight, will you? He told me he was cool with my decision to do this, but I want to be sure."

"No problem. Where is he now?"

I glanced over toward the bar where Austin stood eating a plateful of hors d'oeuvres and sipping on a Pepsi.

"He's over there by the bar. Cadence should be here any minute. He knows she's Kallie's mother, but he still doesn't know my connection to her. He might get curious and ask questions once he sees us together. Until I can work out how and when I can tell him the truth, I have to be careful."

"Have you decided how you're going to tell him?"

I reached up to grip the back of my neck and sighed.

"I don't know yet. Cadence and I are supposed to go out later on tonight to talk about it. It's not going to be easy. I mean, Christ. How in the hell do I tell him he took his sister to the fucking prom?"

"That's no joke, man," Devon acknowledged and shook his head. "Don't worry about it tonight. You've got enough to focus on. Just do what you need to do. I'll take care of the kid. After we get through this dog and pony show, maybe I'll take him to see the new *Avengers* movie or something."

I placed my hand on Devon's shoulder, gave it a brief squeeze, and patted him on the back. I didn't think I'd ever appreciated his friendship as much as I did at that moment.

"Thanks, Devon."

After Devon walked off to be with Austin, I pulled my speech from my breast pocket and skimmed through it once more. Every few minutes, I'd pause to sweep the room for Cadence. I'd expected her to be here twenty minutes ago and began to worry she'd had second thoughts.

"I know who you're looking for. She isn't coming."

I turned to see my father had come up beside me.

"Who do you think I'm looking for?"

"That stupid girl who fucked everything up years ago," he said quietly through his teeth as he nodded politely to anyone who passed by.

"I don't have time for your mind games. I need to think about my speech. I'm supposed to talk in ten minutes." I turned to walk away, but he grabbed hold of my arm and plastered on a smile. To anyone who was watching, it may have looked like he was offering me words of encouragement. However, I was familiar with the malice showing in his eyes. His grip tightened.

"Listen to me, boy. Forget that woman. Do you think her coming back now is a coincidence? Your political career will never survive the scandal she'll bring. It will destroy you."

I released an impatient sigh.

"I don't know what you *think* you know, but what's between Cadence and me is none of your business."

"Oh, believe me. It's absolutely my business. I know all about her and what her endgame is. She's had a hell of a time financially for years—putting that daughter of hers through private schools, starting that ridiculous organization. Because of your obsession, I've had to keep tabs on her. Now she's back and looking for trouble. You've got money and power, and she wants a piece of it."

I froze.

"What did you just say about her daughter?"

"Don't play stupid. Do you honestly believe I wouldn't know about the love child you spawned?"

Ice slithered down my spine as I grappled with what he was saying. I didn't believe his accusation—Cadence wasn't suddenly back in my life for financial gain. I knew better than to believe that to be true. However, his mention about keeping tabs on her raised the hairs on the back of my neck.

"Are you trying to tell me you've known about her daughter —my daughter—for years and you never told me?"

"You fool! Keep your voice down! People might hear," he hissed. Taking my elbow, he led me toward the edge of the rooftop. I went along willingly, needing to find out what else he'd kept from me over the years.

"Answer my question," I demanded through gritted teeth. "Have you always known?"

"Of course. I've known about her since the day she was born. They call you The Fixer, but it's always been me doing the fixing. That Riley girl has always been a threat. You need to cut her out of your life now before she does real, permanent damage."

I didn't want to believe even *he* could lie about something this monumental. His lie was jarring and couldn't have come at a worse time, yet I shouldn't have been surprised by what he'd done. Just when I began to feel like I could put the pieces of my broken world back together, he made room for more devastation by punching right through to the center of my chest and ripping out my bleeding heart. That's what he always did. I didn't think it was possible for me to hate him more than I did at that moment.

"You son of a bitch!" I hissed. "I thought I knew the depths you would stoop to for power, but this is a new low—even for you. How could you keep that from me?"

"It wasn't a matter of keeping something from you. You need to look at the bigger picture. It only takes one person to bring the house of cards tumbling down. This was about protecting you!"

I glared at him, suddenly seeing everything with perfect clarity.

"If you call fucking with my life protection, you really are delusional. I'm out."

"What do you mean you're out?"

"It means I'm not running. I've got seventeen years of catching up to do—no thanks to you—and I don't have time for your games, this campaign, or the Senate. I'm out."

"If you think you're going to pull out of this campaign, guess again. It's time you take your rightful place. The Senate seat is only the beginning." He gripped my arm, and his eyes flashed with something that bordered on maniacal as he raved. "You have the makings of a president, Fitzgerald, and it's high time you realize that!"

I stared in shock, unsure if I should take him seriously.

The fucking presidency?

I nearly laughed, shook my head, and ripped my arm free from his vice-like grip.

"I wanted to do something good—to make a positive change —but there's been something off about this whole damn thing right from the get-go. I'm not doing this with you. Maybe I'll consider again in the future, but I won't be doing it for you. I'll be doing it for me, my children, and my wife." When his eyes widened in surprise, I smiled. "That's right, Pops. I'm going to marry Cadence. It's what I should have done all those years ago."

Turning away from him, I scanned the room for Devon. I needed my wingman now more than ever.

"Devon!" I called when I spotted him. He paused the conversation he was having with Austin and looked in my direction. I motioned my head for him to come over. When he approached, I stared directly at my father when I spoke.

"Do me a favor. Get Austin, take him home or out to see the movie you mentioned earlier. This show is over."

I didn't know what Devon's reaction was because I was too focused on my father's expression. It morphed from shock to anger in a split second.

"Don't you dare do this, boy."

"Watch me."

I walked over to the podium and stepped up onto the riser. For the very first time, I was finally going to take back full control of my life.

28

CADENCE

I spotted Fitz as he took the podium and watched him scan the crowd. There was a gray-haired man standing near him, trying to get his attention. On closer inspection, I recognized the face I'd seen countless times on television.

It was Fitz's father.

My stomach sank, and I tried not to let apprehension get to me. I watched another man approach Senator Quinn and usher him off to the side. It only took me a moment to realize Devon Wilkshire was the second man. Even from here, I could tell the years had been kind to him. He still had that rugged handsomeness he'd had when I'd known him at Camp Riley. The two men put their heads together in quiet conversation and walked away while Fitz adjusted the microphone on the podium and scanned the crowd again.

When his eyes landed on me, a small smile turned up the corners of his mouth. The confidence and ease in which he stood made his presence known throughout the entire rooftop patio. His eyes didn't stray from me, his gaze intoxicating. We stared at each other for a moment, a gentle kind of understanding passing between us. I smiled back encouragingly, silently telling him I had his back. I believed in him with all my heart.

The wind kicked up, blowing my hair across my face. Brushing it aside, I focused on Fitz once more. He was no longer looking at me but up and to my left. I turned toward whatever had caught his attention, only to see a string of oil lanterns break free from the high poles surrounding the patio.

It was like I was watching a video on slow motion. Liquid poured from the lanterns, soaking the white and red sashes lining the glass surrounding the roof before they crashed to the ground. Instantly, the material ignited. In no time at all, the flames seemed to leap from the sashes to the furniture, setting fire to the nearby tablecloths and chair seat cushions.

"Oh my God!" I brought my hands to my mouth in disbelief.

People began to scream. I froze to the spot and stared in horror as the fast-moving fire got closer and closer to the propane patio heaters. Everyone rushed toward the exit on the other side of the room, their once pleasant chatter now cries of pure desperation. I moved forward, intent on following them when someone grabbed hold of my arm.

"Oh, no you don't," said a gruff voice from behind me. I turned around to see Fitz's father behind me, his face glowering with hatred.

"Senator Quinn," I said in surprise. I felt another small gust of wind. Heat licked the back of my neck, and I looked behind me. The flames had already spread across the middle of the rooftop, creating a barrier between me and the exit. Fitz was on the other side trying to push through the surging crowd to get to me. He couldn't break free, so I yelled, "Go with them, Fitz! I know another way out!"

"That boy is pathetic risking his neck to get to you. Goddamn fool!" the Senator spat out. I barely heard his words as I wracked my brain, trying to remember which way I had turned through the maze one floor down.

"Please, sir, we need to get out of here! Follow me."

"Not so fast." Gripping my arm tighter, he steered me back down the narrow hallway and down the stairwell that led to the lower floor. "You and I need to go someplace private and have a little chat first. You're not going to fuck this up for me."

He turned left at the base of the stairs, pulling me along with him. I shook my head, knowing we needed to either continue down the stairs or go the other way to reach the service elevator.

"Senator, I can assure you, I have no idea what you're talking about. There's a fire! We need to leave! This is the wrong way!" I pulled, trying to break his hold, but he only tightened his grip. "Ouch! You're hurting me!"

"Shut up!" he snapped. He continued dragging me down the hall, my feet sliding along the floor as he pulled. I could hear little explosions coming from the roof overhead. I prayed it wasn't the propane tanks. I'd never heard a gas explosion before, but I imagined it would be louder.

When we reached the end of the hallway, he shoved me down a dimly lit corridor and into a dark room. I swore as my ankle rolled all the way to the side, causing me to stumble forward.

"Shit!" I yelped, throwing my hands out to stop myself from falling. I wasn't fast enough. My face collided with something hard that made a loud clanging sound. Pain splintered up my leg and my head rang. I clutched my head to stop the ringing and felt something warm and sticky under my fingers—blood.

I fought nausea and forced myself to turn around. I blinked, waiting for my eyes to adjust to the dim light. Brooms, mop buckets, and other cleaning supplies filled the space. I appeared to be in a large janitor closet of sorts.

"If you care about your daughter at all, you'll keep that bastard child away from my son. Do you understand me?"

Confused by what was happening, I could only stare at the broad frame of Senator Michael Quinn filling the doorway. I barely had time for his words to register before a loud boom shook the entire building. My ears rang, and I screamed.

Propane tanks.

The first boom was followed by a second, then a third. A loud crack echoed through the corridor, bringing with it thick, black smoke. The smell began to get stronger, filling my nostrils until I began to cough. I wasn't an expert, but if I had to guess, the fire on the roof was now on this floor and spreading fast.

Panicked, I lunged and tried to push him out of my way, not caring about anything other than escape. Our bodies collided, and we stumbled against one of the metal shelves causing everything resting on it to go clanging to the floor. I tripped over a bottle of something rolling on the floor. I spiraled down, bringing both of us crashing to the ground.

The smoke was getting thicker and I could barely breathe. He gripped my shoulders and I began to kick and claw, panic and desperation overtaking all common sense.

"Let me go! We have to get out of here!"

"Fucking wild bitch! You've always been wild. Nothing but trash. Your mother was a stage whore and you're no different!"

A loud roaring sound muffled his words and I saw a flash of light. His hold on me slackened and we both turned our attention toward the light. To my horror, I saw flames licking around the edge of the doorframe. I looked back at Senator Quinn and saw his eyes widen as realization of the danger suddenly sank in. Pushing himself off me, he made a beeline for the door. I scrambled to stand up, intent on following him out. My twisted ankle screamed in pain as I got to my feet.

Fitz's father seemed to assess the fire beginning to climb the walls of the hallway before turning back to look at me.

Something evil flashed across his face as he stepped out into the fiery corridor and closed the door behind him. Instantly, I was thrown into pitch blackness.

"No!" I screamed. Moving as fast as my ankle would allow, I reached out to grab hold of a shelf. Using one hand to steady me, the other fumbled through the dark in the direction of the door. When my hand reached the smooth surface, I found it hot to the touch as I skimmed along searching for the doorknob. When I found it, I prepared to rip the door open, but instantly pulled my hand away—the metal handle was fiery hot. The flesh on my hand burned, and I squeezed my eyes closed. I was trapped.

Think! Think!

Falling to my knees, I felt around the floor, pushing through the mess of cleaning supplies until I felt the familiar satin material of my purse. Fumbling with the clasp, I pulled out my cell phone. The screen lit up. Fingers shaking, I dialed 9-1-1.

"Please hold for the next available operator," said a computerized voice on the other end of the line.

"Please hold! It's fucking 9-1-1!" I screamed to no one. Hanging up, I dialed again.

"All circuits are busy. Please try your call again."

God, no. This can't be happening.

Using the flashlight app on my phone, I angled the light toward the door. Fire glowed through the tiny crack at the bottom, and smoke billowed up toward the ceiling. Adrenaline and fear thundered through my veins. Moving the light around the small room, I looked for anything that might help me. I spotted a pile of folded white rags and a gallon-sized jug of distilled water. Staying low to the ground, I crawled over to the items. A fire alarm began to sound, and I nearly laughed, wondering why in the hell it hadn't gone off twenty minutes ago.

My throat and lungs burned as I poured water over the rag.

It was getting hot—so hot I wanted to scream. Covering my mouth with the soaked material, I crawled back to lay against the wall furthest from the door. Sirens wailed in the distance, but I knew they'd never find me in time. The smoke was beginning to thicken, swallowing me whole. Black. Suffocating. I took deliberate, shallow breaths, knowing I had to reserve my oxygen as I tried to call 9-1-1 for a third time.

When I still didn't get through on the fifth attempt, I decided to try reaching the only other person I could think of— the one man who had always tried to save me. I began to cough violently, my lungs burning and fingers trembling as I dialed his number. I could only hope and pray he wouldn't let me down now.

FITZ

I had only made it down two flights of stairs when my phone began to ring. I would have ignored it but knew it was Cadence calling by the ringtone I'd set specifically for her. I struggled to get my phone out of my pocket as I was shoved this way and that by panicked people fighting their way down the stairs.

"Sweetheart, where are you?"

I could barely hear her through the loud rush of the crowd.

"Fitz...twelfth floor...maintenance closet." Her voice was raspy and low, barely able to choke out the words.

"Wait, what?" There was no answer. "Cadence!"

I pulled my phone from my ear to look at the screen.

"Come on, man! Keep it moving!" said some guy from behind me as he pushed me forward. The sudden jolt knocked the phone from my hand, sending it flying until it was swallowed up within the sea of people.

"Shit!"

Panicked, I looked around for Austin. He was well ahead of me with Devon in the hastening crowd.

"Austin, stay close to Uncle Devon! I'll be right behind you!"

Turning back, I ignored the curses from the people trying to get down the stairs as I pushed my way up toward the door that would open up to the twelfth floor. When I finally reached it, I yanked it open as much as I could, slamming into anyone who wouldn't move out of my way and slipped through. Plunged into a wall of suffocating smoke, I brought my arm up to cover my mouth.

I didn't know how she'd gotten to the twelfth floor. The last time I saw her was right after the lanterns fell. My father had been standing next to her, but I'd lost sight of them in all the commotion.

"Cadence! Cadence!" I yelled, then waited a beat hoping to hear her respond. The only thing I heard was the thrumming of my heart and the shrill sound of the building's fire alarm.

Fuck!

The smoke was so damn thick, I could barely see a thing. Feeling my way along the walls, I paused at every door hoping to find her location. None of the rooms were set up as hotel guest rooms, giving the appearance I was on a floor reserved solely for hotel operations. I passed laundry rooms and storage rooms, but nothing that resembled a maintenance closet. Flames glowed brightly up ahead. If she was anywhere near there, I'd never be able to get to her.

I continued to open door after door but no Cadence. My lungs burned, and I began to cough. Stepping into a room filled with rows upon rows of kitchen supplies, I closed the door behind me. The air wasn't as smoke-filled, allowing me a minute to catch my breath.

Running toward the shelves, I began to rummage through storage bins with the hope of finding something to cover my mouth. I just needed to buy time—just a few more minutes of air—so I could find her. I frantically dumped the contents, watching as they scattered all over the floor. The search was futile.

I slammed my fist against one of the metal shelves in frustration. The entire floor was a maze full of shit. There wasn't anything here, and I was wasting time. Inhaling a huge gulp of air, I covered my mouth with my arm once more and prepared to go back out into the smoky hell. As I moved to open the door, something red in the corner of the room caught my eye. I turned and spotted a neat row of at least ten fire extinguishers. Relief flooded through me as I rushed to grab one of them before going back out.

I pushed through the door, only to smash into something. The impact knocked me back into the room, flat on my ass. The fire extinguisher clanged to the floor.

"What the..." I looked up. I didn't run into something—it was someone. My father stood above me, coughing and sputtering as he tried to make sense of who was on the ground at his feet.

"Fitzgerald?"

"What the hell are you still doing in here? Where's Cadence?"

"Forget that damn girl. She's gone," he choked out as I got back to my feet.

"What do you mean she's gone? I saw you with her."

"It means she's gone. I took care of her just like I took care of the last one."

"The last one? What are you talking about?" I asked impatiently as my worry over finding Cadence grew. I didn't want to hear one of his rants. I just wanted to get to her and get the hell out of this inferno.

"I'm talking about Bethany, your drunken little problem. She was a liability—a problem to be dealt with," he paused to succumb to another coughing fit. After he recovered, he glared at me, his gaze maniacal.

"I don't know why the fuck you're talking about Bethany, now of all times. I need to find Cadence! Now, where is she?"

My father ignored me and carried on like I hadn't even said a word.

"I mean, I'll admit I didn't plan on the car accident," he rambled. "That was just a fortunate accident. But getting the pills in her hands was the easy part. That idiotic girl was all too eager to buy pretty pills from a stranger she'd just met."

His mumbled words were incoherent, insane babblings I barely understood. We both began to cough again as I tried to decipher what he was saying.

"You're responsible for what happened to Bethany?" I asked incredulously. There was a loud crack and a hiss to my left, but I didn't bother to look to see what caused it. I was too busy staring at my father who stood there, grinning like a Cheshire.

"Problem solved," he boasted, then brushed his hands together for added effect—like the mother fucking asshole was actually proud of what he'd just admitted to doing. I gaped at him in disbelief as I thought back to that time in my life.

Bethany. Pills. Car accident. Cause of death. The toxicology report.

If what he said was true about Bethany, nothing would stop him from harming Cadence. My fists curled until all I saw was red—thoughts of vengeance and retribution entwined tightly around my heart. I couldn't let him hurt her. Not now—not ever. She and Kallie were innocent pawns in his fucked up game. It was time for this all to end.

"You've gone completely mad! Where is she? What did you do?" I tried to scream the words, but they came our hoarse and raw, my lungs burning from more smoke inhalation. My father coughed again and didn't answer me. Instead, he bent down to pick up the fire extinguisher I'd dropped and took off running.

The problem was, he was headed straight toward the corridor where I'd seen the fire. "No! That's the wrong way!"

I cursed under my breath, trying not to acknowledge the fact the asshole cared more about saving his own skin than anything else and hurried back into the kitchen supply room to get another extinguisher.

When I came back out, there was a deafening boom. Instantly, I was knocked flat again from the impact of some kind of explosion. My body slammed to the ground, knocking what little air I had from my lungs. My ears rang as I struggled to make sense of what was happening.

I heard someone scream, but everything was muffled through an echoing ring. Everything was so hot—so hot I thought my skin would melt from my bones. I rolled to the side and tried to focus.

When my vision cleared, I saw him.

The blast had thrown my father down the hall and back toward the kitchen supply room. He was on his back, still and unmoving as an avalanche of burning plaster and metal collapsed just a few feet ahead of him. I blinked, time seeming to move in slow motion before it rushed back in to match real time.

"Dad!"

I got up as fast as my stunned body would allow and limped over to him. From the looks of it, he'd taken the flash head on. Every part of his exposed skin was charred black and bloody. The pungent odor was unbelievable, and I had to fight the bile welling in my throat as I leaned over him. His eyes moved to meet mine, but his body remained motionless. I watched in horror as a small trickle of blood fell from the side of his mouth. Slowly, he raised a shaky hand and pointed. I looked in that direction, but all I saw was fire and smoke.

"What is it? Is that where Cadence is?" He didn't answer.

His arm fell to the floor and his eyes went vacant. "No! No, no, no! Wake up, damn you!"

I shook his burned body, needing him to tell me where she was. He didn't respond or move and a part of me knew he was already gone. Still, I pressed my fingers to the side of his neck, fighting to ignore the way they sunk inside his charred flesh as I attempted to find a pulse. There was nothing.

My body went still as everything I'd ever felt for him came crashing down around me. I saw flashes of myself as a boy meeting him for the first time. I remembered how kind he'd seemed and how my mother softened whenever he entered the room. Then I remembered how he wasn't there when she died. I remember the early years when I lived with him—the cruelty, the punishments, the way I longed for a parent but got nothing from him. I remembered the fight we'd had on the day I got married. I'd told him I wouldn't go through with it and said I was going back to Cadence. He just issued more threats—more ultimatums. I hated this man with every fiber of my being, but nonetheless... he was my father.

"Ah! Fuck!" I screamed and slammed my fist to the floor. I looked down at his lifeless body once more as the conflict raged inside me. I had to sort out my feelings later. He was dead. There was nothing I could do for him now and I was running out of time. My only hope was to find Cadence.

Leaving my father's body to the will of the fire, I took off in the direction he'd pointed, praying like hell he had been trying to tell me where she was. My lungs screamed as I ran through the smoke, my throat burning despite my arm covering my mouth.

I have to get lower to the ground.

I dropped to my knees and army crawled as fast as I could. The only thing I could see was orange and yellow glowing bright. Everywhere I looked there was fire—in front of me, behind me—bubbling the wallpaper and eating away at the plaster and wood. Panic seized my chest.

"Cadence!" I called out, ignoring the pain the hoarse cry brought to my chest as I moved closer and closer to the flames.

I neared the end of the hall and could see the faint outline of one final door. Flames slithered along the walls across from it, seeming to jump back and forth to teasingly lick its surface. I crawled along the floor and heat moved across my skin—so hot, I wanted to scream. Instinct told me should get out. It wasn't the fire that terrified me, it was the smoke. I wouldn't survive if I breathed it in for much longer. Every second that passed meant I was running out of time.

But desperation made people do desperate things. I had to know if she was there. If I turned around now, then found out that's where she'd been all along, I'd never forgive myself. My only thought was to get to her. She had to be there. I could feel it in my bones like some sort of sixth sense.

Just one more door.

When I got to be a few feet away, I realized the fire damn near surrounded the frame. Pulling the pin from the fire extinguisher, I aimed the hose and squeezed the handle, clearing the flames with frozen snow just enough to close the remaining gap. I reached up for the door handle but jerked back from the burn.

"Fuck!"

I shook my hand, not even thinking about the blisters that were probably forming as I pointed the hose at the area around the doorknob. Disoriented, I tried to focus as I ripped off my suit jacket. Using the material as a shield for my skin, I turned the knob and pushed the door open.

I scanned the dim room lit only by the flames that threatened to burn me alive. Through the smoke, I spotted a head of golden hair, lying motionless against the far wall.

"Cadence! Baby! Sweetheart!" I cried out, shimmying my

body across the floor to get to her. Fear gripped me like a vice as I scooped her lifeless body into my arms. A white cloth tumbled from her hand and her head fell back limp. "No, God no. Please!"

Just as I had with my father, I pressed two fingers against her throat. She had a pulse—weak, but it was there.

I looked back at the door. Flames bloomed and were beginning to engulf the entire opening, radiating heat and asphyxiating smoke. I blinked rapidly, trying to bring moisture to my burning eyes as I glanced around the tiny room that felt like the inside of a furnace. A half empty gallon of water and a pile of rags lay next to where Cadence was. Realizing that may be the reason why she was still alive, I dosed another one for myself. I refused to allow this place to become our hell.

Acting on pure instinct, I grabbed the fire extinguisher one final time. Squeezing the trigger, I screamed through the dripping wet rag and sent white foam to smother every single threatening flame.

My lungs heaved, and I knew I probably only bought us a few minutes. Turning back to Cadence, I stood and cradled her in my arms. Moving as fast as my smoke-inhibited body would allow, I stepped out into the blistering hot hallway and ran toward the direction of the stairwell.

The smoke was thick, and I had to use the walls to find my way. When we finally reached the entrance to the stairs, I pushed through the door and ran down the first flight.

She has to be okay. She has to be okay. I can't lose her now.

I repeated the chant over and over again as I rounded the corner of a landing. Every gulp of air I took was a challenge. Unexpectedly, water rained down from overhead when we reached the tenth floor. I swore under my breath.

"Fucking sprinklers."

I didn't have time to think about why they hadn't been working on the twelfth floor. My only concern was getting

Cadence out of there. It seemed to take forever, but I finally reached ground level and pushed through the emergency exit door to the outside.

Clean, smoke-free air assaulted me. Sirens and flashing lights were everywhere—firetrucks, police cars, ambulances. I barely processed the scene as I collapsed to my knees and gasped for air. I couldn't breathe. Everything hurt so bad as I fought to stay coherent and awake.

I need to keep moving. Cadence needs medical attention.

I knew this, yet I couldn't find the strength to stand back up. Instead, I laid her lifeless body down on the grass. She was still —so still. Her golden hair covered her face—soaking wet and streaked with black. I pushed it aside.

I heard someone yell, "There they are!"

More voices shouted.

I didn't look up to see who it was.

I felt arms come up behind me and pull me to my feet. I couldn't take my eyes off Cadence.

People surrounded her. Someone was doing CPR.

Oh God. Please no!

My already failing heart seemed to stall, and my vision began to blur. I opened and closed my eyes several times in an attempt to keep focus.

An oxygen mask was placed over her face.

That was a good sign, wasn't it?

Someone put one over my face. I batted it away, only for it to be replaced once more.

My vision blurred again, then all went black.

30

CADENCE

I choked and coughed while voices shouted around me. My throat and chest hurt so bad, I felt like they were on fire as I gasped for air. My head throbbed. There was pain in my ankle and leg. And my face—there was something on my face. I reached up to grab it, but my arms felt like lead weights as I attempted to pull it away.

"Oh, no. You need that," said a female voice.

Slowly, I opened my eyes and turned my head toward the sound of the voice. A paramedic was standing to my left and repositioning whatever was on my face. I blinked and tried to get my bearings.

It's an oxygen mask.

I shifted my gaze to the person hovering above me. A very disheveled looking Fitz stood looking down at me. His face was filthy, and his hair was sticking up wildly in all directions. I looked behind him to see flashing lights, more paramedics, and firefighters rushing about. Fitz breathed a sigh of relief.

"You scared the hell out of me, sweetheart," he said, his voice was hoarse and raspy.

"Fitz, I...what happened?" My words were muffled through the mask as I tried to sit up. Pain ripped through my skull in a blinding ache.

"Shhh. Lay down. You don't need to talk now," he told me.

"She got lucky. I don't hear any rattling in her lungs, and there's minimal swelling in her airways," the paramedic said. "I'm going to go see about helping some of the other victims. Please make sure she leaves the oxygen mask on for a little while longer and give me a shout if you need anything. I won't be gone long. Are you sure you don't want a painkiller for that hand? It's a nasty burn."

"I'm okay. Thank you for your help," Fitz said with a nod.

After she walked away, I took in Fitz's appearance again. His white shirt was covered in black soot, appearing burned in some places, and his left hand had been bandaged.

"Are you okay?" I asked.

He lifted my hand with his unbandaged one and brought my fingers to his lips.

"I'm fine. Just a little burn to the hand is all."

That's when it all came flooding back.

There was a fire. I was trapped. Senator Quinn.

I shifted the oxygen mask down so I could speak without restriction. He tried to stop me again, but I pulled my head away and forced myself to sit up. Ignoring the throbbing in my temples, I gripped Fitz's arm.

"Listen to me, Fitz! Your father," I choked out the words, feeling as if I had nails in my throat. "He closed the door on me. I was trapped."

Sadness filled his expression as he reached up to stroke my head.

"I know, sweetheart. But he's gone now. He can never hurt you again."

"What do you mean he's gone?"

"He was killed in the fire. There was a blast..." he trailed off as conflicted emotion clouded his features.

Burning tears formed and blurred my vision as I contemplated everything that had happened tonight. I remembered my mother once telling me God only gives what one person can handle. If that was the case, I'd reached my capacity. I looked at Fitz, my emotions a jumbled mess. All I knew was I needed to be close to him. I needed to feel some flicker of hope to know everything was going to be okay. The welling tears spilled over and streamed down my face.

"Hold me, Fitz. Please, just hold me."

Resting one hip on the side of the gurney, he sat down next to me. He pulled me close and I closed my eyes, giving in to the sobs that wracked my body. Resting in the safety and security of his arms, I tried to find balance and allowed the calmness of his embrace to wash over me. He stroked my back and murmured quiet assurances, his hypnotic and soothing voice chasing away my fears. He was like a snowstorm, blanketing me in white, covering me. I was buried, trapped, yet still warm at the same time. My fingers gripped his shirt, hanging on with everything I had. I never wanted to let go. He was everything I needed at that moment—protector, savior, lover, friend.

Finally feeling like I had an ounce of strength, I opened my eyes again. When I did, I spotted Devon and Austin standing a few feet away. Austin was looking at the ground and toeing his shoe around in the grass. Quickly, I looked at Fitz. He very subtly shook his head.

"No, he doesn't know," he murmured quietly. "But I'm sure he suspects something is up. I'm going to need to tell him soon, but I'll let you call the shots on this one. I've wasted half my life without you. I'm not going to do anything to fuck it up again."

"Mom! Mom, is that you?" I turned my attention to my right and saw Kallie and Joy racing across the lawn. Fitz released his hold on me and stood but kept his bandaged hand on the small of my back.

"Cadence, you scared the life out of us, girl!" Joy exclaimed once she reached my side. "I heard about the fire on the news. When I couldn't reach you, I called Kallie and found out she couldn't get a hold of you either. Neither one of us wanted to sit there and wait, so I picked her up, and we came straight here. But then the police wouldn't let us through the barricade and…"

She trailed off, and her eyes widened as she took in my appearance for the first time.

"I'm okay," I croaked out. Looking to Kallie, I noticed her concerned expression and grasped her hand in mine. "Don't worry. It's just a headache and a little sore throat. Nothing I can't handle. Mom's made of steel."

Her hand tentatively reached up to touch my shoulder.

"I don't want to hurt you or anything, but can I…can I give you a hug?" Kallie asked.

"Of course. Come here, baby girl." Reaching out, I pulled her in as tight as I could. Over her shoulder, I turned my head to watch Fitz's expression carefully. Despite the chaos of the situation, the fact he was seeing his daughter for the first time wasn't lost on me.

After she pulled away, Austin took a step closer.

"Hey, Kallie," he said.

"Austin, what are you doing here?"

"That's, ah…" He pointed awkwardly toward Fitz. "That's my dad. I was here with him for this event thing he had going on tonight."

Kallie looked at Fitz. He just stared, appearing stunned into silence before eventually reaching out to shake her hand with his one good one.

"It's nice to meet you, Kallie. You look… you look just like your mom."

My daughter observed him curiously as she shook his hand, her eyes following the line of his arm that was still resting behind my back. She narrowed her eyes suspiciously.

"Is this him, Mom? The boyfriend you tried to deny having?"

I nearly laughed but instantly found it was a mistake. My lungs screamed. Devon cleared his throat obnoxiously loud and Fitz tossed him a dirty look. The corners of my mouth turned up slightly when I realized how some things never changed.

Batman and Robin.

I looked back at Kallie. Her big, green eyes were full of young, innocent excitement. I had worked tirelessly over the years to protect that innocence. The world was full of ugly truths and I'd always felt she shouldn't be burdened with any of it. Glancing back at Fitz, I realized there was nothing ugly about our truth. She didn't need my protection from this. The love Fitz and I shared should be celebrated. It had lasted the sands of time and everything else in between.

"Well, honey. It's funny you should mention that," I began, struggling to find the right words. I was sitting on a gurney outside of an ambulance in the middle of pure mayhem. This was not the time nor the place for this discussion. "There's a lot I need to talk to you about but not here."

"That's right. Not here," Fitz agreed and wrapped a protective arm around my shoulder. He looked down at me, eyes brimming with a mixture of happiness and worry. "It can wait. You need to go to the hospital and get checked out first."

"I'm fine, Fitz. I'll admit, I'm exhausted, but what I want more than anything is a shower. I just need a few minutes to feel like a human being again. What time is it?"

"It's just after eight," Kallie answered.

"Joy, if you could take Kallie and me home, that would be

great. I'll come back to get my car from the parking garage tomorrow."

"You really should go to the hospital, Cadence," Fitz warned.

"You heard the paramedic. She said I was lucky and appeared to be okay. If I think I'm not for any reason, I'll go." I raised my eyebrows and looked pointedly at him, hoping to convey a message that said I didn't want to put this off any longer. "I need to get cleaned up and get the stink of fire off me. Do you and Austin want to come by the house for pizza in about an hour? I know it might be a little late, but I'm sure nobody has eaten dinner yet."

"I'm up for pizza," Austin said.

Fitz shook his head.

"Why am I not shocked by that?" he chuckled. Looking to me, he whispered, "Are you sure about this, sweetheart?"

"I've never been more sure of anything."

Then, taking me by surprise, he leaned in to place a chaste kiss to my lips.

"Whoa! I knew it!" Kallie exclaimed. "He is your boyfriend!"

When I answered her, I never took my eyes from Fitz. He stared back, making me feel like I was the only person in the world. All I could see, hear, and feel was him.

"No, baby girl. He's not my boyfriend. He's the keeper of my heart."

31

Abingdon, Virginia
3 MONTHS LATER

CADENCE

nxious butterflies danced in my stomach as Fitz drove us down the long stretch of road leading to Camp Riley. The GPS on the dash said we were three minutes away. I hadn't been to the property since my parents died. I just couldn't bear to come here. The place held too many memories I'd wanted to keep buried. While things with Fitz and me were better than ever, it was still hard to visit my childhood summer home and not see my mother and father hustling about in the thick of a musical production.

When the sign for the camp came into view, my stomach dropped. The wood plank that once boasted bright gold lettering was now worn with age and neglect. I should have expected as much but still. I supposed I should be grateful the sign was there at all. So much else had completely changed.

The gravel road that had only been used for pedestrian

traffic or service vehicles was now paved with blacktop. Trees had been cleared to widen the road, leaving room for two-way motor vehicle traffic. To the left of the road, a housing development had been built. Modern homes and lush green lawns took up the space that had once been miles of forest interspersed with quaint little cottages. To the right of the road, the tall moss-covered oaks and pines stood tall and untouched. That portion of the land still belonged to me—even if it was only for a little while longer.

After a long debate with myself, I'd decided to sell it to the corporation that offered me three times the land's worth. Fitz, knowing how hard my decision was, offered to come here with me to finalize the sale. I couldn't in good conscience let sentimental value get in the way of doing what was best for Dahlia's Dreamers. The company was holding up just fine on its own through private donations and my book sales. In fact, *And I Smile* broke my personal record when it hit the *New York Times* bestseller list for the ninth week in a row. However, the office space and furnishings for my non-profit could use some serious tender loving care, but it hadn't been in the budget. It was a reality I had to accept when a client sat down in one of our waiting room chairs only to have it collapse beneath them.

"I don't know who the head of the TDP corporation is, but I wish he wasn't so insistent on meeting me instead of my real estate agent to inspect the property. It's five o'clock in the evening on a Saturday. By the time we get back home, it will be after midnight. We should have gotten a hotel room," I complained. I knew I sounded whiny, but I was too miserable about what I was about to do to even care.

Fitz glanced at me curiously as he maneuvered the Audi down the smooth black pavement toward my parent's old cottage.

"You okay?"

I sighed.

"Yeah. It's so depressing coming here now. It will be strange without my parents. I know selling is the right choice, but that doesn't make it an easier to accept."

"Don't be depressed, sweetheart." Reaching over, he squeezed my leg reassuringly before pointing to a green street sign on the corner. "Look! They used the path names for the street names. It's still Watercolor Way. See? It's like I've said before—everything happens for a reason. Things are going well. The kids are happy, we're both in a good spot professionally, and we're together. Everything will work out just fine."

I looked out the window at the passing scenery without really seeing it. I knew Fitz was right. The ugliness of the past finally seemed to be behind us. We buried Fitz's father with a lot less fanfare than the Senate would have liked. A delegation of Members of Congress wanted the ceremonies to be held within the halls of Congress itself, but Fitz politely declined their offer without revealing his reasons. In private, he told me he didn't think his father—a man fueled by paranoia, grand delusions, and greed—deserved to lay in state in the Rotunda, a place shared with Presidents, Vice Presidents and Generals. I couldn't agree more and supported his decision to hold a smaller affair. We avoided the media and didn't comment when the President ordered the flag to be flown at half-mast over the Capitol Building through the day after the funeral. When the Senate passed a more elaborate resolution on the Floor noting the accomplishments and distinctions of the late Senator Michael Quinn, Fitz turned off the news coverage. Watching *Game of Thrones* just seemed so much more appealing.

Kallie and Austin had taken well to the news about me, Fitz, and our history. Kallie was more accepting than I expected her to be, taking every chance she could to get to know Fitz better. Fitz had been over the top, spoiling her rotten in an attempt to make up for lost time—not that Kallie minded in the least bit. Austin and I were getting along well, but he was a little more cautious. However, it was for reasons Fitz and I hadn't predicted. Austin requested we keep things on the 'downlow' until after he graduated high school. I couldn't blame him. Kids could be so cruel, and he'd most likely get ripped to shreds by his peers for taking his half-sister to the prom.

Out of respect for Austin's wishes, Fitz and I both agreed to keep our relationship quiet. There would be no political campaigns in the near future if at all. Fitz was beginning to learn he could make more of an impact in the private sector rather than the public. As a result, Quinn & Wilkshire decided to spearhead a pro-bono PR campaign focusing on local non-profit organizations to raise awareness. It was set to launch next week.

When the car came to a stop in front of my parent's brown clapboard cottage, I didn't wait for Fitz to come around to open the door for me like he always did. Instead, I quickly climbed out and approached the porch steps. The buyer was supposed to be here in fifteen minutes, and I wanted to get this over with as soon as possible.

The wood beneath my feet creaked as I climbed the stairs. Reaching into my purse, I fished around for the keys to the front door. When I couldn't locate them, I looked back toward the car. Fitz was approaching behind me holding up a silver ring with keys dangling from the end.

"Looking for these?"

"Yeah, thanks. I could have sworn they were in my purse. Where were they?"

"On the floor of the front seat of the car."

Assuming they'd just fallen out of my purse, I took the keys from Fitz's outstretched hand, unlocked the front door, and entered the kitchen. The old table still sat in the middle. Other than the smattering of cobwebs and the dust lingering on the surface of everything, the kitchen looked just as it had the last time I was here—except my parents were missing.

A wave of nostalgia came over me. I expected it to happen, but I didn't expect tears to come along with it. Fitz's strong arms came from behind me to wrap me in his warm embrace.

"I'm sorry," I sniffled. "I don't know why I'm crying. I guess it's because I still miss them so much. I'm being silly when I should be wiping down the table. We can't very well sign a contract on a table full of dust."

Fitz turned me to face him and tilted my chin up with his index finger.

"Sweetheart, I don't mind a little dust."

"You might not, but the buyer will."

Stepping back, he reached into his back pocket to produce a thick envelope and handed it to me.

"Trust me, the buyer doesn't care about dust or anything else. Things are fine just the way they are. See for yourself." His eyes gleamed with the most peculiar look, almost playful. I glanced at the envelope curiously.

"What are you talking about?" I asked as I took it from him.

"Open it."

I sighed, thinking I should be cleaning instead of indulging Fitz in whatever game he was playing. I slid my finger along the seal and pulled out the stack of folded papers. I skimmed through the text and immediately realized it was the purchase contract between me and TDP for the sale of the land. Automatically, my hand dropped into my purse to feel for my copy of the contract. When my hand made contact with the envelope, I knew what Fitz had handed me wasn't mine.

"Why do you have a copy of this?"

"Isn't the buyer supposed to get a copy?"

"Well, yes. But..." My stomach twisted and my eyes widened. "Are you TDP?"

"No, sweetheart. *We* are TDP."

"I don't understand."

He grinned.

"It's kind of a funny story actually. Do you remember me telling you about the night Devon came over and I told him about Kallie? The two of us had been trying to find ways to spin the story with the public if needed."

"Yeah, I remember. Why?"

"Well, we had a few too many beers and one subject jumped to the next. That's always a dangerous combo. Anyway, we got off topic and started talking about our taxes and charitable contributions. Things kind of just spiraled after that. Why don't we take a walk, and I'll tell you about it?"

Genuinely confused, I shook my head.

"I can't go for a walk. They buyer will be here soon and—"

"Cadence, nobody else is coming here today. Now, come with me."

When he took my hand, I eyed him questioningly. He didn't explain further, and simply led me out of the house.

"Where are we going?"

"To the lake."

"The lake! That path has to be so overgrown by now. I'm not wearing shoes suitable for hiking."

He glanced down at my navy ballet flats and shrugged.

"So, I'll carry you if I have to. Now, if you'll stop arguing, I'll explain everything when we get there. Trust me."

32

FITZ

As we walked down the hill toward the lake, birds chirped in the still of the trees overhead. Rays of light streaked through the branches, bending over the path like a living canopy. With Cadence's hand in mine, it felt like we'd walked this way to the secret spot a thousand times. Although I hadn't been here in years, it was still familiar. The path was overgrown like Cadence predicted, but it wasn't nearly as bad as it could have been, and we were able to navigate it with relative ease. I was actually thankful for the overgrowth. With the new housing development not that far away, I worried about the possibility of someone intruding on us. However, it was clear nobody had traveled this path regularly in a long while.

"Fitz, are you going to tell me what the hell you were talking about back there?"

I chuckled.

"I will when we get to the lake."

She pulled her hand from mine and stopped dead in her tracks.

"I'm not walking any further until you tell me what's going on. Who or what is TDP?"

I shook my head and pulled her to me.

"You have no patience," I chided and pecked a light kiss on her forehead. Moving my lips to her hair, I inhaled deeply. Her vanilla scent mixed with the surrounding pines brought me back—way back. "Mmmm... you smell good."

"Fitz, don't you dare try to distract me," she warned.

I laughed again and pulled away.

"Fine. You win. TDP is a brand-new, non-profit corporation. If you flipped through to the back of the papers I handed you, you would have seen your name listed as the president. It's just waiting for your signature of acceptance."

Her brows pinched together in confusion.

"Another non-profit? I'm sorry, maybe I'm a little slow on the uptake here. You'll need to explain better."

"Quinn & Wilkshire was behind on quarterly donations. To catch up, Devon and I decided to donate a big chunk of money to TDP. A large portion of that money was then used to place a sizable offer on this land. I have ties to this place too, Cadence. I couldn't let you sell it. There are enough structural buildings and land left to make this into something again. My thought was to keep it a summer camp, but on a much smaller scale than Camp Riley. It wouldn't be a performing arts camp, but a literacy youth camp for low income families. When we made the donation, we also made sure enough money would be left over to get a new camp up and running."

"But who would run it? I certainly don't have the time. Plus, Abingdon is over five hours away from D.C. As great as this all sounds, I can't be in two places at once."

"I've thought about that too. I went over things with Joy—"

"Joy? She knows about this?"

"Yeah. Your best friend is pretty amazing," I appreciated with a smile. "After talking to Joy, we came up with a plan. With her and Marissa looking to adopt soon, Marissa plans to quit her job and go back to teaching preschool. Since she'll be off during the summer, she's willing to come here to work the youth camp. She actually excited about it. If Joy and Marissa happen to adopt along the way, Marissa will be able to bring their new son or daughter with her to the camp and supplement their income in the process."

"But that would mean summers away from Joy. I can't imagine they'd want to be separated right when they are trying to establish a family, and I can't afford to have Joy take entire summers off from Dahlia's Dreamers."

"That's already been worked out too. We'd keep your parents old place for ourselves and use it as a summer getaway. Joy wants to snag one of the remaining cottages and turn it into a summer home as well, then convert one of the other ones into a satellite office for Dahlia's Dreamers. It's all been worked out, sweetheart. All everyone is waiting for is your stamp of approval."

She shook her head in disbelief as she took it all in. If there was one thing I'd learned over the past few months, it was Cadence was an organized planner. Her ducks were always lined up in a row, and I was pretty sure I just sent them flying all over the place.

"I can't believe you did this. I'm having a hard time wrapping my head around it all..." She trailed off, and her eyes suddenly went wide. She gripped my arm and shrieked, "Oh my God! This means I don't have to sell the land!"

"Well, technically you do, but you'll be selling it to yourself in a way. You just have to—"

My words were cut off as she threw her arms around my neck and rained kissed all over my face.

"I love you, I love you, I love you so, so much!"

"Had I known I'd get this reaction from you, I wouldn't have waited to get the details ironed out. I would have told you two months ago," I laughed.

When she pulled away, her emerald eyes sparkled with delight.

"Thank you, Fitz."

"Anything for you, sweetheart."

I only hoped she was just as excited for the next surprise I had planned. Taking her hand in mine once more, we continued walking to our lake spot.

"What does TDP stand for?" she asked as we approached the end of the path.

"I thought you'd never ask," I smiled and pulled out my phone. Opening the picture app, I scrolled to find the image I was looking for and held it out for her to see. "It stands for The Dahlia Project. This is just a mockup of the sign I had designed, but eventually, it will replace the worn Camp Riley sign out on the road."

Her sweet, sexy mouth tipped up at the corners.

"The Dahlia Project?"

"Yeah, I couldn't help myself. I had a real fondness for that dog. This place isn't quite the same without her. It seemed appropriate."

When the trees parted to open up to the vast lake, the sun was low in the sky, but it hadn't quite fallen behind the treetops yet. I looked out toward the dock and smiled. Joy had set up everything perfectly for me. A beach blanket was spread out and unlit candles surrounded it. Along with the candles, freshly picked dahlia flowers were scattered around the dock. Seeing it all as it had been on the day Cadence first gave herself to me quickened my heart. The only thing missing was the Boombox. Neither Joy nor I managed to get our hands on one, but it was okay. That's what smartphones were for.

I heard Cadence's sharp intake of air when she spotted what was on the dock.

"Fitz, how in the world did you manage to do this?"

"Well," I drawled out. "I had a little help. Joy might have been here already today."

"Might have?"

"Yeah. Just like I might have given her a list of instructions... and she may have made up your old room so we have a place to sleep tonight too."

She laughed as we stepped up on the dock.

"Well, aren't you a little schemer? No wonder you weren't worried about getting back so late or booking a hotel room. Either way, I think it's perfect! It's just like it was when we were younger! Now all we have to do is wait for the sun to get a little lower so we can see all the vibrant colors."

She let out a little squeal of excitement, held out her arms, and twirled around. I thought my heart would burst, seeing her so happy. Grabbing her around the waist, I pulled her into my arms, cupped her face, and our lips connected. Gliding my tongue across that pouty lower lip, she sighed into the kiss. I pulled her closer and pressed deeper, dominating the kiss until she felt like putty in my arms. My pulse raced from the passionate way she kissed me back. This woman never failed to steal the breath right from my lungs.

"I think we might be able to find something to do to pass the time until the sun sets," I murmured against her smooth skin as I nibbled along the line of her jaw.

She pulled back and gave me an impish grin.

"I'll admit, it was sad seeing my parents place so empty, but the lake will always belong to you, Fitz. You didn't have to open an entire corporation just to get me here. If you wanted to do it on the dock again, all you had to do was ask," she joked.

"Do it, huh? Is that what you want to do?" I teased back. I loved when we shared flirty moments like this. It gave me a glimpse into the future and what could be between us.

"Maybe."

I lightly traced the line of her collarbone with my fingertip. "Hmmm...let's see what I can do about that."

I skimmed a hand up her waist, sliding under the loose-fitting material until I could capture her breast. Shifting the cup of her bra down, I rolled the already hard nipple. She let out a little whimper and closed her eyes. Lowering us down to the blanket, I pressed her back to the dock.

I held her face between my palms and pressed my mouth to hers once more. Her lips moved to meld with mine. I kissed her desperately, our tongues sliding deep to clash and taste. She was wearing a pencil skirt—the tight little thing had driven me insane with lust all goddamn day. I could have easily shifted it up and gone right for the gusto. However, I wanted to take all the time in the world to savor her.

As I kissed her, I slowly removed the clothes from her body, only breaking our connection when I had to slip her shirt over her head. Once she was naked, she reached for the buckle on my pants.

"No, sweetheart. Just lay back and let me do the work."

She did as told without question and just watched as I stood to light the candles. Once they were lit, I dug into my pocket for my phone and pulled up the music library. After connecting to the little Bluetooth speaker I'd asked Joy to bring, I selected the playlist I'd made just for this occasion and set both devices down on the dock. The music that sounded in the quiet, early evening air wasn't anything we'd listened to in the past. We may have circled back to where we began, but tonight was about moving forward and making new memories.

Once I was stripped out of my khakis and polo shirt, I laid back down, covering her body with mine. I needed to feel her bare skin against me—the other half of two souls on fire. I could sense Cadence's desire and her longing for more. She purred beneath me as I trailed kisses down each of her thighs, calves, ankles, and toes. This woman was perfection, and she was all mine.

I moved back up her body, my lips trailing over her hips and across her smooth stomach. I closed my eyes and inhaled the scent of her skin, needing her more and more with every breath I took. She squeezed my biceps and urged me closer.

"Fitz, please..." she mewled. I looked into her expressive emerald eyes. She looked so unguarded and exquisitely tender when she whispered, "Take me. I need you."

Her words almost broke me, and my heart began to hammer in my chest.

I took her hands in mine and kissed each of her fingertips before pulling her arms above her head and locking them in place. The weight of my cock pressed against her warm and velvety heat. My blood surged from the desperate need to possess her. Thankfully, Cadence had gone on the pill two months ago. Since then, there had been no more barriers between us. When we connected now, we were truly one.

Her gaze glowed sultry and provocative as I slowly slid into her waiting body. Instantly, I was lost in all-consuming heat. I began to move slowly and deliberately, absorbing every sensation and savoring her every reaction. We made love tenderly, each of us exploring each other as if it were the first time—and in a way, it was. Being together again as grown adults in the place where we first began felt different somehow.

I continued to push into her with long, languid strokes, fighting with every shred of my being to hold on—to wait for her. She felt so damn good. I was so close but knew she wasn't there yet. Knowing what she needed, I increased my pace and her hips rose to meet mine. I could only hope beyond hope she would get there soon.

When her eyelids began to flutter, I knew she was nearly there. Her head dropped to the side and her eyes rolled back, her expression reflecting one of imminent pleasure.

"That's it. Come for me, sweetheart."

I drew back once more, then pushed forward again and again. Her fingernails clawed down my back and I felt her brace beneath me. Our gazes locked and we both launched to the brink of ultimate pleasure.

At her shattered cry, my orgasm burst forth in an explosive stream of both agony and ecstasy. I choked out a strangled moan, pouring myself inside her. It was a moment of derailing intensity, a perfect blending of heart and mind.

I collapsed down on top of her, careful to balance my weight so I didn't crush her. My cock jerked as she vibrated around me, still giving up the last remnants of our release. Once our breathing returned to a steadier rhythm, I reluctantly withdrew from the heated clutches of her body and pulled the excess blanket over to cover us. We laid there for a while, listening to the music as the sun dropped low behind the trees.

"Do you love me?" I asked her.

She tilted her head up to look at me. Skimming a finger along the lines of my tattoo, she smiled softly.

"You know I do."

"Hmmm... I'm not so sure. Let's see if you can prove it." Pulling myself up to a sitting position, I reached for my pants and dug in the front right pocket until my fingers connected with a folded-up square of paper. Tugging it out, I handed her the origami fortune teller. "You up for a game of questions?"

Her eyes sparkled with humor, and she sat up.

"I don't know what you're up to, but I'll play." Plucking it from my hand, she laughed as she placed her fingers under the flaps. "Okay, pick a number, Mr. Quinn."

"Four," I said right away, knowing it didn't matter which number I picked. Everything would lead to the same question.

She counted the origami four times and held it out to me once more.

"Pick a color."

"Green, sweetheart. Always green."

"G-R-E-E-N."

Once the origami landed on its intended destination, she shifted the paper to unfold the flap. As she read the question, her hands began to shake.

"I would have gotten down on one knee, but we're already sitting down so..." I trailed off, trying desperately to read her expression. Her eyes were still fixated on the origami and she had yet to look at me. Reaching for my pants once more, I dug into the left pocket and removed the tiny black box. She looked up and our gazes locked. This wasn't a silly game of questions from years past. This was the real deal.

"Fitz, I..." she whispered, bringing a trembling hand to her lips.

"Nearly two decades have passed, but when I look back, I can remember every single moment of the first summer we spent together. It was a time I'll always cherish because it brought me strength through the years when I needed it most. I didn't plan on falling in love with you back then, just as I don't think you planned on falling for me. But once we met, it was clear we couldn't control our feelings. We both fell in love despite the obstacles. For me, a love like that has happened only once. When I got it back—when I got *you* back—I vowed to never let that love go again. What we have is rare and beautiful, sweetheart. I can't replace the time we lost, but I want the chance to be your Colonel Brandon and everything else in between." Taking a nervous breath, I asked the most important question of my life. "Will you marry me, Cadence?"

33

CADENCE

He sat a foot away from me, his eyes searching mine. Every time I looked at him, something deep twisted in my heart. A shiver raced down my spine and energy crashed through the air like a thunderbolt. My love for him was bigger than anything else I'd ever felt. It was intense and potent—just like he was. As I stared into his expressive pools of gray, I saw something in our future that would go on forever.

I wanted to leap into his arms and scream yes, but we both had to remember we weren't alone in the decision to make a lifelong commitment.

"We should talk to the kids about this, Fitz."

He grinned sheepishly.

"I already did. I asked Kallie's permission first. Once she gave it, she, Austin, and I went ring shopping."

"You went shopping for a ring with them?"

My heart wanted to explode with love. The fact he'd asked Kallie made my heart swell. Tears of joy filled my eyes.

"Yep. Austin wanted me to get this gaudy solitaire while Kallie was eyeing up too much bling. In the end, I chose this."

He flipped open the lid of the small box in his hand. I gasped. Nestled in a bed of black satin sat a princess cut diamond set in an intricately twisted vine of gold and pavé diamonds.

"Oh, Fitz! It's beautiful."

"It reminds me of the braids you always wear."

"My braids? I didn't think you really noticed the way I wore my hair," I laughed.

"I always notice you, sweetheart. Even when you think I'm not looking." He paused and inhaled a shaky breath. Taking the ring from the box, he held it out. "I've loved you for more than half my life. You are my forever. I want us to be a family—me, you, Austin, and Kallie. So what's it going to be, sweetheart?"

Tears began to fall freely without any chance of stopping. I don't know how it happened, but we were really here. I glanced out over the lake, taking in the picturesque scenery. The trees were dense, and the rolling hills were just as breathtaking as ever. The sun had finally dropped to the perfect level, leaving pink and orange hues to paint the sky. It made everything around us feel warm. I allowed the heat to encompass me and looked back at Fitz. This wasn't a dream, but my perfect reality. Second chances don't happen often, and I would forever be grateful for ours.

"I love you, Fitzgerald Quinn. I've loved you since I was eighteen years old. From the very first kiss we shared, I've been yours."

"Is that a yes?"

I pressed a hand to his heart.

"With you, it will always be yes."

Taking my hand from his chest, he slipped the ring onto my finger. It was a perfect fit. Years of wrong suddenly shifted to right, and it was because of this man. I had no reservations. Without him, a piece of my heart had been missing. Now that my keeper had put the piece back, there was no doubt—he defined me.

To be continued...

Thank you for reading *Defined*! The story continues with Kallie in *Endurance*, a sexy emotionally-charged sports romance that will keep your heart racing!

It was time to prepare for a new kind of race—the race to Kallie's heart.

Sloan

As the son of a Formula One racer, the need for speed was in my blood. But in the blink of an eye, my life in the fast lane came to a screeching halt.

That's when I met her—Kalliope Benton Riley.

She wasn't my usual type at all. She was a total hippie, packaged to perfection with flowy dresses and rainbow-colored hair wraps. She had outlandish ideas about the stars, the moon, and predetermined destiny. Ridiculous.

Yet, I couldn't turn away from her mesmerizing green eyes.

She was more than a pit stop.

She was my addiction—my checkered flag.

Kallie

A psychic gypsy once told me I was cursed when it came

to relationships and romance. She was right. But her warning only prompted the universe to say, "Hold my beer."
Enter Sloan Atwood.
He was arrogant and cocky. Avoiding him should have been easy, but all his sexy rough edges were impossible to ignore.
Before long, my heart knew I couldn't box this lap.
There would be no winners in this race.
Total shut down was the only way to prevent permanent damage.

One-click ENDURANCE now!

If you loved *Untouched* check out a some of the other books in my catalogue!

The Stone Series
If you haven't read my books, *The Stone Series* is my first book series and is still my number one bestseller. This sexy, billionaire romance was literally my whole life for over three years. It's a complete trilogy and it's available on all platforms!

The Sound of Silence
Meet Gianna and Derek in this an emotionally gripping, dark romantic thriller that is guaranteed to keep you on the edge of your seat! This book is not for the faint-hearted. Plus, Krystina Cole from *The Stone Series* has a cameo appearance!

For more titles, please visit www.dakotawillink.com.

SUBSCRIBE TO DAKOTA'S NEWSLETTER

My newsletter goes out twice a month (sometimes less). It's packed with new content, sales on signed paperbacks and Angel Book Boxes from my online store, and giveaways. Don't miss out! I value your email address and promise to NEVER spam you.

SUBSCRIBE HERE: https://dakotawillink.com/subscribe

BOOKS & BOXED WINE CONFESSIONS

Want fun stuff and sneak peek excerpts from Dakota? Join Books & Boxed Wine Confessions and get the inside scoop! Fans in this interactive reader Facebook group are the first to know the latest news!

JOIN HERE: https://www.facebook.com/groups/1635080436793794

MUSIC PLAYLIST

Thank you to the musical talents who influenced and inspired *Defined*. Their creativity helped me bring this story to life.

"Mamma Mia" by Maryl Streep *(Mamma Mia! The Movie Soundtrack)*

"Feel Again" by OneRepublic *(Native)*

"Could You Be Loved" by Bob Marley *(Uprising)*

"Out of the Dark" by De Lune feat. Jason Zerbin *(Out of the Dark)*

"With or Without You" by U2 *(The Joshua Tree)*

"Waka Waka" by Shakira *(This Time for Africa)*

"Dangerous Night" by Thirty Seconds to Mars *(America)*

"Hi-Lo (Hollow)" by Bishop Briggs *(Church of Scars)*

"Shots" by Imagine Dragons *(Smoke + Mirrors)*

"Love Don't Run" by Steve Holy *(Love Don't Run)*

"The One" by Kodaline *(Coming Up for Air)*

"A Thousand Years" by Christina Perri *(A Thousand Years)*

LISTEN ON SPOTIFY

ABOUT THE AUTHOR

Dakota Willink is an award-winning *USA Today* Bestselling Author from New York. She loves writing about damaged heroes who fall in love with sassy and independent females. Her books are character-driven, emotional, and sexy, yet written with a flare that keeps them real. With a wide range of publications, Dakota's imagination is constantly spinning new ideas.

Dakota often says she survived her first publishing with coffee and wine. She's an unabashed *Star Wars* fanatic and still dreams of getting her letter from Hogwarts one day. Her daily routines usually include rocking Lululemon yoga pants, putting on lipstick, and obsessing over Excel spreadsheets. Two spoiled Cavaliers are her furry writing companions who bring her regular smiles. She enjoys traveling with her husband and debating social and economic issues with her politically savvy Generation Z son and daughter.

Dakota's favorite book genres include contemporary or dark romance, political & psychological thrillers, and autobiographies.

AWARDS, ACCOLADES, AND OTHER PROJECTS

The Stone Series is Dakota's first published book series. It has been recognized for various awards and bestseller lists, including *USA Today* and the *Readers' Favorite* 2017 Gold Medal in Romance, and has since been translated into multiple languages internationally.

The *Fade Into You* series (formally known as the *Cadence duet*) was a finalist in the *HEAR Now Festival Independent Audiobook Awards*.

In addition, Dakota has written under the alternate pen name, Marie Christy. Under this name, she has written and published a children's book for charity titled, *And I Smile*.

Also writing as Marie Christy, she was a contributor to the Blunder Woman Productions project, *Nevertheless We Persisted: Me Too*, a 2019 *Audie Award Finalist* and *Earphones Awards Winner*. This project inspired Dakota to write *The Sound of Silence*, a dark romantic suspense novel that tackles the realities of domestic abuse.

Dakota Willink is the founder of Dragonfly Ink Publishing, whose mission is to promote a common passion for reading by partnering with like-minded authors and industry professionals. Through this company, Dakota created the *Love & Lace Inkorporated* Magazine and the *Leave Me Breathless World*, hosted ALLURE Audiobook Con, and sponsored various charity anthologies.

The Dahlia Project

Thank you for your contribution!

The Dahlia Project is not just something I wrote about in *Defined*, but a real-life charity inspired by my daughter.

A portion of the proceeds from some of my books go to various non-profit organizations. To read more about participating books and the organizations The Dahlia Project will give to, please see the Dakota Gives Back tab on my website. Your purchases help make a difference in a very real sense.

By supporting The Dahlia Project, you've helped make the lives of these people a little better. Thanks for your support! To stay up to date on its progress, subscribe to my newsletter by clicking HERE.

Dakota Willink

SUPPORTED ORGANIZATIONS

Kiva

Kiva is an international nonprofit, founded in 2005 and based in San Francisco, with a mission to connect people through lending to alleviate poverty. By lending as little as $25 on Kiva, anyone can help a borrower start or grow a business, go to school, access clean energy or realize their potential. For some, it's a matter of survival, for others it's the fuel for a life-long ambition.

100% of every dollar you lend on Kiva goes to funding loans. Kiva covers costs primarily through optional donations, as well as through support from grants and sponsors. To learn more, click HERE.

Room To Read

Room to Read seeks to transform the lives of millions of children in low-income communities by focusing on literacy and gender equality in education. Working in collaboration with local communities, partner organizations and governments, they develop literacy skills and a habit of reading among primary school children, and support girls to complete secondary school with the relevant life skills to succeed in school and beyond. You can read more about Room To Read by clicking HERE.

Made in the USA
Monee, IL
05 November 2023

45813209R00166